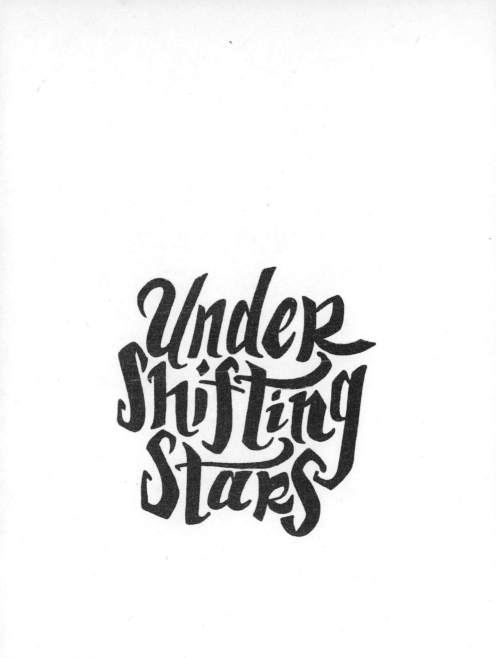

By ALEXANDRA LATOS

HOUGHTON MIFFLIN HARCOURT
BOSTON   NEW YORK

The text was set in Arno Pro.
Hand-lettering by Andrea Miller
Cover and interior design by Andrea Miller

Library of Congress Cataloging-in-Publication Data
Names: Latos, Alexandra, author.
Title: Under shifting stars / by Alexandra Latos.
Description: Boston : Houghton Mifflin Harcourt, [2020] | Audience: Ages 12
and up | Audience: Grades 7–12 | Summary: Twins Audrey and Clare grapple
with their brother Adam's death as well as with the need to belong.
Identifiers: LCCN 2019039955 (print) | LCCN 2019039956 (ebook) |
ISBN 9780358067757 (hardcover) | ISBN 9780358067818 (ebook)
Subjects: CYAC: Twins — Fiction. | Sisters — Fiction. | Grief — Fiction. |
Belonging (Social psychology) — Fiction. | Family problems — Fiction.
Classification: LCC PZ7.1.L378 Un 2021 (print) | LCC PZ7.1.L378 (ebook) |
DDC [Fic] — dc23
LC record available at https://lccn.loc.gov/2019039955
LC ebook record available at https://lccn.loc.gov/2019039956

Manufactured in the United States of America
DOC 10 9 8 7 6 5 4 3 2 1
4500803258

For my children—
I'll love you always
and forever.

Audrey

I raise my hand. Ask if I can go to the bathroom.

Take a bathroom pass, he says.

The pass is a necklace, but the white string has turned gray so I put it in my back pocket. Then I'm gone. Skip one two three, it's good to be free.

A pipe burst above the coatroom last week. It's not the first time. Floor tiles have bent together to form a mountainous ridge that leads to the bathroom. I follow the path, leap over one peak, then another, and back again. Three times for good luck. Pause to make funny faces in the mirror before using the toilet. There are no new comments on the stall. I stand up to flush.

This is not ideal.

The bathroom pass is floating in the bowl. It must have fallen out of my pocket.

Do you know the names of all the germs lurking in the average toilet? I do. In grade five I did a science-fair project on germs. I was surprised to discover the school water fountain had more, but I'd already looked up toilet bowl germs and their related afflictions.

The answer is: E. coli, salmonella, norovirus, staphylococcus, shigella, and streptococcus. The first three are relatively minor and cause diarrhea, abdominal cramps, and vomiting.

But staphylococcus can cause impetigo.

Shigella can cause dysentery.

Streptococci can cause a skin infection commonly known as flesh-eating bacteria.

These are all worst-case scenarios, I agree. But I think it's better to err on the side of caution.

The first flush is unsuccessful. The pass dives like a manta ray, its body struggling to escape into a cave. Then it bobs back up again. The second and third flushes are a repeat of the first. Dive and bob. Dive and bob. The fourth time, I hold the flusher down, close my eyes, and pray. Come on, little manta ray, you can make it. Count to ten. Open my eyes.

The manta ray has indeed made it into the cave. But now the bowl is very full. Too full for the next person to use. Being considerate, I flush again.

For a second it seems like the situation is resolved, and I breathe a sigh of relief. Then the water returns and keeps rising and doesn't look like it's going to stop. It reaches the edge of the toilet seat and spills over the lip of the bowl and onto the floor.

The manta ray does not come with it.

I wash my hands and hurry out of the bathroom before the event can be linked to me. The water has already seeped out from under the stall.

I have every intention of returning to class, I do, but then I happen to look out the window of the side door. The one that faces the playground. I'm not sure how long I'm out there before he finds me. I'm hanging upside down on the monkey bars and the first thing I see are his shoes. I know they're his because he never wears socks.

You're supposed to be in class, I hear him say.

Let's have class outside today.

We can't.

Why?

Because we have to follow the rules.

But *why*?

Pourquoi êtes-vous si difficile?

I flip off the bars and land on my feet in front of him. Perfect dismount. I'll answer your question if you answer mine, I tell him.

Monsieur Martin exhales like a whale and pinches his nose. It leaves a red mark like he was wearing sunglasses.

Because I said so. Besides, you lied to me. I trusted you to go to the bathroom.

I did! I did, but then I came out here.

I see that. Where's the bathroom pass?

In the bathroom, I say because it's the truth.

Shortly after we return to class, Lydia screams in frustration and throws her workbook across the room. Monsieur Martin and Marianne the teaching assistant take her to the back of the room while the rest of us continue our work and pretend it isn't happening.

George is picking his nose. I watch as he wipes his finger clean on the lip of his desk drawer.

Outside, the sun is shining and the birds are chirping.

My math book has a large 9 on it. I'm supposed to be doing the end-of-chapter French questions, but Martin *est préoccupé* so I pull out my sketchbook and draw the playground instead.

Playgrounds are very hard to draw. There is a lot to remember if you're not lucky enough to have a view of one outside your window, and there are a lot of lines. Plus all of these lines have to have the right *perspective*. Ms. Nguyen, the art teacher, taught us how to draw with perspective.

You put a little *x* on the page to mark your horizon, and then you take the corners of your object (say, a box) and draw toward the *x* so that they connect there. Next you draw horizontal and vertical lines where you want the box to end and it will look 3D.

Or you can leave them so it looks like the box is coming right at you, like a train.

The playground isn't progressing as hoped so I continue work on my underwater scene involving dolphins. I once heard dolphins are the only mammals that have sex for fun, besides humans. How do they do it? To avoid the question, I draw them holding hands (fins).

Fin. La Fin. The End.

Audrey! Monsieur Martin is at the front of the room again. You're not paying attention.

I am too! To what?

To me. To what I'm saying.

I am. I only looked out the window for a second. I feel like adding, What did I miss? But I can tell from his expression that it wouldn't be appreciated.

He marches to my desk and there's no time to close my sketchbook.

Looks like it will be a frownie-face day. When the bell rings, I watch him draw it on my chart in permanent marker.

To make matters worse, my parents get a phone call. This isn't the first time, but I doubt they ever get used to it. Clare goes to a different school and they never get phone calls about her.

In the car Mom looks like I've broken her heart. Again? she asks.

Apparently, I say.

They think you flooded the bathroom.

It was already flooded.

So you didn't? She sounds hopeful.

4

I didn't say that.

Mom shakes her head as she drives. She can't even look at me. What's going on with you?

Nothing. (Avoiding: And you? Don't be cocky.)

When we get home, I go straight to my room. There I pull out my sketchbook and draw angrily. In haste. *Rapidement.* According to Ms. Nguyen, my fast sketches look like images from a 3D movie without the glasses. Or photos from a multi-pinhole camera. I wouldn't know.

At some point Dad knocks on the door. Audrey?

I throw the book under the bed, pretend I've been thinking about what I did wrong.

Come in.

He sits beside me on the edge of the bed. There's a moment of silence in which we both just look at our hands, and then he asks, Is there something you want to tell me?

You came to see me, I say.

Tell me what happened at school today.

I sigh deeply. Dramatically. You split me and Clare up, I tell him.

Do you miss Clare?

That's not the point. The point is that you split us up. I'm at Freak and she's at a normal school.

Honey, no one thinks you're a freak. His thick eyebrows are curled toward each other and I can tell he's saying the truth. Not everyone in the world thinks the same way and that's a good thing. A lot of the kids at Peak have extremely high IQs like you.

Most of them are weirder than me!

You aren't weird, Audrey.

I am too and you know it!

Dad puts a hand on my shoulder. Honey, calm down.

We look at each other for a moment. A standoff.

Then he exhales loudly, rubs his hand along his spiky chin the way he always does when he doesn't know what to do. Are you saying you acted out today because you and Clare were split up? Because, honey, this behavior started years ago.

But I'm at Peak because of Adam.

That's not true. Your teachers recommended it years ago because they thought you needed more one-on-one attention. And yes, we're worried about how you've been coping. We thought Peak might help you more now.

But *now* I feel even more alone than I did before. Get it?

Another chin rub. I've given him something to think about.

George glued his desk closed with snot today, I tell him to strengthen my case.

The side of Dad's mouth twitches. That could happen in public school too, but I'll talk to your mother. All we want is for you to be happy.

A door slams downstairs. Clare's home.

I take the stairs two at a time and run into the kitchen, where my sister is already sitting at the table. Her hair hangs over her face like a curtain, the side with the thick blue streak facing toward us. She dyed it after Adam died and touches it up at school where Mom and Dad can't stop her.

Mom tries to pass me a plate of spaghetti but I race past her. Embrace my stunned sister.

Clare, I'm coming back to your school in the fall! Isn't that grand?

She turns a bewildered face to my mom, who looks just as shocked.

Dad arrives at the door just then, his breath a bit wheezy. That's not quite true, he tells them. I told her we'd *think* about it.

I watch Clare's face. Look for traces of similarities between us. We aren't identical: her hair is light and mine is dark. She was born under the earth sign Taurus and I was born under the air sign Gemini. People say fraternal twins are just regular siblings, but I know differently. We shared a womb. You can't get closer to someone than that.

I watch Clare's face, and it crumples.

She might be coming back to my school? Her voice rises to hysterical. *Mom?*

Both of my parents just stand there.

She takes off. As she runs up the stairs to her bedroom, I hear her wail: As if things weren't hard enough at school. Thanks a *lot*! Her bedroom door slams shut. Walls rattle.

Tears gather in my eyes. They sit there in my eye sockets until everything goes blurry. I can't move. I just stare at the carpet where she used to be standing. There's a chunk of mud that could be mistaken for chocolate. I feel the familiar weight of my dad's hand on my shoulder and shrug it off.

I'm going outside.

The sun is already beginning to set pink orange purple over the hill beside the park. I climb onto the swing. Tilt back and look up at the sorbet sky.

Clare and I used to do this. We used to swing side by side until the sun set.

Beside me the swing is empty.

I'm going to get her back, I say out loud. I'm going to prove I can be like her.

I start to pump.

At the top of my swing, there's a face watching me from the basement window. When I come back to the ground, it's gone.

Clare

My name is Clare. According to Baby Names R Us or whatever stupid website my friends were dicking around on, it means "illustrious." I wasn't entirely sure what that meant so I looked it up.

1. Highly distinguished, renowned, famous;
2. Glorious, as deeds or works;
3. Luminous, bright.

My brother's name was Adam. It means "of the earth." I can't even explain the feeling.

We were in the library. We were supposed to be doing research for our project on Canadian identity, but of course my friends had no interest in doing what we were supposed to be doing, so they started looking up names instead. Adam. When the screen loaded, all I could see was *in the earth.*

Next they looked up Audrey, even though I told them I didn't care. *Noble strength.*

"Yeah, right." I rolled my eyes. "Let's spell it 'Oddrey.'" *We're sorry, there were no results for baby names starting with ODDREY.*

My friends laughed, like I knew they would. I looked back at my screen. *Luminous, bright.* Perhaps my light died with you, Adam.

Oh well, I can still remain highly distinguished, renowned, famous, and glorious.

✦ ✳ ✦

That probably makes me sound mean. Sometimes it feels like girls in grade nine have two choices: be mean or be a loser. So I pretend to be mean, only sometimes I don't know if I'm pretending anymore.

After The Accident, my parents suggested I see a therapist. I told them *No F-ing way.* Audrey sees a therapist. So they talked to my teachers and it was "mutually agreed upon" that I would visit the guidance counselor once a week starting in September. You know, so I don't get behind on my studies. It was a valid concern considering I had no motivation to do anything, let alone schoolwork, but I'm not going to give them that.

It's now May, so for the last eight months I've spent an hour a week with a bearded man who insists I call him by his first name, Kyle, and who tries to act like he's one of us even though he was a teenager in the eighties. His "office" is located right beside the front door and used to be the front-hall closet. That's just my theory, but I bet I'm right — there's no window and I think he has to crawl over the desk to get behind it. Sometimes I wish the fire alarm would go off just so I could solve that mystery. The extra-shitty thing about this already-shitty situation is that in order to not disrupt my core courses, they schedule my appointment during my option, which also happens to be my favorite class and the one in which I have the highest grade: graphic design and media.

And I never end up talking about Adam. I always talk about Audrey.

It's been three days since I found out Audrey might be returning to my school. Every afternoon, I've hung out as long as possible with my friends before going home and heading straight up to my room. When

Mom calls me for dinner, I lie and say I already ate or that I'm not feeling well. It worked for the first two days, but now they've caught on.

"Come down anyway and spend some time with us," Dad says.

So I do, but I don't say anything. I hold a hot mug of tea in my hand and stare at the liquid's surface. I act mean.

"It's not Audrey's fault," they tell me in private. I never would have gotten away with this behavior before. They have to be careful what they say around her now. She's struggling the most with Adam's death. She's trying, and I need to be more supportive and try too. She's my sister.

After three days, however, they've had enough.

"For God's sake, Clare! What's wrong with you?" Mom's face is red and she's gripping her utensils like that's all that's stopping her from throwing them at me. "I hope this isn't the person you're going to grow up to be."

I sneak a glance at Audrey. Mom's mini-me — that's what everyone calls her, because it's freaky how much they look alike. She's eating her lasagna slowly. She doesn't show any sign of understanding, but I know her better than anyone.

It's hard to believe, but when we were little, Audrey and I used to be inseparable. We used to *want* to be inseparable. We were each other's first friends, and the other kids were jealous we always had someone to play with. Audrey was always the imaginative one, the free-spirited air sign as opposed to the grounded earth sign, the twin who was coming up with new games and was willing to do things that were exciting, even dangerous, like attach three Slip 'N Slides together down the large hill in the park. The other kids in the neighborhood loved Audrey and were always knocking on the door asking if she could come out — they didn't give a care if I was around or not. But then those kids and I grew up, and Audrey just . . . didn't.

Take sexual education class, grade seven. Billy is sitting in the back row. He's the most popular guy in our year because he's cute and not afraid of anyone, so everyone's afraid of him. Even the teachers are afraid of him. Last week he threw Craig's binders out the fourth-floor window and Ms. Johnson just kept on marking papers like she didn't even notice.

Mr. Bailey: A girl's first period usually occurs at about age twelve, but some girls experience their first period much earlier.

Billy: I don't trust anything that bleeds for five days and doesn't die.

The guys laugh. Mr. Bailey titters nervously.

Me (in my head): An ancient *South Park* reference. I hate *South Park*.

Audrey (out loud): Clare's had her period, but I'm still waiting.

Even now, the memory still makes me cringe. Not just because it was completely embarrassing, but because after Audrey said that everyone started laughing and calling her weird, and as her face turned red and her eyes filled with tears, I felt trapped between my own humiliation and a feeling of helplessness to protect my sister, even though she'd put me in the position in the first place.

It's not my problem. It doesn't have to be my problem. But even as I tell myself that, I feel the guilt rise up, and I have to shove it back down. My family assumes I'm embarrassed of Audrey the way older siblings are embarrassed of a clingy baby sister. They have no idea what it's actually like for me, and they don't care enough to try to find out.

Mom's still giving me stabby eyes.

"I don't know what you expect from me," I tell her. "I'm down here spending time with you. Isn't that what you wanted?"

Dad sighs loudly.

Mom just shakes her head in apparent disappointment and goes back to her lasagna. Her dark hair is up in a messy bun and she's not wearing any makeup, but she doesn't have to. She's gorgeous with her long, dark lashes and bright blue stabby eyes. It doesn't even matter that she's wearing the most hideous wool sweater in the world — one she made herself — over a pair of faded leggings. She pulls the working-artist look off perfectly.

A few years ago, Mom started a store on Etsy making custom toys, and she's actually pretty popular. She runs her business out of the attic, which isn't technically legal. The floor used to alternate between rafter and drywall but six years ago Dad spent a weekend lining up boards on top of the rafters and nailing them down. It's probably not legit and it definitely didn't look like it, so they bought a few area rugs to cover it up. Every morning at seven a.m. the ladder's down and blocking the entrance to the one bathroom we all share and I know she's working on a knitted blue elephant that doubles as a ball or something.

Dad works downtown as an accountant. It sounds like the most boring job in the world. I think he finds it boring too, which makes me wonder why he'd even bother to go into it in the first place. He works long hours and we can't go on vacation certain months of the year because it's "high season." What's really annoying is that he doesn't get extra time off during "low season." It's practically free labor, but if you tell him that, he'll give you a lecture about having a good work ethic and how much it pays off. Yet every year he's disappointed with his bonus. He has to go into work crazy early just so he can be home for dinner with us.

We've always lived in the same house. It's super skinny and tall, like an old man of a house, with a party-hat roof and a crooked fireplace. We live on a street full of houses like ours: old and outdated but in a good neighborhood that's close to downtown, so they're now worth millions of dollars. Developers buy two houses and knock them down to put up three infills, which are these long homes with no backyards to speak of, but they have the good neighborhood thing, so they go for double the millions. I kind of wish that would happen to our house: that I'll wake up one morning to see one of those big wrecking balls outside my window, and my parents will say, *We feel the same way as you, Clare. We can't live here anymore.*

The tea burns my throat on its way down.

Adam was seventeen. Two summers ago he decided he needed his own space from his parents and little sisters. He preferred to live in a creepy basement in a room with shower curtains for walls than upstairs with us. He said if he moved down there, Audrey and I could have our own rooms. He wanted a drum set. He wanted to impress his new girlfriend, Dahlia, who was gorgeous. He was saving up to buy a car and working at a warehouse late into the night and he didn't want to wake us up when he got home.

Of course, he didn't share all his reasons with Mom and Dad, but I knew them. There were times, usually playing Nintendo in the basement together, that he would show off about his girlfriend and I would listen to him, a lot of what he said going over my head, but too cool to let him know. Adam was my hero and I wanted to be exactly like him. In fact, I wished *he* could be my twin.

This is the first semester Audrey and I haven't been in school together. I want to keep it that way. I'm not going to let myself feel guilty about her anymore.

Not since she killed Adam.

✦ ✳ ✦

Even though it's Friday night, I tell my friends that I'm not in the mood to go out. Sharon tells me not to let Audrey coming back ruin my life. Sharon is my best friend and the only other person in the world who understands what I go through with Audrey. The only person who recognizes how guilty I feel about wanting to be my own person, separate from my twin, and who sees how hard on me my family can be. After The Accident, I moved in with Sharon's family for two days because it hurt too much to be home. Sharon did everything she could to make me feel better. She asked her mom to buy my favorite foods. She let us watch my favorite movies. The morning of Adam's funeral, she braided my hair and painted my nails so I'd look better than I felt.

Tonight I just want to be alone, but I need to feel close to Adam, so I hang out in the basement and play Nintendo until I can't see straight. Adam and I used to play all the Mario games together, old-school and new, and sometimes *Mortal Kombat*.

It's way past midnight when I drag myself off the couch and cross the basement toward the stairs. Something flickers in the corner of my eye and my head whips toward it. One of the dark curtains that makes up Adam's room is fluttering. The bottom edge lifts, almost as if beckoning me to enter.

"Adam?" I whisper.

No, it's just a breeze from the vent. *You're alone, Clare. It's okay.*

Shivering, I hurry out of the basement and to the second floor of the house, which is dead quiet. My parents like to watch renovation shows before bed, but they would have turned off the TV hours ago. There's no light under Audrey's door either. I brush my teeth, change into pajamas, and then climb under the covers.

But I can't sleep.

So I sneak back into the basement and stand outside the curtains again. I've been hanging out in the basement almost every night since Adam died, but I've never gone into his room. Not even when he was alive. It's always been Adam's private space, and I've never had the desire to see it until now.

Mom and Dad told me they haven't moved anything in his room. I know it's partly because they can't look at his things without crying and partly because they want to preserve him, like some kind of Museum of Adam. That's how I feel when I push aside the curtain and step inside: I'm a visitor, an outsider, hoping to understand my brother better.

I kind of expect it to feel like a hospital with the curtains, but instead it feels more like a tent. He's attached band posters to some of them too. It's a small space with only a bed, two nightstands, a dresser with bookshelves covered in books and trophies, and a small rack of clothes. The rack used to hold his suit, but he was buried in that.

My stomach rolls and I sit down on his bed.

For a while I just sit there, looking around. This is where Adam used to spend his time. Where he used to sleep. This room is all we have left of him.

On one of the shelves there's a framed photograph of Adam, Audrey, and me, taken about seven years ago, when Adam was in grade six and Audrey and I were in grade three. Every year on the first day of school, Mom took a picture of us at the front door. In the photograph Adam is standing in the middle with an arm around each of us. His sandy hair is long, and he's smiling with his mouth closed to hide his braces.

It's too painful to look at, so I tear my eyes away to where his phone is lying on his nightstand. The police found it in his pocket and gave it to us in a plastic bag, along with his wallet. It took my parents days to crack the code on his phone, but they were determined, as if it held some last piece of evidence, some small glimmer into his last moments on earth.

The code was 2021, for the two dates in May when Audrey and I were born.

They downloaded all his photos and saved them in a folder on the family computer to look at once they could handle it. Then they put the phone back in his room. For me to find.

I roll across the bed to grab it. Of course it's dead, so I have to plug it into the charging station on his desk and wait a few seconds before the apple icon flashes, followed by the home screen: a photo of Adam and Dahlia, both of them smiling, Adam's arm around Dahlia's shoulders. Yuck.

I never really liked Dahlia. She always talked down to us like we were little kids, and they spent most of their time in the basement, which kind of meant we weren't allowed down here. I blamed that on her. I hated hearing her voice when she called on the landline — which she only did when she was desperate. Usually they were having a fight or they hadn't talked in a mere hour because he was in the shower or something. She was annoying.

I open Adam's photos. At first glance most of them are of skateboarding. After dinner Adam and his friends would ride rails, aka the handrails of the elementary school. Our old principal hated skateboarders and put up signs all over the premises saying NO SKATEBOARDING. The first picture I open is of Cody skating the handrail at the front entrance. Next: Akish skating the rail directly above the sign, flashing a hang ten.

Watching Adam and his friends growing up, I was always kind of jealous of the boys. They had it so much easier than us. They yelled like maniacs on field-trip buses; they acted dumb on purpose; they got dirty on purpose. No one expected them to be anything but wild, dirty idiots. *Boys will be boys,* the teachers said. It seemed so free. I'd get on my bike and ride past the school, catching glimpses of Adam flying off the rail and landing perfectly before coasting to a stop. His friends would cheer, holding up their phones to film it.

I pick and choose pictures to open, skipping over the repetitive skateboarding ones. Drunken group shot in a field, looks to have been taken in the spring. Cody riding a large blow-up zebra in a pool and howling, a beer held high above his head. Dark photos taken at night: groups of guys and girls with their arms around each other looking half-cut, Adam kissing Dahlia's cheek while she holds up his phone to snap a picture. It's a good thing the 'rents haven't seen these.

Next I scroll through the album of videos: Adam skating rails, his buddies skating rails, stupid Dahlia roller-skating down the street, Adam and stupid Dahlia cheering at a concert . . . Until I see one of just Dahlia. It looks like she's wearing one of his collared work shirts and that's all.

I hit play.

The video was taken in this room. I recognize his bookshelf in the background, against the curtains. Dahlia is standing on top of Adam on the bed. He must be lying on his back against his pillows, because from this angle, her bare legs stretch sky-high. As I watch, she begins to unbutton her shirt. My breath catches and then I'm holding it, waiting. She's moving slowly, teasing him, and my heart begins to pound, and I can feel sweat gathering under my armpits and a strange tingle at the back of my neck. I know what's going to happen next. I know I should turn the video off, that it's wrong to keep watching, but I don't/do.

Adam laughs low and tells her she's sexy. Her eyes narrow on him seductively, her tongue tracing the top of her lip . . .

I watch the entire thing. She undresses until she's only wearing a pair of black panties. She's thin with large boobs.

Adam starts breathing faster.

"Do you like what you see?" Dahlia asks, swaying on the spot.

His arm whips out and grabs her. There's a squeal as the phone bounces on the bed before the video freezes on the play button.

I hit it again.

This time I lie back on the bed against the pillows and hold the phone up, the way Adam must have done. I don't want to watch as Adam's little sister this time. I want to watch like Adam.

I pretend I'm Adam and my girlfriend's stripping for me. I hold the phone up and imagine she is right in front of me, dancing and stripping, and that at the end of the video I'll reach out and grab her and pull her to me.

They've taken a lot of videos and I find them all. I make a new folder called *skateboard decks* and move them there so he'll never get caught.

In one she's completely naked with a bandanna around her eyes.

"You better not be filming this!" she giggles. "I'm going to check your phone later."

"You won't find a thing."

"You're a pervert."

"That's what you love about me."

Then the video ends, and I'm left sitting there with the phone in my hand, all alone in the dark.

Audrey

Clare doesn't want to be twins. (Not anymore.)

In grade six she told me, We weren't even supposed to be twins. Adam told me that Mom really wanted a girl so they did IVF.

What's IVF?

In vitro fertilization. They picked two female embryos and both of us implanted. We're petri-dish babies.

How do you grow babies in a petri dish?

Clare made her frustrated noise. Never mind. The point is, it wasn't natural. We're like GMO twins.

The next day at school she told her new best friend, Sharon.

It must make you feel better, Sharon said to Clare. It would make me feel better.

Why?

Sharon looked at me like she was surprised I'd asked. Because you're weird.

Clare said, What the hell, Sharon.

I said, What makes me weird?

The fact that you don't know you're weird.

That was very confusing. For the rest of the day I wondered why I was weird and not Sharon.

When Mom picked us up from school, Mrs. Crawford came running over. She was gasping like a fish out of water. Her white arms were spotted with red marks when she leaned them on the open window. I was sitting right beside Mom, and Clare was still talking to the girls at the front door. Her friend Charlotte was putting lipstick on over and over again.

I wondered what had happened to Lip Smackers. Those tasted good and you didn't have to worry about missing your lips the way Charlotte did.

Mrs. Crawford looked at me and asked, Can I talk in front of her?

Of course, Becca. Mom sounded annoyed.

Okay. But she lowered her voice anyway. Margaret, I didn't know you had — her voice lowered even more — IVF. But not for the regular reason.

Mom laughed but it sounded weird. Too high. She tucked her hair behind her ear and checked the rearview mirror even though she wasn't ready to back out yet. It's hot out, Becca. You should get back in your car.

I'm so sorry if I embarrassed you. I just kind of thought it was something you would have told us. We're in book club together.

I guess I just thought it was personal, Rebecca.

Oh, it is. And we would never tell anyone outside of book club. Don't worry about that.

Mrs. Crawford shifted like she might walk away, but then hung on to the open window instead. I guess I just don't understand why you thought having another boy would be such a bad thing.

I didn't think it was a bad thing. I just wanted to have a girl as well.

Isn't IVF for gender selection illegal?

Now Mom was mad. I could tell because she was holding the wheel with both hands. And her hands looked very white.

Not that it's any of your business, but I went to the States.

But what about God's will? Mrs. Crawford asked. Maybe Adam was supposed to have a brother. As a mother of four boys, I can tell you that there is nothing stronger than the brother bond. Mrs. Crawford looked straight at me. I can't help but wonder if these sorts of things happen when we mess with nature.

Then she was rushing away across the street again. The back of her dress was soaked.

What a nasty person. Mom said it so quietly I could barely hear. Then she looked at me out of the corner of her eye. What did you think of that? (When my parents want to know if I understand something, they ask what I think of it.)

Clare told everyone this morning that we weren't supposed to be twins, I said. Something about an unnatural dish.

Mom sighed and rotated to face me. It doesn't matter how you came to be. What matters is that you did. You're here. And I'm grateful every day.

The way she said it let me know she was saying the truth and it was something I should never forget.

Okay. So am I.

Good. She squeezed my knee and then rolled down the window. Put her head out.

Clare, get in the car! *Now!*

Clare waved to her friends and darted to the van. As she passed my window I gave her a wave too, but she didn't even look at me.

✦ ✳ ✦

Like every night after dinner, Clare goes to the basement. She always liked it down there. She and Adam. I used to go down sometimes to watch them play *Super Mario Brothers* and *Mortal Kombat*.

Now I hate it.

I stand at the top of the stairs. Debating. I can hear the Mario music and it makes me feel dizzy.

I'm holding the bannister Dad put in when Adam moved down there. It's just for show. Dad had this thing with a light that was supposed to turn on and beep when it found a stud. But he dragged it over the entire wall and nothing. And then I dragged it over the entire wall and nothing. So Dad screwed the bannister in and told me not to rely on it.

I count the steps as I go (just for fun because I already know the answer). There are twelve steps down to the basement. There are fourteen steps on the main staircase. I haven't counted the steps to the attic because I don't need to know.

We'll never go up to the attic in a blackout.

If a tornado is coming, we'll go to the basement.

If there's a blizzard, we'll stay on the main floor and burn wood in the fireplace. (This will never happen. Schools are never closed for snow days. People would rather crash their cars than miss work.)

I think it's good to be prepared. There's a flashlight plugged into an outlet in the kitchen. There are boxes of matches in the drawer beside the sink. No one's allowed to touch the crate of water bottles in the furnace room. *Get a drink from the sink, you princess!* I tell them. On a trip to Costco I made Mom buy a box of nonperishable food items to keep with the water.

Calgary's safe from natural disasters, Mom told me. We're inland so we'll never have a tsunami or hurricane, and the mountains protect us from tornadoes.

What about the ones that hit Priddis? And Tornado '87 from the song?

The ones in Priddis were small. We won't get an F5 like Edmonton because of the mountains.

It could still happen.

Mom let out a sigh. Yes, anything could happen.

✦ ✳ ✦

As I was saying, there are fourteen steps on the main staircase and only twelve here. Here the stairs are thin and steep and you have to wear socks because you can get a splinter. At the bottom the floor is cold uneven concrete. I step onto the path of rugs that lead to the couch. Take a deep breath.

Look up, Audrey. Be brave.

Clare doesn't notice me. Adam turns his head in my direction and gives me his best lopsided grin.

My heart pinballs against my ribs.

He's sitting with his hands behind his head and his legs stretched out onto the ottoman. Beside him Clare is completely absorbed in her game. In front of them is the large TV Adam bought. Mario is dodging fireballs on the screen.

Clare?

She jumps and looks at me, and a fireball hits Mario in the face. Burn. What the hell? she yells. What are you doing down here?

I came to see you.

Her face scrunches like a paper ball. You haven't come down here in months. The blue streak disappears as she turns to the wall. Look, she says, because that's how she always starts sentences with me now. (Look, what do you want? Look, I'm busy.) I kind of like this being my space now.

I don't know how to respond. I want to tell her to be happy I might come back to her school. I want to ask if she remembers when we used to be best friends. I want to tell her how much I miss being twins with her.

But I can't get the words out.

Clare rolls her eyes and picks up the remote. Aims it at the TV. Mario is resurrected again, floating down from heaven in a bubble.

Look, I'm in the middle of a game, so unless you have something to say, leave me alone.

Adam smiles and pats a spot on the couch beside him.

I turn and go back up the stairs.

Mom and Dad are in the living room. They each have a glass of wine and the fire's going so they want to be alone. I go upstairs to my room and close the door.

At first I was happy when Adam moved downstairs. I wanted my own room. In my own room I could do the things Clare made fun of me for doing. I'm too old to play with toys but I still do it sometimes. In secret. I take a bunch of toys that don't belong together and act out a scene.

Now I miss sharing a room. It meant Clare had to talk to me.

At my desk I turn on the lamp and open my sketchbook. I like all breeds of dogs. I didn't even want to buy an expensive breed because I've heard of puppy mills. I wanted a rescue dog. But Mom and Dad said no, so I started drawing the dog in the sky that belongs to everyone. Sirius the Dog Star is the fifth nearest star known to man.

The hardest part about drawing Sirius is that he needs a background or he'll disappear. His fur is white and fluffy like a teddy bear. I like to bury my face in it and pry apart his puppy finger pads. He's never scratched me. Not even once.

I tell Sirius the things I can't tell anyone else. He's my only friend now.

A tear hits the page and I wipe it away.

Sometimes I wonder if Clare would like me more if we were identical twins. It seems like such bad luck that we aren't. Clare and I weren't even born on the same date. We don't even share the same star sign. Only I was born under the twins. Clare was born under the bull.

Maybe there was a mistake in the hospital and my identical twin is with Clare's identical twin right now.

The first night Adam babysat, the three of us watched a documentary on the Dionne quintuplets. The Dionne quintuplets were the very first quintuplets known to have survived infancy. They lived in a nursery for only the five of them and wore identical dresses in five different colors. At night they slept together in a long room with five identical beds. The room was full of toys. People came and watched them play on the playground from behind a glass mirror. It was called Quintland. They became instant stars.

After that I thought people might be interested in us.

I asked Clare, Do you think people would pay to see us?

She blinked at me.

It was because they were identical quintuplets, Adam said. That's very rare.

I meant if we were identical twins. Do you think they would then?

Clare blinked at me again. She was doing it on purpose.

That was a long time ago, Adam said. Things have changed. There are laws against that kind of thing now.

Oh. I was kind of disappointed.

It's messed up, Adam continued. The Ontario government made them "wards of the king" and took them away from their family and put them on display like animals. They made money off them as a tourist attraction.

Still, I liked the idea of being famous. But maybe I already was. Maybe there was a hidden camera floating above my right shoulder. When Clare wasn't with me, I skipped to school sometimes. So it would be more entertaining to watch. I picked flowers and talked to them so the viewers could know what I was thinking.

One day I was bending over the garden talking to a flower and someone said, Are you talking to yourself?

I looked up and the sun was in my eyes, but I could tell it was a group of girls in my grade and the grade below me.

I'm not talking to myself. I'm talking to the flower.

They all started laughing.

That is so weird, Sharon said. You know flowers can't understand you, right?

I didn't want to explain I was pretending about the camera so I just walked away. But after that all the kids started calling me weird.

You don't want to be like everyone else, Mom said. It's a good thing to be yourself.

It was the first time she didn't tell me the truth.

ClaRe

After Audrey leaves, I pause the Nintendo and just kind of stare at the screen. Then I throw my controller onto the floor. I know I'm being a jerk, but I can't stop myself. Now when I see Audrey, I just fill with rage.

Not that I was a particularly good sister before. Adam used to tell me to be nicer to Audrey. One time she tried to join us when we were playing Mario Wii and when I told her we were busy trying to pass a level, Adam jumped in and stuck up for her like he always did. He told her she could play instead of him.

"That's okay," she said, and went back upstairs.

After the basement door closed behind her, Adam said to me, "You shouldn't act like that. She looks up to you."

I rolled my eyes. "You mean she looks up to *you*."

"No, I've seen it. She idolizes you. She wants to be like you."

My hand kind of faltered on the button and Mario plummeted to his death. It was like Adam was saying she *couldn't* be like me. Then Mario returned to the screen, floating in a bubble. Adam-as-Luigi jumped up and freed him. I started playing again.

"You don't understand," I said finally.

"You're embarrassed of her. I get it. Mom and Dad make you take care of her all the time, and your friends bug you about it."

I wanted to tell him that it wasn't that simple, that I wasn't just trying to be cool. Sure, it bugged me that whenever I went out, Mom said *take your sister* like she was a friggin' jacket, but that was the easy part. The hard part was that I cared about Audrey so much, it hurt. I flinched whenever she was called on in class because I was terrified of watching the other kids make fun of her. Audrey is my *twin*. I feel her pain like my own, and sometimes it's a lot to bear.

But I didn't know how to explain any of that, so instead I said, "It's not that simple. You all think of me as some popular girl. You don't get that I'm just trying to survive."

"We all feel like that, Clare," Adam responded. "But it's not worth hurting people you care about just to fit in."

"Stop judging me."

"I'm not judging you." He shoved a hand through his hair and glanced at me out of the corner of his eye. "I guess I'm just saying life is short. Don't look back and have regret."

"I'm not being mean to her," I muttered, hating the idea that Adam was looking down on me.

"You're not being nice, either. And one day you might actually miss her."

I purposefully jumped off a cliff and tossed the controller aside, ending that particular conversation. But Adam never stopped trying to make us get along. Behind me the curtains around his room flutter, and it feels like he's here with me again.

"Adam?" I whisper. "Can you hear me? If you can, give me a sign."

The curtains continue to flutter, fed by the vent, and I feel my heart sink because I'll never be able to talk to him again. I'll never be able to ask him.

Now that he's dead, does he finally understand how I feel?

✦ ✳ ✦

The next morning, I wake up to Mom banging on my door. It's the same routine every school day: my alarm goes off, I hit snooze after snooze until Mom eventually bangs on my door and yells at me through the wood that I'm going to be late. She doesn't understand I'm a normal teenager because Audrey wakes up at 7:00 a.m. sharp every single morning.

The first thing Mom says when I walk into the kitchen: "You're not wearing that to school."

I feel my entire body tense and grip the handle of my bag tighter. "What's that supposed to mean?"

"Let's start with the shorts."

"*Everyone* wears these shorts."

Mom leans back against the kitchen sink and crosses her arms. "Ripped shorts with the pockets hanging out? I doubt it."

I plaster on my fakest sweet smile. "Well, maybe when you drop me off at school, you can take a moment to look around a bit."

It's meant to be a jab. Mom has spent the entire semester focusing on everything Audrey — talking to Audrey's teachers and making sure Audrey's doing okay. She's always worried about Audrey "doing okay," as if she's afraid Audrey is somehow going to get worse. I don't even see how that's possible.

Mom mimics my fake-pleasant smile. "Well, things might be changing. Then I can keep an eye on both my girls again." She glances over at Audrey, who is wearing a sweater Mom knitted for her and baggy jeans and staring at the back of the cereal box. Her mouth is moving slowly, but no words are coming out. She's probably trying to read the French.

Mom looks back at me and frowns. "You're wearing too much eye makeup."

"Seriously?" All right, so when people say Audrey and I look nothing alike, it's because she's the pretty one. Like Mom, Audrey is super cute with her large blue eyes, long eyelashes, and thick dark curls. I'm gangly with thin blond hair to match, and small brown eyes you can barely see without liner.

But that's not why I'm wearing it. I'm wearing it because it's my war mask.

"Yeah." Another glance at Audrey. "You should dress more age-appropriate."

Now it's taking all my energy not to flip out. Audrey *can't even wear buttons.* The mere thought that the buttons on her coat might not be spaced exactly the same distance apart triggers a panic attack, so Mom can only buy her coats with zippers.

When Audrey gets up and leaves the kitchen, I let out an exasperated breath, letting my eyes roll back in my head. "Are you actually telling me that I have to change so I fit in with *Audrey*?"

"This has nothing to do with Audrey."

That was a lie. Everything has to do with Audrey.

"She probably won't wear makeup until . . . well, ever."

The moment I say it, I realize how ridiculous I sound. I was implying that she's immature, but really she'll never wear it because she doesn't need it.

"Aaaaghhhhh!" I scream and stomp out of the kitchen.

Upstairs in my room I open up drawers and yank clothes out, drop them on the floor. I'm trying to make a mess for Mom, but if she calls me out I'll say I was stressed finding a new outfit. I toss the shorts into the corner, then pull on the jeans version of my shorts but with even bigger holes. Ha!

The joke's on Mom. The joke's on everyone. Because that girl downstairs, the one who yelled about wanting to be like every teenage girl . . . she doesn't really exist. She's a role in the movie of my life. I've gotten pretty good at playing her too. But if that version still isn't good enough for Mom, I might as well show her the real me.

So I change into the clothes I actually want to wear rather than the ones I wear to look like every other girl. I peel off my sheer, sparkly black shirt and replace it with a black zip-up sweatshirt over my tank. Mom hates this sweatshirt. She hated it when Adam wore it, said it made him look like a lowlife. It has a skeleton tree on the back. He gave it to me years ago, after he grew out of it. I wipe the majority of the eyeliner off but slip the pencil in my pocket.

My hands are shaking and I have to ball them into fists as I go back downstairs. I'm so angry. I've felt angry for so long, I can't even remember what it feels like to not feel angry. To not want to break the world around me, rip the sky into pieces and toss them back again. Kyle thinks everything I feel is completely normal. He claims anger is one of the stages of grief and that's why I'm "laying unwarranted blame on Audrey." Whatever, dude.

When I enter the kitchen again, Audrey is climbing into the car. Mom pauses halfway out the door, and her eyes widen when she sees me. I grab an apple from the bowl on the counter and take a bite, my eyes locked on hers as I silently dare her to say something about this outfit. If she does, I'll throw back that nothing will make her happy.

Instead she turns away and says, "Your lunch is on the counter."

Audrey's in the front seat and I'm in the back. It's always like that with the three of us now. When we were little, we used to fight over who had shotgun. Now we climb into our usual seats and no one suggests we do anything different. Mom is probably relieved she doesn't have to talk to me. I don't know if the two of them talk either, because I put in my earphones and stare out the window the entire drive.

I suppose I have to get to how it happened. It's not enough to say Adam died, even though that's all I've been able to tell anyone who asks. If they push, I might be able to add *car accident*.

A few months before Adam died, the 'rents decided to send Audrey to a shrink. She was always in her head and disrupting class. She wasn't growing out of the behavior like they'd hoped. Dr. Jackson tossed around a bunch of theories, including attention deficit hyperactivity disorder and autism spectrum disorder, before deciding he needed to spend more time with Audrey in order to settle on a diagnosis.

Then one day he suggested she try more extracurricular activities. She wasn't any good at sports, and T-Rex was a better ballerina. She wanted to try karate. So Mom bought her a karate gi and a white belt, and they dropped her off at her first class and went out for dinner. About fifteen minutes into the class, the house phone rang. It was Audrey. The collar of her gi was rubbing the back of her neck. She wanted to come home.

Adam didn't want to interrupt Mom and Dad's date night, so he said he'd pick her up. I told him not to and make Audrey deal, but he wouldn't listen to me. He said he had his new car and was happy for an excuse to drive.

He never made it there.

+ ✻ +

The first thing I do when I get to school is go to the bathroom and apply the eyeliner again. Charlotte and Rhiannon stay outside to have a smoke in the courtyard, but Sharon follows me. She leans a hip against the sink beside me, arms crossed over a bra stuffed with gel packs.

"What's up with your outfit today?" she asks. "Ripped jeans and a sketchy sweatshirt? Really?"

"It was my brother's."

"You look emo."

I laugh darkly and apply the liner to the other eye. "Good."

"That's not a compliment."

I ignore her and step back to study myself. I look badass. Tough. The dark, smoky eyes are in stark contrast to my blond hair with the thick blue streak. All I need is a bunch of piercings and black lipstick, and then Sharon really will have something to complain about.

"I mean it," Sharon says as we leave the bathroom, "you're going too far into this 'I'm depressed and want the whole world to know it' emo act. It's making the rest of us depressed."

Am I really hearing what she's saying correctly? Because it sounds like she's saying my mourning phase is bumming her out.

"Seriously," she continues, "it's been, like, three months."

I stop in the middle of the hallway. Directly in front of me is the fire hose wrapped up in its protective glass case. I imagine breaking the glass and wrapping the hose around Sharon's neck over and over and over again . . .

Instead I turn to face her. "You know *ten* months isn't a long time, right? Like in the span of our lives, not just stupid high school?"

She glances around, obviously afraid all the people walking past us in the hall are going to overhear. "I'm not saying you should be over it or anything. But there's a way to handle stuff like this."

"Is there?" I hear my voice rising. "And you would know, right? Because you've been through it before."

Sharon's cheeks turn pink, but she's not embarrassed. At least not about being a complete ignorant asshat. About the students who are definitely starting to look? Maybe.

"I get it sucks that Audrey might be coming back, and I totally feel for you because that girl is messed, but I'm trying to give you advice. As your friend. The other girls think you're changing." The threat is there behind her words: *Soon you might not fit in with us.*

Too bad I already don't.

+ ✳ +

It's Taylor's turn to present.

The name is called and there is an audible inhale, like the class is sucking in one breath. Fluid as a dancer, Taylor stands and moves to the front of the classroom, wearing ripped jeans, a clunky metal wallet chain, a backwards baseball cap, and an open black leather jacket over a white T-shirt with a golden lion's snarling face. There's something about the way Taylor moves that makes you take notice, but it's the haircut that fascinates me the most: long on top, short on one side and shaved on the other. It's tough and daring and everything I wish I had the guts to do.

A few desks over, Billy lounges back in his seat, slips a pen between his teeth. He's grinning, there's a twinkle in his eye, and I feel my forehead break into a sweat.

Biology on Tuesday and Thursday is the only class I have with Taylor, but I'm well aware of the rumors. According to Sharon, the Matthews family moved here from the UK at Christmas and Taylor is an only child. But that's not the crazy part. The crazy part is that no one seems to know if Taylor is a boy or a girl. No one. Supposedly Taylor has been known to use both bathrooms and is pushing the principal to add a gender-neutral bathroom. When the teachers talk about Taylor in class, they use the pronouns *they* and *their,* which always makes the students snicker and some of the teachers turn red.

Another glance at Billy confirms he's grinning mockingly. Waiting.

My fingers knot together under the desk as my breathing becomes shallow. It's a weird feeling, almost like I'm worried *for* Taylor. The very same clenching of the gut I get when Audrey is about to do something weird. But why do I care? Taylor has nothing to do with me.

34

When they begin to speak, the room immediately quiets. That accent. It makes the back of my neck tingle, and the tingle travels all the way down my spine. Halfway through the presentation, I realize that I have no idea what the topic is — something to do with plants? — because I've been so focused on the sound of their voice.

Then Billy coughs. It's a simple clearing of the throat but enough to make Taylor pause and glance up. Billy's still smiling his usual mischievous smile, the one he busts out when he's about to make fun of someone, but as I watch, he pulls the pen from his lips, runs it along his tongue seductively. Then his eyes close and he starts pumping it in and out of his mouth.

I sputter-cough, masking my shock. My heart's thumping and it's like my eyes are glued to Billy and the way he's making out with the pen. The hairs on the back of my neck prickle and my arms break out in goosebumps. *Billy's tongue, Taylor's tongue.* The thought pops into my head and it won't go away and I feel the heat crawling up my chest and into my face. I pray no one looks at me.

Beside Billy, Jason covers his mouth with his fist. His shoulders are shaking with smothered laughter. Billy flips the pen, starts from the other side, his eyes still locked on Taylor.

The room suddenly goes strangely silent, and I follow Billy's gaze to see that Taylor has stopped speaking and is smirking instead. The expression is unfazed — daring, even. It says they aren't going to be intimidated.

"Taylor?" A voice breaks through the fog. "Are you finished?"

Ms. Dunphy is standing at the back of the classroom. I don't turn around to look at her. I can't.

Out of the corner of my eye, Billy taps the desk with the pen. Once. Twice.

"No," Taylor says in that sexy British accent. "I'm not even close."

Then their gaze shifts to land on me, and I smile in what I hope is a reassuring way. As they start speaking again and our eyes lock across the room, I feel a strange sensation, like our bodies are linked as well. Like when my breathing slows, their breathing slows. It doesn't matter what is happening in the rest of the room. Taylor's words vibrate down through their body, through the floor and up my legs.

When the presentation ends and Taylor breaks eye contact, I feel cold. Instead of walking down Billy's row, Taylor walks down mine. I quickly look down at my desk and hold my breath, but I still feel them pass, still smell the leather mixed with — what? My face is burning. I just focus on my desk, willing my breathing to slow. Emotions tumble through me: relief, excitement, fear.

Someone else's name is being called — Stan — and now a gust of Axe body spray hits me instead. My heart is still slowing, my fingers are sore from gripping the desk so tightly, and all I want is to escape from the room. I should ask for a bathroom pass but I'm too afraid to stand.

My legs are shaking.

+ ✳ +

At lunch I walk with Sharon & Co. to the park a block from school and sit on the baseball bleachers. Sharon and I sit on the top row because we're "best friends," and Charlotte and Rhiannon sit on the row below us. Sharon claims this is so we can all see one another better.

It's one of those perfect May days that feel like summer, even though we're not immune to a freak snowstorm — you never know what to expect with Calgary. Some winters we have a white Christmas, and others we have a chinook — a warm wind that blows down the Rocky Mountains and into the prairies — and all the skating rinks melt.

We take off our sweaters and lean back in the bleachers like we might actually get a tan.

"Who's going to the year-end dance?" Sharon asks.

I don't say anything. I'm still annoyed at Sharon for her earlier comments. I'm also not interested in a stupid dance.

"I'm going with Jacob!" Rhiannon announces, and bounces on the bench. "He asked me this morning."

Charlotte kind of deflates. "I'm going with Sam. But I, uh, kind of asked him."

"Burn," Rhiannon says.

"Shut up, Rhi. Everyone knows guys are scared to ask the hot girls. I'm going with Jeff." Sharon turns to me. "What about you, Clare? Hoping for Billy to ask you?"

As soon as she says Billy, I think of the way he sucked on the pen in front of Taylor. Then I'm thinking about the way he kissed me at the dance last year. It was the sloppiest, most disgusting experience of my life — like kissing someone whose tongue had been frozen at the dentist. I think I vomited in my mouth.

"I don't want to go," I tell her.

She rolls her eyes at Charlotte and Rhiannon in a way that implies they saw this coming. Like I'm determined to just stay at home and be sad. But it only lasts a second before she switches the conversation back to herself, biting her bottom lip the way she does when she has juicy gossip. "I'm gonna go all the way with Jeff."

Charlotte's mouth falls open at the same time Rhiannon says, *"What?"*

I'm just as shocked as them. It's no secret her and Jeff have done more than kissing, but is she ready to have sex with him? They only started dating last week.

"Yeah. We're fifteen now" — Sharon pauses to look at me — "well, most of us are. We're not kids anymore. Back in the day women had children at our age."

"That's gross," Charlotte says.

Sharon shrugs. "Our bodies are ready. I feel ready. Jeff is the guy."

I have trouble imagining Jeff as the guy. He still looks like a boy to me. He wears pants that are two sizes too big for him and always has an unlit smoke between his lips. Has anyone ever actually seen him light the smoke? Anyone?

"Only you know when you're ready," Rhiannon says wisely. "Let us know how it is." Then she follows it up with one of her hyena giggles.

I bite the straw of my juice box hard. "Hey, have any of you talked to Taylor?" I try to ask it casually, but from the way Sharon's eyes narrow, I know I've done a poor job.

"Why are you asking about that weirdo?"

I shrug. "I guess because of what Billy did in bio."

Sharon throws her head back in laughter. "Oh my God, I can't believe I almost forgot about that." She turns to Rhiannon and Charlotte. "Billy was, like, deep-throating a pen while Taylor was giving a presentation."

Charlotte busts out a laugh. "Oh my God, I wish I'd seen that."

I laugh too and then instantly feel bad about it. Why? What's going on with me?

Sharon isn't smiling anymore. In fact, she looks like she can read my mind.

"Don't tell me you actually feel bad for that freak. What does *it* expect?"

I stand up, squishing the sandwich my mom made through its plastic bag. "I'll see you later." I toss the bag into the garbage at the bottom of the bleachers, miss, and walk away anyway. I can't get away from them fast enough.

"Where are you going?" Sharon yells behind me, but I ignore her. I put the sweatshirt back on, pull the hood up over my head, and shove my hands into the front pockets. I don't know where I'm going. I just know I want to be away from those girls.

Halfway across the park I realize there's nowhere to go but back to school. I don't have a car. The only friends I have with cars are talking about losing their virginity to guys — an idea that makes my skin itch. I know it's going to have to happen at some point in my life, but the last thing I want to think about is some heavy, sweaty guy on top of me.

I enter through the side entrance to the school and am bombarded with noise and people: students slamming lockers, yelling at their friends, walking side by side so they block the entire hallway, hanging off door frames. There's a staircase to my right that leads to the wrestling pit, and I duck down it. At the bottom, the door to the pit is locked, but extra wrestling mats are stacked in a pile in a corner. Perfect. I lie down on them, put my feet against the wall, and close my eyes.

There's a pleasant weight on my lower abdomen. My skin tingles as my hand moves to the right pocket of my sweatshirt to pull out Adam's phone. I shouldn't have it, I should have left it in his room, but I like having it with me. I know it's obsessive — *odd,* even — but I can't help it.

I click off the volume, scroll to the first video, and push play. Dahlia is on top of me again. She's swaying and speaking, and even though I can't hear the words, I know them all by heart.

Audrey

Like every morning, we drop Clare off at school first. She's not wearing her usual clothes today. She's wearing Adam's sweatshirt, the black one with the tree made of bones. She's only a few feet up the path when Sharon and the others swarm her.

Clare in her new life without me.

My stomach tightens. Like every morning.

We drive past the diner on the way to Peak. Mom always keeps her eyes on the road and talks to me or hums when we pass it. After Adam died, she asked if we could drive a different route. She didn't wait for my answer and just turned onto a different street. Just like that. I had a panic attack and we had to drive home and then back again with the proper route.

I'm sorry, she told me. The diner reminds me of Adam.

We have to go that way. It's important.

Mom nodded and we didn't talk about it anymore.

Today I wait until the diner is the size of a toy in the rearview mirror. Then I ask Mom for her and Dad's decision.

You've had nine days to think about it, I tell her. (Eight hours

40

and thirty-five minutes short of nine days, but hopefully they're not counting.)

Not yet, sweetie, she says. It's a big decision. She runs teeth along her bottom lip. We need to consult Dr. Jackson, and you just saw him the night before you asked to switch schools.

Why?

Why what?

Why do we have to consult Dr. Jackson? This should be a family decision.

It's not that simple. Sometimes parents need advice. Despite what kids think, we don't have all the answers.

We're silent for a while. I count seven dogs during this silence. That is very good luck because seven is a good-luck number. They are the following breeds:

1. *Wiener dog* (these always make me smile)
2. *Labradoodle* (Labrador and Poodle baby)
3. *Schnauzer* (or maybe a Scottie?)
4. *Greyhound* (like on the buses)
5. *Shiba Inu* (like Menswear Dog on the internet)
6. *Miniature poodle* (mini clouds glued together)
7. *A breed I can't remember but it has a very big head*

Dr. Jackson will say no, I tell Mom. A neon sign with the single word flashes behind my eyes.

NO. N-O.

Mom looks at me. For a long time. It's kind of scary because she's not looking at the road. Not necessarily, she says.

I can tell she isn't saying the truth.

And it makes me mad.

You're lying! You're lying to me right now! My eyes flood with tears until the road in front of us blurs. I feel my chest tightening and expanding until I can hardly breathe. I can't breathe at all now. The air in the car is too close, too tight. The car no longer has any oxygen! It's full of carbon dioxide! Help! Help! I grab at the door to open the window.

Shh, sweetie. Calm down. Mom pulls over to the side of the road and turns on the hazards. She reaches across me to open the glove box, pulls out one of the brown paper bags.

Deep breaths, Audrey. Deep breaths.

I hold it to my mouth and breathe in, breathe out. A long time passes.

I take the bag from my mouth. Mom is sitting with her hands in her lap and staring straight forward. There are tears in her eyes.

I'm sorry, she says without looking at me.

I'm still upset but I tell her I'm okay so she'll start driving again. She doesn't say another word about Dr. Jackson.

Nous sommes arrivées. Mom comes to a stop the closest she can get, which isn't very close. Cars and vans idle while parents and nurses help kids from cars. That was my first hint that everything was going to be different. But on my first day, I missed it. At that point I was just scared about not going to school with Clare. We'd gone to school together our whole lives. We'd always been in the same class, too.

Now it's like going to school without the other half of my body.

Mom?

Yes?

I look down at my sweater. Pick at a loose thread. I wish I hadn't spoken because now she's waiting. I can't ask why Clare doesn't want me around. I already know the answer.

Sometimes I wish I could be Clare, I say.

Mom sighs and rubs my back. Oh, sweetie. You're turning fifteen. It's a tough age, but it's also very special. You're straddling childhood and adulthood. The only difference between you and Clare is that she's already made the leap.

Is that it? Is that what's wrong with me? I wonder. Maybe in a few years I'll feel like I want to grow up. Then everything will change.

Mom gives me a kiss on the head. Time to get out.

✦ ✳ ✦

After Adam died it was decided. New school for a new semester. I would attend Peak. (The name is meant to inspire our highest potential. But no one reaches their highest potential at Peak.)

Sharon told me people call it Freak. She said, Oh my God, you're going to *Freak*? Well, I can't say I'm surprised.

I made the mistake of asking what she meant.

Basically everyone calls it that because only *freaks* go there.

That's not true, I told her. It's a school for gifted students too. Not everyone learns the same way, you know.

She laughed. Yeah, right. That's just what parents tell their kids so they don't feel bad about themselves.

Mom and Dad didn't want to send me to Peak. Not at first. At first they just took me to see Dr. Jackson because Ms. Pearl said I needed an assessment. Ms. Pearl was my grade eight science teacher. She looked like a pinhead with eyes like a fish.

And she hated me.

She hated when I talked to friends in class. She called me loud. She called me obnoxious. She yelled at me in front of everyone when I came back late from lunch. I always stopped to pet the neighbor's dog. When I drew in class, she ripped the pages out of my notebook.

I was afraid to go to school. I always made a mistake.

Mom asked Clare to stop going to friends' houses at lunch and come home with me instead. She wanted Clare to walk me back to school so I made it on time.

Clare yelled, She's ruining my life!

One day Ms. Pearl called home and gave my parents the bad news. There was something wrong with me.

Mom was on the landline in the kitchen and I snuck upstairs to listen in.

Ms. Pearl said, I've done everything I can but it's just no use.

What's that supposed to mean? Mom asked.

I think you should take her to a children's psychologist.

Are you saying there's something wrong with her?

You need a professional opinion.

Mom was pretty upset after that conversation. I remember she cried.

I suspect she has ADHD, Dr. Jackson said. Then he gave me a million tests and asked me a zillion questions and told me to play while he watched. Afterward he determined I didn't pass but I didn't fail.

Only that didn't matter in the end.

Fit is important, Dad told me after Adam's accident. You'll be happier in a new school.

I knew what he meant. I'd finally failed the test.

+ ✳ +

The other students are at their desks when I enter the classroom. Marianne is making the rounds greeting everyone with her usual smile. Monsieur Martin is at the back of the room doing his paperwork. I go to the back and stand over his desk. Clear my throat. He doesn't look up.

Bonjour, Monsieur Martin.

Bonjour.

I'm thinking of switching back to public school.

Is that so? He still doesn't look up.

My parents and sister know but I'll need your cooperation.

Now I have his attention. He puts down his pen and looks up at me. My cooperation?

Yes. I know you like having me here about as much as I like being here.

He rubs his nose with finger and thumb. The gesture makes him look old. He's one of the youngest teachers I've ever had.

Which isn't very much, I take it?

I don't answer because it feels like a trap.

Audrey. He says my name like the effort of vocalizing it makes him very, very tired. I don't dislike having you here. It *disappoints me* that you push back against the very people who are trying to help you. It disappoints me further that you continue to treat this school and everything it stands for with derision. It is one thing for outsiders to treat our students with a lack of respect, but it's quite another coming from you.

At the end of his speech he gives me a hard look.

I'm sorry, I say. I just want to return to school with my twin.

He studies me for a long time. I fidget with my hands, wondering if I should apologize for calling the school Freak. But does he know about that? I can't be certain.

Eventually he sighs. How do you require my cooperation?

Well, I assume my parents will ask for your opinion on the matter, I say, trying to sound as professional as possible. I would like you to tell them I am ready to return to the regular school system. *S'il vous plaît.*

I'd considered saying the entire thing in French because I knew it would impress him more, but the risk of losing my message was too large.

You feel you're ready? Audrey, I called home just days ago. I found you outside on the playground in the middle of class. Then I found you drawing said playground instead of listening to the lesson.

Those are very good points and I apologize.

How can I possibly recommend that you're ready when you haven't mastered the basic rules of the classroom? That is pillar number one.

I knew he'd say that, so I have my reply ready.

I'm going to be the perfect student from now on and show you I can follow the rules. Then we can both be free of each other forever.

I don't know why you would say something like that, Audrey. I don't dislike having you here.

But think about how much easier your life will be! I make my voice sound upbeat and excited like he won a prize. Then I return to my desk so he can't accuse me of being late.

At lunchtime I decide to do something *mature* (the meaning is the same in French as it is in English). I decide to leave the school grounds during my lunch hour like I've seen other kids at Peak do.

I always eat my lunch under the tree in the southeast corner of the schoolyard. My forehead begins to sweat as I pass the tree. My hands start to shake as I go through the gate. On the main street the cars that pass are very loud. I count two red, one black, four silver. Then I cut off the main street and arrive at a park. There's a homeless man asleep on a bench. I take a deep breath and run past him. To be safe. When I look back he's still asleep.

I'm walking along the path that cuts through the park when I see the yellow string. It's a few feet ahead of me. No, not string. Tape with CAUTION written across it in bold letters. It's attached to a black block. I squat and peer at it. On its surface is a wire contraption like a mousetrap.

What is that? I wonder out loud.

Gopher trap, says a voice behind me.

I jump to my feet and turn around. The voice came from a guy about my age holding a long wooden stick tied to a smaller stick. It looks like a cross. He has blond hair that sticks up all over the place and is wearing a T-shirt, long shorts, and flip-flops.

What does a gopher look like? My voice sounds small. I'm afraid of sounding ignorant.

But he just smiles. Like squirrels but cuter. People say they're a pest because they leave holes everywhere.

Panic seizes me. We can't let them kill them! These holes are their homes.

I look at his stick. Let's stop them.

He looks at it too. Shrugs and passes it to me.

I approach the first box slowly. *Timidement.* I hook the stick under the wire and close my eyes. Take a deep breath. Then I flick the stick up.

The block unearths itself to reveal legs and a tail.

I scream and drop the stick. Now I understand how it works. The trap sits on top of the hole. It gets them when they're trying to exit. When they want to see the sun or go out and run.

I imagine myself as a gopher. Leaving my family in the den to travel the tunnels and risk going outside for food. I swear this is the way out. Why is it so dark?

Hey now, the boy says and takes a step closer to me. It's okay. There might be others we can save. Look at that one. The trap hasn't snapped yet.

He gently takes the stick from me and lifts the trap away. See? When the wire is down, the trap is empty.

There's still time.

We run around the park removing the traps. There is only one other gopher that we don't save in time.

We should say a few words, the boy says. It's only right.

Goodbye, Mr. Gopher, I say. I hope you're in heaven with your gopher friends.

Build tunnels in the clouds, Mr. Gopher.

I smile at the boy and he smiles back. Indents appear at the sides of his mouth. Dimples. His eyes are a soft brown like puppy fur.

You're kind of cool, he says.

Really?

I think the gophers would tell you that you're the coolest person in the world for saving their lives.

I laugh. You saved them too.

That's true. In that case, I guess I'm kind of cool too.

He grins at me and then something really weird happens. My cheeks get kind of hot. And then it feels like I can't control my face. I turn around so he can't see and put my fingers to my lips. I'm smiling super large. My lips are stretched out and I can't stop.

I pretend I turned around to walk back to the playground. The boy follows. I can control my face again by the time we get to the swings.

What's your name? he asks. He swings slowly from side to side rather than forward and bumps into me softly.

Audrey.

I'm Calvin.

I like the name Calvin, I tell him. I swallow and look at my shoes. I don't just like his name. I like him. I don't remember the last time I felt like this. It must have been in elementary when I still had friends.

Why aren't you in school? I ask him.

I don't go to school. I'm homeschooled. I live right there. He points at a little white house across from the park.

He asks if I go to Clare's school and I don't respond, but I'm on an upswing and he takes it as a nod. I don't correct him. I don't want him to think I'm a freak like the other kids do.

Calvin begins to pump. So, Audrey, what do you like to do when you're not protecting the little guy?

I don't know how to answer the question. I know normal fourteen-year-olds don't play scenes.

I like to draw.

What do you draw?

I wish I could lie and tell him I draw a lot of stuff. I like to draw me and my dog.

Oh, you have a dog? I wish I had a dog.

I wish I had a dog too. That's the truth. Calvin frowns and I can tell he's confused.

Why are you carrying a cross? I ask quickly.

Oh, this? It's actually a sword. Ever heard of LARPing? I shake my head and he says, Live-Action Role Playing. I'm hoping to participate in a LARPing event soon. I've been practicing with my friend Frank.

Practicing what exactly?

Sword fighting. Basically it's a game where players act out their characters and have battles and stuff. I've seen them dressed like sword fighters from medieval times and practicing in the park. There's a lot of grunting.

So LARPing is kind of like playing make-believe?

Totally. It's like when grownups started telling us we were too old to play pretend, LARPers asked why. Calvin grins and tilts his head to the side. Are you scared now? Are you wishing you were anywhere but here?

I'm not. I'm realizing Calvin might be like me. I want to tell him that I play scenes but the words don't come out.

The other players are a bit older than me, probably in their twenties,

Calvin says. They have swords and full costumes that probably cost them a lot. I don't have anything so I have to practice with this stupid stick. My mom doesn't let me bring "weapons" into the house, though, so I have to hide it under the pine tree in front of our house.

The front door of the house opens and a large woman comes out. She cups her mouth and yells, CALVIN!

Calvin's face turns a bright red and he jumps off the swing, stands so that's he's blocking the view of his mom.

I've gotta go, he says. But can I have your number?

My what?

Your phone number. His face turns even redder. He pulls a cellphone out of his pocket. What's your phone number?

I give him both numbers.

But I never use my cell, I tell him, and quickly look down so he can't see that I've turned red too.

I'll call you, he says. Then he runs away across the park.

My face is still hot when I arrive back at the path with the uprooted gopher traps lying beside it. There's a warm feeling in my stomach too.

Did that just happen? Did a boy just say he's going to call me?

I can't stop smiling.

Clare

On the weekend of Audrey and my separate birthdays, Mom announces we'll be celebrating on the same day. She's making banana bread when she tells me this, as if the smell will warm me up to the idea. Banana bread is my favorite, especially hers because she doesn't cook it long enough so it's super gooey.

"Seriously?" I explode. I feel like I say that all the time now. *Seriously? Are you serious? You can't be serious.* I'm living in a nuthouse.

Mom continues to mix the raw banana goodness, not giving my outburst the attention it deserves. "You two are twins. Your father and I thought we could start a new tradition. It will be a good bonding experience."

A good bonding experience. Being forced to share a birthday is going to be a good bonding experience. And where was her urge to start new traditions at Christmas when Dad wanted to go to Mexico? Instead we sat through dinner trying not to look at Adam's empty spot at the table. A month later we did the same thing on the date Adam would have turned eighteen.

"I just want to have my own day."

Mom turns away to scrape the mixture into a pan. "You're never happy, Clare. Everything is always a fight with you. Have you noticed that? Audrey's happy to do anything, but you're so difficult."

"That's not true." My voice breaks, and I'm glad her back is to me so she can't see how much her words hurt me. Baking banana bread together was supposed to be *our* bonding experience. Audrey is on a walk with Dad.

"It is. It's like you want to fight."

"Why would I want to fight? No one *wants* to fight."

"You're fighting me right now!"

"Because you're being unfair!"

Mom opens the oven and shoves the bread inside. "I'm making you banana bread and you're picking on me."

Inside my head, I'm screaming. I'm whipping banana peels at the windows. Hurling the empty mixing bowl at the dining room table. Sweeping bags of sugar and flour onto the floor and then scooping handfuls of white and tossing it into the air over and over again, coating everything in a dusty, sparkling white. Christmas is here again.

In real life, Mom closes the oven, and before she can turn around, I go to my room and throw my pillow instead.

Sunday night I go to Sharon's for a sleepover to celebrate like we always do, but it doesn't feel the same. Even though I've been there tons of times since, Sharon's room still reminds me of when I stayed with her after Adam's death. And when the others basically repeat the same conversation they had a few days ago on the bleachers, I kind of wish I'd stayed at home.

Because my actual birthday comes first and falls on the holiday Monday, we go for our family dinner that night. Audrey wants pasta and I want seafood, so we go to Red Lobster where they have both. It's one of those gorgeous spring evenings where the sun doesn't set until close to 9:00 p.m., and Red Lobster is like entering a dark ship. By the time the food comes, Audrey and I are bouncing in our seats we're so excited. It feels like when we were little kids. We notice each other doing it and laugh. She gives me a few scoops of her Alfredo and I give her a crab leg. I catch Mom watching us and give her a tentative smile, but she looks back down at her meal.

Is she still angry with me? I feel a pang in my chest. This is how it always is with us now. She and Dad are always rooting for Audrey to succeed and never see me as a separate entity. To them I'm just there to help Audrey too. They're always trying to understand her, yet they have no idea who I am.

Communicate, Kyle always says to me. *Tell them how you feel. How can you expect them to understand what you're going through if you don't tell them?*

Mom excuses herself to go the bathroom.

Let them see you, Clare. Give them and yourself a chance. You deserve it.

I sit there for a few seconds, staring at my empty plate, and then I make a decision. I get up and follow her.

The restaurant is packed now. There's a huge crowd by the front door, and a group of kids are ogling the lobsters in the tank. I narrowly miss running into a server as I try to catch up to my mother. I see her disappear into the bathroom, the door swinging closed behind her. Inside, two out of three stalls are occupied. I have to use the bathroom too but I don't want to miss my chance to talk to Mom, so I wait by the sink. The woman in the other stall comes out first, washes her hands, and leaves. Then it's just Mom and me.

She looks a bit surprised when she sees me standing there. "Have you been waiting for me?"

"I wanted to talk to you."

It's clear she doesn't like the idea. She goes to the sink and washes her hands.

I take a deep breath. "I'm sorry I got upset when you brought up sharing our birthday. I want to explain why."

"I know why you got upset. You're always upset if I do something for Audrey."

"See, that's the problem. You think I'm mean to Audrey all the time. You don't remember how I stopped going to friends' houses at lunch and went home with Audrey instead. You asked me to stop going so I could walk Audrey back and she wouldn't be late."

Mom rolls her eyes. "Was that really a big deal, Clare? You spent time with your friends all the time."

"I'm trying to explain how I want to be seen as a separate person. As Clare."

"Everyone sees you as a separate person, Clare." She rips a paper towel from the machine. "That isn't an issue."

"It is for me." I take a deep breath. How can I explain to her that I want space to be my own person, especially now that I'm trying to figure out who that person is? That watching Adam's videos was like going down the rabbit hole and I need to look after me for once?

"I've finally had a chance to be on my own and now all of that might change."

Mom squishes her paper towel into a ball and leans against the sink in an action that's meant to tell me I'm going too far. But I can't stop.

"It's always about Audrey."

There. I said it.

"Sometimes one child needs more help than another child, and the parent has to give it to them."

"That's the thing: Audrey *always* needs more help."

Mom frowns. "I'm disappointed in you, Clare. I thought you'd be more gracious. Is this really the person you want to be?"

"I'm not a bad person for telling you my feelings."

"What if it was you? Would you rather *you* were the one with the problem?"

"Of course not." My cheeks burn with embarrassment. I can't believe she'd ask me that question.

"Then show some compassion. This is the last thing I need after ten months of hell." She tosses her paper towel ball in the garbage and leaves.

I don't go after her. I stand in the bathroom alone feeling horrible and rotten and guilty.

+ ✳ +

When we get home, I go straight to bed. Above me are the glow-in-the-dark stars Audrey and I stuck on the ceiling. Mom never noticed.

When did life get so hard? I don't feel like I fit in anywhere anymore. My parents are acting crazy even considering letting Audrey come back to my school, and all my friends care about is trying to find a boyfriend. Do I want a boyfriend too?

I close my eyes. I'm playing the video again, but this time it's in my head. I see Dahlia on the bed, only it doesn't have to be with Adam. It can be any guy I want. A fantasy guy.

Think of a fantasy guy, Clare.

None come to my mind so I go with KJ Apa from *Riverdale* because I like the show and my friends are always talking about how hot he is. And, yeah, he is pretty built in the scenes where he takes his shirt off.

You just haven't wanted to think about it because the guys at school are all pimply and pubescent, I tell myself. *You just need a hot, older guy.*

So KJ Apa is lying on the bed and I'm Dahlia, standing above him. I press my eyes closed tighter and try to put myself in her sexy body. I'm swaying above KJ Apa with my perfect boobs — man, Dahlia's boobs are so perfect — and I'm hot and wet and I want him. I imagine my long legs, the feel of his shirt against my skin, my fingers on the buttons as I slowly reveal myself to him. Like I'm a present I'm offering to him. I try to imagine his face, the way he'd look, wanting me, aching for me . . .

But all I can see is Dahlia. In fact, I can't see KJ Apa at all. I try to fight it, try to shift views, but it's too late — I'm back in his body. I'm watching the strip show and I do feel all hot and wet, but for all the wrong reasons, and all I want is to let it keep going, to keep watching her. Always her.

I stop fighting it.

✦ ✳ ✦

I feel sick in the morning.

The alarm goes off at 7:00 a.m. and I slam a hand down on it, pull the pillow over my head. A while later Mom walks through my door without knocking — surprise surprise — and announces I'm late, as if I didn't already know.

"I'm sick," I tell her. "I'm not going to school."

She stands at the end of my bed and crosses her arms. "It's Audrey's birthday. Are you actually sick?"

Of course she doesn't believe me. She's probably still angry with me for last night. "Yes," I snap. "I'm *actually* sick."

Leaning down, she puts a hand on my forehead. "You feel fine. What is it? A cold? Flu?"

General unwellness. Being completely F-ed up. "I just feel off. Like I might puke," I add so she'll let me stay home.

"All right." She sighs and straightens. "I'll go get you some water and then call the school."

Finally, after a night of tossing and turning, I drift off to sleep.

I wake up four hours later. I can hear music playing above me and know Mom's in the attic. There's a large glass of water on the night stand, as well as a bottle of Tylenol and a peanut butter and jelly sandwich. Man, how I love Mom's PB&J! I scarf it down and am just starting to feel better when, *BAM*, last night's events hit me in the face again.

What's wrong with me?

A deep shiver runs through me and I look at my arm. It's covered in little red dots, like a rash. I put both hands to my cheeks. They're hot. Burning.

All of this happened so quickly. I found the videos and I watched them, and I didn't even think about what watching them meant. Obviously I'm not attracted to my brother, so what? Do I want to *be* him?

Maybe.

I don't know.

I'm so messed up.

I mean, yeah, there's a part of me that has always wanted to be him. But I think when I'm watching the videos and imagining Dahlia is above me, I'm not Adam. I'm me.

Mom's singing along to her music now, totally lost in her artistic creation, so I know she won't be coming in anytime soon. I grab my laptop from my desk and return to bed, balance it on my lap. It feels like I'm doing something bad just by going to Google. I type in *Am I a lesbian?*

The first result is a quiz: *Am I a lesbian?* I click the link to open the page, and it's immediately obvious another teenager made it.

Question 1: What do you think this quiz is going to tell you?

    a.   I'm a lesbian

    b.   I'm bisexual

    c.   I'm straight

I click *a*.

Question 2: Have you ever thought about kissing a girl?

    a.   EW GROSS NO!

    b.   Yes

    c.   Girls and Guys

I click *b*.

Question 3: Do you find yourself wanting to do sexual stuff with a boy?

    a.   No only girls

    b.   What was the question? I was thinking about boys

    c.   Mostly both I guess

    d.   Mmm BOYS so hot

I think about Billy. In grade seven, Sharon asked Charlotte, Rhiannon, and me which boys we had crushes on. They all had their answers ready. Charlotte and Sharon liked more than one guy and could rank their crushes in order. Rhiannon only liked Adil but *really* liked him. Like I was kind of scared for Adil.

When they asked me, I told them I liked Billy. I didn't even know why I said him. Probably because he was, and still is, the most popular boy in our grade. Ever since then, they've thought I have a thing for him. At last year's school dance they even went so far as to tell him that I liked him, and he asked me to dance. That's how we ended up having our disgusting kiss.

The quiz tells me I'm 70% lesbian.

Wouldn't that mean I'm bisexual? The quiz is as useless as expected. Frustrated, I open a blank Word doc and mentally go down the rows of students in my bio class, making a tally: *Who would I get with?*

The problem is I know these people, and I don't like most of them. So yeah, while they might be good-looking, there's no way I'd want to spend more than five minutes with them. Rhiannon? Skip. Charlotte? Ew, gross. Billy? If we'd kissed again it might have been better, so I put a check in the *M* for male column and feel better because the *F* column is getting pretty long.

Then I get to Taylor and it's like my whole body reacts. My heart beats faster, my palms get sweaty, and I can feel my cheeks heat. Suddenly I'm afraid my door will swing open and Mom will waltz in. My hand hovers, switching between the two columns until I settle on placing a checkmark in both.

I go back to my Google results, but all I get is link after link about how lesbians are women attracted to other women. I open each website in turn, reading the same thing over and over again until I see one that says, *How do I know if I'm straight, gay, or bisexual?*

I begin to read.

> Trying to determine whether or not you are attracted to someone of the same sex can be very confusing and often overwhelming. It is important to remember that the process is different for everyone. Some lesbian, gay, and bisexual people know from the time they are young; they report "feeling different." Other people don't

discover their attractions until puberty, late adolescence, or even adulthood. This can also depend on the amount of support and acceptance they have received or can expect to receive from family and friends. It isn't uncommon to feel attracted to someone you admire, like a close friend.

Do I admire Billy? Maybe that's the real reason he came into my mind instead of any of the other guys. He's so *there,* he's such a guy, and I like that about him.

Do I admire Dahlia? This is harder. I don't know her very well, but what I do know about her is kind of annoying. The more I think about it, the more I have to admit I'm attracted to Dahlia entirely because of her body. Is it possible that's because I want to have her body?

My head feels like it's going to explode. I keep reading.

If you're feeling confused, try to remember you're not alone and it is not a rush. **Sexual orientation** and **gender identity** develop over time.

What's the difference between sexual orientation and gender identity? I search the website and learn that *gender identity* is described as "one's concept of self as male, female, a blend of both, or neither." It goes on to say there is a misconception that sexual orientation and gender identity are connected, or even the same thing, but that's not the case. A person who transitions from female to male and is attracted to women would typically identify as a straight man, but a lot of people would mistakenly label him gay. So maybe a better way to think of it is that sexual orientation is who you like and gender identity is who you are.

In that case, who am I? I'm attracted to Dahlia, but it's not as simple as that — not even close. Because I'm also the guy in that fantasy. And wanting to wear Adam's clothes doesn't have anything to do with Dahlia — it has to do with me. Does that make me transgender like the example on the website?

I attack Google again, this time typing in *female transgender,* and it quickly becomes apparent that I needed to type it in the other way around: *male transgender* or *female-to-male transgender.* In the middle of the page is a link to a page called Extremely Handsome Men (FTM). I click on the link and my jaw drops open. The first guy is dressed as a cowboy with a mustache and a broad torso covered in tattoos. The second guy has finer facial features, but his body is all man — strong shoulders, thick arms, and thighs that could snap me in two. The third man has a closely shaved head, stubble around his jaw, and a major six-pack with a smattering of chest hair that leads to his treasure trail.

I once stole boxer briefs from a store and wore them to bed, but I never wore them to school or anything. I wear Adam's sweatshirt, though. And looking back now, there was that one time after a party, when some guys walked us home to Sharon's house and one of them gave me his jacket. We moved through the streets like a pack, and I felt more comfortable in that jacket than I had all night, found myself slipping to the back of the group to walk with the single guys. Maybe I even started to feel like one of the guys, because when I got home and looked in the mirror, I was surprised to see such a feminine face staring back at me.

But some days I wake up and feel really feminine, too. It's like I never know how I'm going to feel one day or how long it's going to last. How can I possibly label my identity if my identity is always shifting?

Frustrated, I slam the lid of the laptop closed and slide it under the bed. Pulling the covers over my head, I burrow down into the middle of the mattress. I wish I'd never looked that stuff up. I wish I'd never touched Adam's phone and found Dahlia's striptease. I shouldn't even be watching the videos without her permission.

Before I'm tempted to change my mind, I dig Adam's phone out of my sock drawer and delete the videos.

Audrey

It's my birthday. At exactly 6:25 I jerk awake from a grainy nightmare in black and white. Like an old-school film.

Adam lying stiff as a board on his bed.

Adam zombie-jerking through the basement and up the staircase.

Adam floating through the hall and up to the second floor. Pausing at the top and glancing right toward Clare and then left toward me.

I woke up too soon, but I know he chose me.

I have the same dream every few days. I've had it for ten months.

My eyes are still full of sand. I dig it out with my fingers. Then I toss the covers to the side and get up.

It's a message. I'm the reason he's still here. Adam has been down there waiting for me.

Somehow I turn into a zombie too, because I'm standing at the top of the basement stairs but can't remember getting there. I take a deep breath and descend. I don't realize my eyes are shut tight and I'm finding my way by count until I'm at twelve and my foot touches the concrete.

He's sitting on the couch again, staring at a dark TV. He turns his head to look at me, only this time he doesn't smile. His expression is blank.

I came to see you, I tell him.

He doesn't react. He just sits there. Waiting.

The basement is cold. Colder than I ever remember it being. Goose bumps have broken out on the exposed skin of my arms and neck. I wish I'd stayed in my warm bed and ignored the message. I'm starting to think Adam might be angry with me. I'd be angry with me too. The events of that night have been burned into my memory. If I let them they'll replay over and over again, which is why I never talk about Adam.

But I have to say this.

I know you would have been safe at home if not for me, I tell him.

Tears fill my eyes and I close them, smear the wetness across my cheeks with the back of my hand. I drag in a long breath and finally say the words I've wanted to say.

I'm sorry, Adam. I'm so sorry.

I'm looking away toward his bedroom, but as I apologize for the second time, I dare myself to look him in the face. For a moment he continues to sit there. Then he stands, stretching up six feet two inches. He doesn't look dead. He takes a step forward and then another until he's standing right in front of me.

Now something is wrong. He's staring down at me with an expression I've never seen before. I take a step back but it's too late. Adam opens his mouth and at the same time his eyes open wider. They're mouths now too and all three of them are impossibly wide and all three are yelling the same thing. Over and over again.

It's all your fault. It's all your fault. It's all your fault.

I close my eyes to block out the image.

I'm sorry, I yell. I'm sorry! Tears stream down my cheeks as I say it again and again. I'm sorry, Adam! I'm sorry!

Sorry doesn't fix anything.

I don't know if he says it or I think it. It doesn't matter. It's the truth.

I wish I could take it all back, I tell him. I would do anything. I'd die in your place.

Audrey?

My head jerks up. Adam is gone. The voice is coming from the top of the stairs.

Audrey? Are you okay?

I race to the bottom of the stairs. Mom is at the top holding a cup of coffee. Her expression tells me she's been there a while. She looks more tired than usual. There are dark smudges under her eyes.

Come upstairs, Audrey.

In the kitchen she tells me Happy Birthday and gives me a kiss. Then she pulls out a frying pan and says, I'm going to make eggs. Clare's sick, so it's just you and me.

My heart stutters in my chest. Clare's sick? *Clare's sick!*

Mom cracks three eggs and pours their insides out.

Is it a cold? I ask.

I don't know.

Flu?

I don't know.

Did you take her temperature?

No.

Why not?

Because I suspect she just doesn't want to go to school.

Not everyone exhibits flu-like symptoms, you know. It could even be something more serious like the Ebola virus.

Ebola isn't in Canada.

Yet. It isn't in Canada yet. For all we know it is already here but we haven't received the memo.

Clare is fine, sweetie. She hasn't traveled anywhere.

But someone at school could have. Then they could give it to her. And on and on. That's why it's called an epidemic. We should take her to the doctor just in case.

Mom drops the spatula in the pan. She grabs the counter with both hands. Tilts her face to the ceiling as if the air is better up there. I count nine seconds. Then she turns around to face me.

I understand why you're worried, sweetie. Adam's sudden passing shook us all. But you don't need to worry so much about germs or natural disasters. Bad things happen in life, and no matter how prepared we are, we can't always prevent them.

But we can try.

Mom smiles but not with her eyes. How about I keep an eye on her and take her this afternoon if she's not better. Deal?

Deal.

Mom turns back to the eggs again. Who were you talking to just now? I mean, who were you talking to in the basement?

Uh-oh, a direct question. A direct question requires a direct answer. The situation is fraught with peril.

I was talking to Adam.

Mom freezes in the middle of poking the eggs. Then she flips them over and scoops them onto two plates. She pushes a plate toward me across the island.

I thought so. I thought I heard you apologize to him. Is that what I heard?

Another direct question. This time she's looking right at me.

I thought if I apologized he would be able to move on and leave the basement.

Move on?

Yes, to another astral plane. Or wherever ghosts go.

Mom takes a bite of her eggs and chews for a really long time. Twenty seconds at least.

Sweetie, I know the last ten months have been very hard on you and that you don't like to talk about what happened, but I think talking about it would be healthier than playing make-believe.

Make-believe?

Pretending Adam is still in the basement.

So that's what she thinks. I sit there. Debating. Then I decide not to say anything. Whether I'm playing make-believe or still believe in ghosts, I'm immature.

Audrey, if you ever want to talk, I'm here for you.

The feeling develops in my stomach. The feeling that always develops when someone suggests we talk about Adam. Like my stomach is swallowing itself.

Mom waits for a moment. I don't say anything. She turns around again and starts making my lunch.

I shove my eggs away. I don't want to eat. There's nothing for us to talk about. Everyone thinks it's my fault. They just don't know I think so too.

+ ✳ +

This time when we pass the diner, I watch Mom's face really carefully to see if she reacts. She doesn't. Not a twitch.

We used to go to the diner every Sunday and always sat in the same corner booth. The owner sat us there because he knew I liked it. The booth had two windows and the couches squeaked when you sat on them. Clare and I always ordered the Belgian waffles with whipped cream and berries.

One time Dad said, No waffles today. They aren't healthy.

I always have waffles, I said. I could feel the panic rising. I was about to get really upset but Clare did first.

Don't claim it's because they're not healthy, she said. That's bull.

Careful, young lady.

Just tell the truth. Audrey wants the truth, right? The doctor doesn't want Audrey having sugar and I get to suffer.

There are tons of other choices, Mom said. How about bacon, eggs, and fruit?

Yeah, because bacon is healthy, Clare muttered. I don't know why I can't have the waffles just because Audrey can't.

I was using my menu to block everyone except Adam out. There were a lot of choices. Too many choices. Under the table, someone kicked me. I looked up to see Adam making a funny face. I made one back.

Dad turned to me. It's true, Dr. Jackson recommended we reduce your sugar intake to help with your concentration. He also suggested you find an extracurricular activity to focus on. Are you interested in any extracurricular activities?

Playing scenes. Only I knew that wasn't what he meant so I didn't say it. The server came along and Adam ordered the breakfast scramble. Then Dad ordered the everything omelet. It was my turn next and I hadn't decided. I felt myself start to panic.

And what would you like? the server asked.

I said the first thing under the bacon section. I'll have the farmer's breakfast. Please.

Would you like toast or pancakes with that?

Pancakes!

Mom looked at Dad the way she did when she wanted him to say something. But he was reading the menu again. So she spoke to me. That isn't the healthy choice, Audrey.

I ordered the eggs and bacon, I said. That's what you wanted me to do.

Clare said loudly, I'll have the Belgian waffles. Extra whipped cream and berries.

Clare! Mom said. Do you have to be so difficult?

The server looked back and forth between them. No one said anything. Eventually she jotted it down on her pad.

I don't know why you want that crap anyway, Adam said. Hash browns are the best. And coffee. Can I get a coffee please?

Dad turned to the server. No coffee for him.

You're Ruiners of Fun, Adam said, and gave me a wink.

Yes, your parents who love you and take you out for a nice breakfast are Ruiners of Fun. Mom snapped her menu closed. She ordered a yogurt parfait and a coffee. Her cheeks were red.

The server left and we sat in silence for a long time.

Dad cleared his throat. So, a new extracurricular activity, Audrey. Any ideas?

None.

How about ballet?

I made a face.

Okay, are you interested in any sports?

I used to like playing Four Square at school.

Four Square isn't a sport, honey.

It should be. It uses all your muscles.

Adam was stacking creamers into a tall tower. How about karate? Audrey meets *Mortal Kombat*.

Spinning bird kick! I cried in a high-pitched voice.

Adam laughed.

Dad looked to Mom and shrugged. Karate?

She shrugged back. Karate.

Karate it is, then. It will be good for her. It's good for young women to learn self-defense.

I was pretty excited about karate. It meant I could beat up my enemies. Or at least scare them away. I imagined doing spinning bird kick on Sharon and instantly felt better.

No one wanted to mess with spinning bird kick.

So Mom signed me up for karate in the summer and took me to buy a gi and a white belt. But karate was not what I expected. It wasn't even in a real dojo. It was in a gymnasium at the health club.

We started off the class running lines. There were court lines painted on the wood and we ran to the first line and back. Second line and back. Third line and back and I wanted to fall over and die.

Then he said, Ten pushups!

Everyone dropped to the floor. The girl beside me was doing real pushups, not the ones they let the girls do in school. I did the same. Afterward I could barely breathe.

The instructor pulled what looked like thick pillows out of the closet. He pushed them farther into the gym.

We're going to do sets of ten punches, he said.

Beside me there was a super-tall and wide guy. He looked like he could be a character in *Mortal Kombat*.

Get into pairs, he said. One of you holds the bag, the other punches. Then switch it up.

Everyone ran away from the big guy. Everyone except for me. He looked down at me and shrugged. I shrugged back. He picked up a punching bag.

The teacher walked over to us. I'll demonstrate.

The big guy held up the bag. The instructor punched like he was trying to do it in slow motion.

Both hands are in a fist. Stand facing the bag with your hips shoulder-width apart. Bring one arm forward and, at the same time, bring the other arm back. See? It's all about maintaining self-control. As your punching arm comes forward, it rotates into the punch. *Kiya!* Slow and controlled. Can you do ten?

Everyone was watching.

I stepped up in front of the guy. Adam would call him a meathead. He smiled at me and I felt bad for thinking it.

Anytime, Audrey.

I mimicked what the teacher did. One arm forward, the other arm back. My fist hit the bag softly.

Good control. Now hit a little harder, and this time, as your fist makes contact, shout *Kiya!*

Everyone was still watching.

One arm forward, the other arm back. Kiya!

Come on, Audrey. You could barely hear yourself.

I took a deep breath. Fine. I'll do it right. This time I moved faster, harder, and punched the bag with all my strength. *Kiya!*

His lip did a twitchy thing. He put a fist to his mouth and coughed but it didn't trick me. I knew he was laughing at me.

All the guys were smiling.

I wished I could spinning bird kick through all those smiling faces.

I finished my ten punches and then took the bag. It was even worse. Meathead crouched down and tapped the bag lightly. Like he was afraid I'd fall over.

Then we switched back and practiced kicks.

Rotate at the hips. The top of the foot, not the toes, makes contact with the bag. Like this. He demonstrated with Meathead again.

Luckily he didn't watch me this time.

My karate gi was stiff. It rode up when I kicked and the collar scratched the back of my neck. It was itchy. I hated it. I wished I could be home on the couch with Adam playing *Mortal Kombat* instead.

I said I had to go to the bathroom but I didn't go. Instead I went to the information desk and asked to use the phone. I called Mom but no answer. I called Dad but no answer. So then I called home.

Clare answered.

Can I talk to Mom or Dad?

Aren't you in karate right now? I could hear Mario being played in the background.

Yeah but I hate it. My karate gi is too stiff. It keeps rubbing the back of my neck.

Silence. Then: They're out for dinner. You know, on a *date*.

I need to come home, Clare.

No, you don't. Just handle it. Okay? There was a shuffling noise and then Adam spoke. Audrey? You okay?

I just want to come home. I could feel the tears pricking my eyes. I was always the crying one.

What happened?

I just hate it. Karate. I want to come home.

I'll be right there. Wait by the front doors.

The call ended and I went straight to the front doors. I didn't bother telling the instructor I was leaving. I'd never see him again anyway.

There was a bench by the door and I sat down there. The sky had lines of orange and purple. It was pretty.

I wasn't sure how long I waited. I didn't have a watch. The lines were gone and the sky was dark when people I recognized started coming out of the building. They were wearing normal clothes now. The real-pushups girl. The meathead.

He stopped beside me and frowned. The lines in his forehead frowned too. Everything okay?

I nodded because I was too scared to speak.

Waiting for someone to pick you up?

I nodded again.

Okay. He disappeared into the parking lot.

Mom and Dad's car sped up to the curb and stopped. Dad jumped out, his face flushed. Hey, honey, sorry we're late. The bill took forever.

Adam's supposed to pick me up, I said.

No he's not. We are.

I called him to come early.

Why?

I didn't like it.

I see. Dad pulled out his phone. Yeah, there's a voicemail from him. I'll call back and tell him we've got you. Get in the car.

The moon was surrounded by dark clouds, like it was Halloween instead of July. I climbed into the back of the car. Dad called Adam three times but there was no answer. He frowned down at the phone.

That's weird. Adam called forty minutes ago. Why isn't he here yet?

Why would Adam be here? Mom asked.

Audrey called him to pick her up early. She didn't like karate.

Mom twisted around to face me. Why didn't you like karate?

This was why I didn't do extracurricular activities. I didn't answer. Mom turned back around.

Should we wait for Adam? she asked Dad.

No, he probably got sidetracked. I'll send him a text letting him know we got her and we're on the way home.

Traffic was stopped by the Safeway. Dad rolled down the window and stuck his head out.

Two cars went through the light. That's it! *Two measly cars!*

There must be an accident, Mom said.

My stomach was sore. I tried to remember if I'd eaten dinner. Right, I'd had macaroni and cheese with Clare and Adam.

We waited. Another two cars went through the light. We inched forward.

This is ridiculous! It's going to take us hours to get home.

Another two cars. More inching. Dad's road rage increased. He let out a string of curses. Mom turned around in her seat and asked me again why I didn't like karate.

The gi was itchy and they laughed at me when I punched.

Sweetie, it was your first time. You just need practice. Don't let them upset you.

Finally we made it through the light. Dad let out a little cheer. Traffic was slow but at least we were moving. We turned the corner and finally we could see the flashing lights. There were two cop cars and a fire truck but we couldn't see the accident.

That was because the driver's car had rolled down the hill into the river.

We'd just pulled up to the house when Dad's phone rang. There he is. Dad answered, speaking louder. Hey, buddy! It's okay, we've got your sister.

Someone else responded. I could hear it even from the back seat. Someone with a much deeper voice than Adam.

What? What are you talking about? He just left to pick up my daughter.

The deep echoing voice responded.

How do you know? How do you know it's him?

Stewart? Mom put a hand on his arm. What's going on?

Dad's face was white. His hand on the phone began to shake. He pulled it away from his ear and I thought he might throw it. Instead Mom took it from him.

Hello? Hello? This is Margaret, Stewart's wife. Who is this?

Dad was lying against the steering wheel. Both his hands were tangled in his hair. His shoulders began to shake.

Mom's voice pierced my ears. No. No, I don't believe you. *Tell me he's going to be okay!*

I looked up at the house. Clare threw open the front door to see what we were all doing still in the car. As she approached us, her smile faltered. She looked first at our parents.

Then she looked at me.

+ ✳ +

Now I slouch in my seat so I can't see out the window. How stupid I was then. How immature. To think I would be good enough at karate to scare Sharon out of bullying me.

Life isn't a movie, Audrey.

The only way you're special is that you're weird.

I ball my hands into fists. Thumb on the outside like karate taught me. If I'd known what taking up karate would cost, I would have tried ballet. Gymnastics. Curling.

I'm sorry, Adam. I say it again in my mind. The image of three screaming mouths returns just as we pull up at Freak.

Things get worse when I walk into the classroom. If you can believe it.

First of all, Marianne is sick. This is bad news because I like Marianne.

Second of all, Marianne is sick. Monsieur Martin is always in a terrible mood when he has to teach us by himself.

Audrey! he says the moment I walk into the classroom.

I'm hanging up my coat and can't hear him. But I know he has already said my name when he says it again louder. AUDREY.

I check the wall clock. It's 8:39. One minute to spare. I'm not late. I check to make sure I have my backpack. It's heavy so I know I have my books, too. My shoes are already off and lined up in their cubby.

Come to my desk, Audrey. I know he's angry because he's pinching his nose.

I'm having an OFF day, I tell him when I get there. To be safe.

Why is that, Audrey?

Because every day can't be an ON day.

Right. Audrey, this morning the gym teacher brought to my attention that you were late for gym last Thursday. After lunch.

I was late? I repeat what he said in my mind. The light above me is making a buzzing sound. It's very distracting. How could I have been late after lunch? The bell rings and I follow everyone into school. I go into the locker room and get changed for gym.

Audrey, what were you doing on Thursday that made you late?

Oh. That's right. Thursday was the day before the long weekend.

I was late because I left the school grounds, I tell him.

Monsieur Martin's eyes open really wide. He puts his glasses back on and wipes a hand along his mouth. You left the school grounds?

Yes. I went to a park. I met a boy there. His name is Calvin.

Monsieur Martin blinks at me. He blinks again. Then he smiles. It's the largest smile I have ever seen on Monsieur Martin.

Congratulations, Audrey! This is great news.

It is? Monsieur Martin is still smiling. What made you leave?

I wanted to be more mature.

Génial! Monsieur Martin claps his hands together. Do you know what this means? The significance? You broke your routine, Audrey.

But I was late, I say. I broke the rules.

Ça n'a pas d'importance, he says. Then he shakes his head. I mean, rules are important. Yes. You should follow them and I'm going to have to give you a tardy. I'm not happy that you were late. I'm happy that you stretched yourself. Life isn't always black and white, Audrey.

When he finishes talking I go back to my desk. I sit and stare at the board until I'm not sure if it's black with white words, or white with black painted around all the letters.

+ ✳ +

Even though we already celebrated our birthdays last night, we have cheese fondue followed by chocolate fondue for dessert.

The fruit is very healthy, I told Mom and Dad when they asked what I wanted. And cheese is full of protein. It's my birthday.

I can only play that card once a year.

As I'm about to dunk a slice of banana into chocolate lava, the phone rings.

Aren't you going to get that? Mom says to Clare. It's probably for you.

Clare shakes her head. She looks white like her plate. She didn't care what we had for dinner because she said she was too sick to eat anyway. I suggested taking her to the doctor but Clare said that I go to the doctor over every little thing. Then she called me a hypochondriac.

Mom answers the phone and her eyes widen. It's probably Monsieur Martin calling to tell her I was late. My hands start to shake. If he tells Mom, Mom will tell Dad. Then they will "discuss."

I think of Mario falling off the cliff. Game over.

Mom has a strange expression on her face. I'm not sure what it means. Audrey, she says. It's for you.

It's for Audrey? Dad is surprised. I can hear it in his voice.

It is. Mom's voice sounds the same as Dad's now. And *it's a boy!*

I don't get up. I don't know what I'm supposed to do.

Mom clears her throat and says into the receiver, Can I ask who's speaking and what this is in regards to? Then she covers it and says, His name is Calvin and he just wants to talk. He's probably calling to wish you Happy Birthday!

I feel my face go hot again and cover it with my hands. Through my fingers I can see Clare staring at me. Her mouth is set in a straight line so I can't tell what she is thinking.

Finally she says, You like a boy named Calvin?

I slide under the table and onto the floor.

Audrey can't come to the phone right now, I hear Mom say. Can I take your number?

I hear her hang up and then everyone starts talking. But no one is talking to me because I'm still under the table. There are a few pieces of food under here. Maybe they should reconsider getting a dog.

Is Calvin a boy from school? Dad asks.

No, I know most of the kids, Mom answers. I've never heard of a Calvin.

It's probably for a school project, Clare says. Don't make such a big deal out of it.

He didn't say it was for a school project. He said he wants to *talk*. This is the first time a boy has ever called the house! Mom elicits a very high-pitched sound that makes me jump and hit my head on the table.

Dad's head appears in front of me. A floating head like he has a go-go-gadget neck.

Kiddo, do you have a boyfriend you haven't told us about?

I turn and crawl away from him as fast as I can go.

I think we embarrassed her, I hear Mom say.

Upstairs in my room I close the door and pace back and forth with my hands covering my face. Still hot. Does Calvin expect me to call him back tonight? I can't do that. I'm not very good at talking on the phone. I don't know when it's my turn to talk and I always interrupt. Dr. Jackson says I require "facial cues," but he also says I miss those.

Sometimes it feels like I can't get anything right.

I didn't expect Calvin to call. He said he wanted to talk but why? Maybe more gophers needed saving. Maybe he collected all the traps and threw them into a dumpster.

Maybe I should go back and do that.

There's a sound outside my door. I freeze. A piece of paper slides under the door. I know what it is right away because it's all numbers and two words.

Calvin Hilton.

That is a very good sign. Like my name, it can be broken into two groups of six, three groups of four, or four groups of three. Personally, I like to break sentences down into as many groups as possible.

(Cal)(vin)(Hil)(ton).

I wish Mom had thought to ask his middle name too.

Dad asked if Calvin is my boyfriend. Is he my boyfriend? How does he become my boyfriend?

If Calvin becomes my boyfriend, we can go to movies on Saturday night. I won't have to stay at home and read alone.

If Calvin becomes my boyfriend, I can update my Facebook profile and everyone will know. They won't think I'm weird anymore.

Calvin is the most exciting thing to happen to me in a long time.

But what if I call him back and he finds out I go to Peak? Then he won't want to be my boyfriend or even my friend. And Calvin is the first potential friend I've had in years.

I fold the paper carefully and slip it into my sketchbook. I want it to be closest to the most personal part of me.

Clare

After Audrey goes upstairs, my parents get stupidly excited over the fact that Audrey got a phone call. Yeah it was a boy, but whatever. I seriously doubt this Calvin was the first boy to call the house.

But then I think about it and realize the 'rents are right. Calvin was the first boy to call. Worse, I might actually be feeling jealous of Audrey. Not because I actually want a boy to call me but because my parents seem proud of Audrey, and I don't think they would be proud of me if they knew I've been watching Dahlia's videos.

Calvin. He must be a boy from school. How else would she have met him? When we were little kids I would have asked her about him, and maybe even been excited for her, but now I don't know how. It feels like it's been forever since we were *us*: Clare and Audrey. I don't know if we can ever go back.

I help the 'rents clean up after dinner and then announce, "I'm going out for a bit."

"With your friends?" Is it my imagination or does Mom actually sound hopeful?

"Yeah," I lie, which makes me feel worse.

"I thought you were sick today." Dad gives me a stern look. "Does this mean you'll be going to school tomorrow?"

I pretend I didn't hear him as I slam the back door.

The sun has already set, so it's dark and the creep factor is high. Beside the door a light bulb hangs from the ceiling and you have to pull the string to turn it on. Then it swings in the darkness, casting light over one half of the garage and then the other.

I make my way over to the skateboards leaning against the wall. Four skateboards, lined up back to back. All of them covered in dust.

The first three Adam's, the last one mine.

One of the nights I rode my bike past the school to spy on Adam and his friends skateboarding, they caught me. What did I expect? They were just standing in a group at the bottom of the stairs and yelled at me to come over.

"We know you have a crush on Cody!"

Followed by Adam telling them to shut the f up.

I turned around and biked home as fast as I could. At home I dumped my bike in the farthest corner of the garage, like it was damning evidence or something.

Adam got home early that night. I was in the family room watching TV and he sat down beside me. The entire couch dipped with my heart.

"Why do you ride by all the time?" he asked.

I felt like such a loser. What had I looked like to them, circling by over and over on my pink bicycle?

"I don't like Cody," I told him. "I like skateboarding."

"You like watching us?"

"Yeah. Except I want to do it too." *I want to be like you.*

I kind of expected him to laugh it off, maybe tell me I'd get hurt and act like I was "just a girl." Instead he got super excited.

"You want to learn? That's awesome. I can make you a board right now."

So that's what he did. He let me choose which deck I wanted from three of his old ones, and then I watched as he added the trucks, bearings, and wheels. As he worked, he told me about how Dad wanted him to be into sports like baseball and hockey.

"Sometimes it feels like I'm a huge disappointment," he confessed.

"Dad loves you no matter what," I told him.

"Oh, don't worry about me. I'm happy." Adam grinned and held the board out with two hands, as if bestowing a gift upon me. "Ready?"

I accepted the board. "Ready."

He grabbed the helmet hanging off the handlebars of my bike and I groaned.

"Don't worry, we'll practice in the alley. No one will see you."

Skateboarding was terrifying. The moment I put the board down on the pavement in front of me, I realized how intimidating a skateboard actually was. It took me an hour to get used to the pushing. I went all the way up the alley and back, Adam cruising beside me like it was the most natural thing in the world, before I finally got my back foot on for more than a few seconds. The board veered wildly to the right and I almost took out a garbage bin before I biffed it.

Adam fist-pumped before yanking me to my feet again. "You did it!"

Oh man, if that was something to celebrate . . .

"It's hard to learn. Especially since you're not a little kid. Kids have no fear and are close to the ground and fall all the time. You have to get over that mental hurdle. Don't think about hurting yourself."

I laughed. "That's exactly the kind of advice Mom wouldn't want you to give me."

"I know."

I stepped on the end of the board, faced it down the alley again. "Let's keep going."

I practiced like that every night of the week after dinner until I could actually ride the board up and down the alley, weaving back and forth, avoiding cracks in the pavement.

"Next we'll teach you to ollie," Adam said. "Then you'll be legit."

As I rode, I imagined cruising up to the school, the surprised look on Sharon's face. I imagined shredding the stupid image I'd created for myself and becoming a skater instead. That would test whether or not Sharon really liked me! But I knew I would never be brave enough — I needed my friends too badly. So it was Adam's and my secret, and I kind of liked that.

Now I pluck my skateboard out from between the others and take to the streets, pulling my hood up to hide my long hair. It's completely dark save for the streetlights, but no one driving by spares me a second glance as I place the board down on the road, put my foot on it. I feel the power in my veins the moment I push off. This is the first time I've skateboarded since The Accident, and it's exhilarating to be out again, but mostly to think people might mistake me for a guy in this sweatshirt. If someone were to see me out their window, would they think I was Adam? Probably not because I'm hella rusty. On my first push, I veer wildly to the right, correct myself so I don't crash into a BMW. Overcorrect and almost plow into an oncoming Audi. Laugh to myself. Adam would love it.

"They just leave them parked on the street," he'd say. "Then they wonder why someone stole the hood ornament off their Jag."

The 'rents have by far the most modest cars in the neighborhood. Mom drives a van even though she swore she'd never get one. First she tried a Highlander with the third row that folds down, but it got too annoying that Adam had to climb over the back seat. *That's how you sell out,* I thought when she told me. *You try to be your own person but life forces you to change.*

Dad drives a Mazda 6 because it's sleek but also affordable, with high fuel efficiency. High fuel efficiency is very important to Dad. Efficiency in general is very important to Dad.

Adam had a really old Jeep TJ with a convertible top that leaked in the winter. It didn't matter how much he cranked up the heat because it all disappeared. He always drove wearing gloves, and I sat on the edge of the passenger seat to be as close to the vents as possible.

Of course, that Jeep doesn't exist anymore. Like Adam.

I falter a little as I take a ramp up onto the sidewalk. I need to get out of my head. That's what Adam always did. *Don't overthink it.* He just saw a ramp and knew he was gonna ride that. Of course that was after years of mastering the small stuff first.

The cool night air hits my face as I gather speed. I'm completely alone in the dark, but I don't have to be afraid. At the park I carry the board across the grass to the tennis courts. Adam told me the people who live across the street hate it when kids skate on the tennis courts, but the skaters never listen because the surface is rubbery and perfect for practicing small tricks, like ollies. I never did learn how to do one. Maybe now's the time.

After closing the gate, I cruise to the far side of the courts, behind the nets that were just put up last week. I stand on the board in the darkness, looking out at the houses across the street through the trees that line the edge of the park. This is where Adam learned tricks under the stars. He probably stood in this very spot with this very board. Maybe he was even wearing a hoodie like this one. Suddenly it feels like I'm in some kind of time bubble and I've gone back six or seven years. I imagine I'm young Adam, learning how to ollie for the first time, and old Adam is in the sky looking down at me and telling me I've got this.

I can almost feel his arms reaching down to hold me as I slide my right foot back so my toes are on the edge of the board. I take a deep breath. Then I ball my hands into fists, and I ollie.

The board rises into the air maybe a centimeter before flying out from under me and into the nets. Awesome, they're good for something. My butt hurts, however, so the rubber is overrated.

I retrieve the board and try again and again and again.

And again.

Two hours later, I haven't ollied, but I've flipped the board completely around. *The trick is in the landing.* It's way past curfew so I jump on the board and speed home, and it's the best ride I've ever had because I'm not focusing on skating, I'm worried about how late it is and how Mom is going to kill me because she's been waiting for an excuse to kill me, and as I pull up to our house I don't even think about it — I do an ollie and jump the curb! Follow it up with a dive-roll onto the grass. I'm laughing and brushing myself off and the skateboard is rolling backwards from where it hit the edge of the lawn. Still elated — I ollied! I actually ollied! — I grab the board and run to the garage to stash it before the 'rents can find out what I'm up to.

The house is dark, save for the hallway light the 'rents always leave on when I go out. I climb the stairs slowly so that I won't make a noise and wake anyone up, but it doesn't matter because they're waiting up for me. Their door is partly open and I can hear the television. I take a deep breath and step into their room, my excuse already on my lips.

"Hey, sorry I'm late, Charlotte was having trouble with a school assignment so I was helping her out and lost track of time."

Neither of them looks impressed. Mom sits up higher in bed. "We were worried about you. I texted to see if you were okay."

"I forgot my phone." That's a lie — I always have my phone. "Which is also part of the reason I was late."

"You look . . . flushed."

"I rushed home when I realized the time." At least that part is true. I quickly shut the conversation down, claiming I'm tired and need to get to bed.

In my room, I open the window curtain and gaze out at the street I was just skateboarding. Now I finally understand the significance of all those nights watching Adam and his friends from the sidelines. For me, wanting to skateboard like Adam wasn't as simple as a little sister looking up to her big brother. When I spied on Adam and his friends, I not only wanted to be like them, I wanted to *be* them. I just hadn't made that distinction yet.

+ ✳ +

In the middle of the night, I sneak downstairs to Adam's room. I sit on the edge of his bed in front of his dresser. My heart is racing so fast, I think my parents can hear it two floors above. Am I really going to do this?

The idea came to me an hour ago. I was lying awake and everyone else was asleep, and I realized I could try. It would be easy. No one would even know. All his stuff is still here. It's the perfect opportunity.

I pull open the top drawer. It's all underwear and socks. I close it quickly and pull open the second. T-shirts. That seems like a good place to start.

Putting on a larger shirt than the one I'm wearing doesn't feel that different, so I grab a leather bracelet and a baseball cap off his shelf and put them on too. But it's not until I pull on a pair of Adam's jeans that I start to feel like I'm playing dress-up. The pants are way too big. I roll the bottoms under and cinch the waist tighter by holding it at the back. Then I look around. No mirror.

I do have my phone. The light is bad in here but I can use the flash. I set it up on his dresser and turn on the timer. Then I stand in front of the bed and wait.

The first shot just gets my legs. I move the camera back as far as it can go on the dresser, but I can still only fit my legs and part of my torso. So I stack a bunch of books up and lean the camera on an angle against them before climbing up onto the bed.

Finally, finally I get a full body shot, and I look like a kid wearing clothes two sizes too big for him. There's also something about the light hair coming out from under the cap . . . Adam had hair to his shoulders up until four years ago. People always told Adam and me that we looked like our dad and Audrey looked like our mom, but I'd never seen the resemblance between Adam and me until now. Apparently all it took was dressing in his clothes.

Adam's wallet is still sitting in its spot on the top of his night table. I root through it until I find what I'm looking for and hold it up to the light. His hair is short in the photograph, but I could totally get around that by tucking my hair into a beanie. Plus I'd pass any interrogation a bouncer could give me because I already know his birthday, address, and height by heart. My pulse quickens as I pop off my iPhone case and tuck Adam's ID in behind it. It would be so easy. All I'd have to do is dress up as him, and I could hit up the bars as Adam.

The ceiling creaks above me and I jump off the bed, tear off all the clothes. I change back into my pajamas and stuff the ball of Adam's clothes into one of the drawers just as Mom calls down the stairs.

"Audrey, is that you?"

Why would Audrey be in the basement? I run to the bottom of the staircase before Mom can come down and investigate. "No, it's me. Clare."

Even standing a floor above me, Mom looks fragile in her bathrobe. "What are you doing down there? You should be in your room."

My shoulders tense in irritation. Soon she'll have me punching in and out. "I was having trouble sleeping," I snap. And before I can think it through, I'm giving her the excuse: "I was thinking about Adam."

"Oh," she says in understanding, and guilt settles into my bones. "I see."

"I feel like I could be closer to him here." *I feel like a terrible person.*

She crosses her arms and leans against the door frame. "Do you want to talk about it?"

I do. I want to talk about what's really going on so badly, it's killing me. With her, with someone, with anyone. But I can't.

"Not really," I say, and start climbing the stairs. "I just have some stuff I need to figure out on my own."

"All right." She puts an arm around my shoulders as I approach. "But if you ever need to talk to someone besides that guidance counselor, I'm always here."

She sounds rejected, and it makes me feel sad and angry at the same time because I know she's thinking the same thing as me. When I was little, I told her everything. I asked for her advice, too. I climbed into her bed for a morning cuddle and opened my arms as wide as they could go, but it was never enough to show how much I loved her. Now our relationship is more bipolar than Calgary's weather, and I have to keep myself hidden so she doesn't realize the truth.

Audrey isn't the freak.

Audrey

Have you ever noticed the stars on the backs of your eyelids? When I can't fall sleep, I close my eyes and look at the stars. Thousands of pinpricks of light. If you look closely, you can see they're connected like a web.

When I was little, I used to dig my knuckles into my eyelids. Then I'd follow the changing patterns on an intergalactic voyage. That was before I knew to be afraid of going blind.

I'm answering English questions when a star slips across my eye. More like an eclipse. A black globule surrounded by a circle of light. I close and open my eye a few times and it disappears.

Maybe it was a bug. Or a bacteria blob. Hopefully I blinked it out.

Trying hard not to think about my sketchbook, I complete my first lesson and move to the next. And so on. And so forth.

I finish an hour early, so I ask Monsieur Martin permission to sketch until the end of class.

You've finished all of your reading?

Yes.

And your end-of-chapter questions?

Yes.

So you have no homework?

No.

Please bring me your workbooks.

I bring him the books and he flips through them, grading them on the spot. I stand there and wait while he does it. He looks young again today. He's wearing a short-sleeved shirt with a collar and he hasn't shaved. I try to guess how old he is. Thirty? Thirty-five? Maybe even in his twenties. I'm bad at guessing the ages of older people.

Finally he sits back in his chair and kind of squints at me. I'm impressed, Audrey. Lately I've been seeing a side of you I've never seen before. You've shown us that you can indeed reach your highest potential. I just wish you weren't motivated to leave us. If you continue on this road, you could be one of our star students.

I just stand there.

What are you going to sketch? he asks. If you'd like, I can call Ms. Nguyen and ask if you can spend the rest of the day in the art room. Perhaps we can work out an extra time period for you to work on your art. Maybe every Monday, Wednesday, and Friday.

Thank you but no, I say. I'll just draw at my desk.

Are you sure? You can use the art supplies.

I'm sure.

I quickly take my books back to my desk. The way he's looking at me makes me nervous. Like if I'm too good I'll never get out of here either.

For the next three days I'm the perfect student. I make sure to listen to him when he's at the front of the class. I finish all the questions in my workbook. I ignore the playground and the lonesome swing blowing in the wind. In fact I ignore the window entirely. Marianne smiles and tells me I'm doing a great job today. At the end of the week she puts three gold stars on my chart.

How many gold stars will it take to outweigh Dr. Jackson?

Marianne doesn't have enough stickers in her pad.

(New goal: to be such a good student, Marianne needs to rush out and buy all the stars.)

✦ ✹ ✦

Mom picks me up from school and I can barely contain the news. School went really well today, I tell her. I got a gold star. Three gold stars!

That's great, sweetie! Mom sounds genuinely happy. Are they your first?

I think one time I got a silver. (That's a lie. The most I've ever gotten is a bronze.)

A gold star means it was a full-potential day. You have to meet all five pillars to get a gold star on your chart. I followed the rules of the classroom. I was respectful and helpful with my teachers and fellow students. I participated positively in class discussion. I excelled in all my subjects.

Well, I'm very proud of you, Mom says.

I'm really happy then. Not just because she might consider letting me go back to Clare's school. It's been a really long time since Mom was pleased with me. I consider talking to her about Calvin, but when I think about him, my face turns red again.

We drive a few blocks and then Mom pulls over in front of a house with a huge stone wall. It looks like a castle.

Can we talk for a minute?

I bounce a little in my seat as I turn to face her. Finally. She's going to tell me the good news.

It's about your sister.

The balloon in my stomach deflates. Of course. They talked to Clare and she made them change their minds.

Mom takes my hand. This might be hard for you, and you might not even have an answer. I don't know how close you two are these days. But have you noticed Clare acting differently?

Yes.

In what ways?

She's dressing differently.

Is that it?

She seems angry. Angrier.

Mom nods. Slowly and then faster. She sits back against her seat so hard it shakes. She's still holding my hand and squeezes it. It worries me that she stayed home from school on your birthday. She used to be so social.

Social. That is one of my least favorite words. Mom and Dad always use it to describe Clare, not me.

I don't think she was really sick, Mom says. And I don't think she went out with her friends that night either. I think she lied to me.

Why don't you ask her?

She sighs. Then she sighs again. I don't know how to talk to your sister, she says. Whenever I try, she just gets mad at me.

I don't know how to talk to her either.

Mom kisses my hand and lets me go. She starts driving again.

Now that it's safe, I pull out my sketchbook. It falls opens to a page with a bookmark in it.

No, not a bookmark. Calvin's number.

I close the notebook fast but not fast enough.

Did you ever call that boy back? Mom asks. Calvin?

I haven't had time, I say.

Sweetie, you need to make time for people. A five-minute call is all it takes. Maybe the two of you could go for coffee.

I don't drink coffee.

You could get one of those iced things that kids who don't actually like coffee always drink. Coffee slushies! No, wait. Those are full of sugar. How about tea?

And then what? I ask.

Well, then you could drink your tea and talk. Mom clears her throat.

Or I could just call him? I ask.

Or you could just call him.

That seems like the easier choice. But thinking about calling him makes my hands feel sweaty. Sweatier than the time Sharon yelled *Freak* at me across the playground. Sweatier than when everyone laughed at me in karate class. What if he finds out I go to Peak? Then he'll call me a freak like the other kids.

How about you call him now? Mom says as we pull up at the house. Just get it over with, like ripping off a Band-Aid.

I don't get what Band-Aids have to do with this.

You're right, that was the wrong analogy. Talking to Calvin is going to be FUN and easier than you think. HE called YOU. He likes you, Audrey. You know that right? He called you three days ago now and is probably sad you haven't called him back. Three days is a long time to wait for someone to call you back.

He's sad?

He might be. He might think you don't like him.

I imagine Calvin sad because of me. I see him at the park, swinging alone with his stick sword. Crying large tears into the dirt. The image makes my stomach clench.

Okay, I say. I'll call him.

Mom grins and pats me on the knee. Atta girl!

We go inside and Mom says she's going to give me space. I hear her pull her ladder down and climb into the attic.

My phone is dead, so I plug it into Mom's cord in the kitchen. Then I sit at the counter and look for patterns in the granite while I wait. A teddy bear. An alligator wearing a cowboy hat.

To avoid any unwanted conversation topics (Peak), I compile a list of questions for Calvin.

1. *How old are you?* (My answer: Just turned fifteen.)
2. *What is your full name?* (My answer: Audrey Elizabeth Arnold.)
3. *What is your favorite subject?* (My answer: Art.)
4. *Which natural disaster scares you the most?* (My answer: A tie between tsunami and tornado but tornado wins because it could actually happen, despite what my mom says.)
5. *Do you like television shows and books?* (My answer: Yes.)
6. *What is your favorite television show and book?* (My answer: I don't have a favorite television show. *Anne of Green Gables* for books.)
7. *Have you saved any more gophers?* (My answer: No.)

That is all I can think of. I write down my answers too in case I get nervous and forget.

When I'm ready, I pull Calvin's number out of my sketchbook and carefully enter the numbers. The phone rings once and I hang up.

I pour myself a glass of water. Enter the number again. This time it rings twice and I hear a click as Calvin answers.

I hang up.

Then I remember cellphones have caller ID and Calvin will know it was me. I hit redial. My heart starts beating faster. It's beating too fast, like it's going to run away from my body. My hand starts to shake and the paper shakes with it.

I can't read it. I can't read it and Calvin is going to be on the phone soon and I'm not going to know what to say.

Hello?

It's him. It's Calvin.

How old are you? I ask.

Who is this?

This is Audrey. My full name is Audrey Elizabeth Arnold. What is your full name?

My hand is sweaty now. I don't think it's ever been this sweaty. It's hard to hold on to the phone. We're already on question number two and I haven't gotten the answer to question one.

Audrey! Calvin sounds excited. Then he laughs. I thought you were a telemarketer and I had to be eighteen or something.

Are you eighteen?

No, I'm sixteen.

I didn't think so. You wouldn't be homeschooled if you were eighteen.

I'd hope not. I'm in grade eleven. And my full name is Calvin Montgomery Hilton. What grade are you in?

I'm in grade nine and my full name is Audrey Elizabeth Arnold. What is your favorite subject?

Um, I don't really like school but I guess it would be language arts.

He doesn't ask me back so I move on to the next question. Which natural disaster scares you the most?

Which natural disaster? Why do you ask?

I'm just making conversation.

Oh. Okay. I guess I've never thought about it. Earthquakes are supposedly pretty scary. What about you?

I consult my piece of paper even though I haven't forgotten. I would never forget the answer to that one.

It's a tie between tsunami and tornado. Do you like television shows and books?

Of course.

What is your favorite television show and book? I like *Anne of Green Gables*.

Calvin laughs again. Audrey, are you really nervous or something?

My hand shakes harder and the paper slips out of my fingers. It glides back and forth but misses the counter. I slam my phone on the granite as I bend to pick it up.

Ouch! Audrey? Are you still there?

Got it. I pick up the phone again. What question are we on again? The last one.

Have you saved any more gophers? I ask.

No, I haven't. Do you think ... do you think maybe we should get together and save some?

Or we could go for coffee.

Calvin doesn't say anything. I'm worried we got disconnected. I'm worried he hung up. Maybe he doesn't like coffee either. Maybe he doesn't like *me*.

Then he says, Audrey, are you asking me out on a date?

He says the word *date* funny. Like he's laughing at me.

My face feels hot. Burning. I feel stupid. I shouldn't have called.

Because I'd like to go on a date with you, Calvin says. How about we go for coffee on Tuesday the 28th?

I nod.

Audrey?

Yes, I say. It sounds like a grunt so I clear my throat. Yes.

Awesome. Starbucks in Britannia at seven?

Seven at night or seven in the morning?

Seven at night.

Okay.

I chose that date because I have a surprise for you.

Okay.

Calvin chuckles. I'm hanging up now.

Okay. I clear my throat again. I need to say something else. Goodbye, Calvin.

See you Tuesday, Audrey.

Then there is silence. Calvin is gone for real now.

I hit END and then my face does the super-large smile again.

I'm going on a date. That's what Calvin called it. A date. A coffee date.

I'm going to be like the other girls who buy *Seventeen* magazine and look for advice. The normal girls. The girls who get off the phone with a boy and immediately call their best friend to tell them about it. But my best friend used to be Clare.

Should I tell Clare about my date? Maybe she can tell me how to act so I don't ruin it.

I work on my homework in the kitchen and wait for Clare to come home. Mom comes in to make dinner and asks how my call went.

Fine.

Fine as in good?

Fine as in good but you're not a teenager so you can't help me.

Mom looks confused but luckily doesn't ask any more questions.

Clare is taking a long time, so I go upstairs to wait in my room. I check my email on my phone. Nothing but spam.

Next I check my Facebook. There are three notifications. I click on the icon to view them.

Sharon has mentioned you in a post.

Sharon? Sharon has never mentioned me in a post. No one mentions me in anything. I click on the notification and the words fill my screen.

Audrey we're so FREAKING excited to see you in the fall!!!

Why would Sharon be excited to see me? Sharon hates me.

Then I get it. I get the joke.

The light of the screen is too bright. I try to delete the post but can't. It's on Sharon's wall.

There are already seventy-one likes on it.

All I can do is untag myself.

Did Clare have anything to do with this? Does she know about it? She must. She's on Facebook and Sharon is her best friend.

I toss my phone across the room.

ClaRe

It's Friday night, which means my curfew is extended to midnight. I've been looking forward to this all week.

I barely listen to the 'rents at dinner. Mom asks Audrey if she wants to tell us about her day and then gives her a look that's supposed to telepathically communicate something, but Audrey just shrugs and looks down at her food. I tell them I'm going to Charlotte's and get out of there as soon as possible. Only instead of walking over to Charlotte's house, I take a bus downtown.

There's a Tim Horton's a block away from my destination, so I duck into the bathroom there, pull Adam's clothes out of my backpack, and quickly change into them. The other night, I snuck back down into Adam's room and grabbed some more sweatshirts as well as an old T-shirt that didn't entirely engulf me like the rest. I also found an old sports bra in my underwear drawer that's so tight, it flattens my breasts against my chest. I tie my hair up into a bun at the top of my head and pull a beanie on. I don't realize the flaw in my plan until I step out of the stall.

A woman is washing her hands at the sink. She glances up, and when she sees me in the mirror, she gets pissed.

"What are you doing in here? This is the women's bathroom."

"Sorry," I mumble, and rush out.

I'm feeling good, though. I'm feeling pumped. I mean, that was a good sign, right?

There is no bouncer yet, so I walk right through the open doors and onto a landing, where a half staircase leads up to the club and another half staircase leads down to a basement where the bar hosts smaller events. Framed advertisements line the walls: a Gothic-inspired burlesque show, the Pride Weekend party, karaoke Wednesdays, eighties night, and various DJs.

Upstairs the club is surprisingly empty, probably because it's only eight p.m. A large rainbow flag is suspended on the wall, below which disco lights spin alone on a dance floor being pumped full of dry ice. Three cage swings hang from the ceiling alongside the dance floor, two of them occupied: one guy on a phone and a woman curled up asleep. To the left is a modern-looking wood bar, the glass cabinet behind it full of bottles of liquor lit from below by multicolored lights.

When I see the bartender, my mood instantly deflates. He's broad and built, wearing a tight black T-shirt that shows off his sleeve tattoos and an expression that signifies he doesn't take shit from anybody. There's no way he's going to serve me. The old Clare . . . maybe.

It's now or never. Adjusting my shoulders and adopting a more confident swagger, I stride up to the bar. The bartender looks up from the drink he's mixing and his eyebrows bend close together as he studies me.

"Right," he says after a moment. "I'm going to need some ID."

My real ID burns in my pocket as I dig out the wallet. He watches me struggle to pull the ID out — it's wedged in so tight! My hand shakes as I finally hand it to him, and I try not to smile stupidly as he looks at the ID, then at me, then back at the ID again. It's clear he's skeptical, but I can't tell whether it's due to my age or the way I look.

Finally he passes it back to me and asks, "What can I get you?"

Malibu is on the tip of my lips, but I quickly change it to a beer.

"All right . . ." He gestures at the taps. "We have Canadian, Coors, Village Blonde, Original Sixteen, Wild —"

I cut him off and order Canadian. Bad choice. I've tasted beer at parties and it's never tasted like this. Maybe because by the time I've tried it, I've already been tipsy on Malibu and orange juice.

More people are filing in now. I'm not going to stay long enough to talk to anyone, but I don't care because it's a high just to be here. At school most of the kids dress like everyone else, but here people are clearly not afraid to wear exactly what they want, even if that's a tutu with a corset and butterfly wings. I watch the girl wearing the wings throw her head back in laughter before wrapping an arm around someone's shoulders.

At some point when I'm halfway through my beer, someone slides onto the stool beside me.

No way. Keep it together, Clare! Keep. It. Together.

"I'll get a Blonde," Taylor says to the bartender, and then winks at me.

The hand that's holding my beer shakes and I spill a quarter of it onto my shirt. Smooth.

Taylor passes me a bar napkin that was originally imprisoned under a cup of cocktail swords. "Come here often?"

"First time." I realize my voice sounds extra high-pitched and try to lower it. "You?"

Taylor accepts a pint from the bartender and takes a deep drink while looking over the rim at me with the stormiest eyes I've ever seen. Light gray around the pupil growing darker until there is a ring of almost black around the iris, they are hands-down the coolest eyes ever.

They extend a hand. "I'm Taylor."

I blink. Does Taylor really not recognize me in these clothes?

We've been in class together for five months now. It's dark, I suppose. Plus they've met a lot of new people in the last few months. I probably blend in.

"I'm Cla —" I hesitate for only a second and then finish: "Clay."

My heart palpitates with the lie and I hold my breath and wait to get called out, certain they must be able to feel my pulse racing through my palm, but that doesn't happen. Instead they release my hand, down the rest of their beer, and ask, "Wanna dance?"

"Uh . . ." I glance out at the dance floor. I can count the number of people dancing. Five. Two couples and a straggler.

"Come on, it will be fun."

Taylor jumps off the stool, and before I have time to think it through, I'm following them through the crowd, taking sips of my drink for confidence, and the disco lights are leaping off the people we pass, obscuring their faces like masquerade masks. I'm so out of my element, yet I know it's exactly where I'm supposed to be.

I usually only like to dance when the floor is packed and I can blend in with everyone else, but the moment we step under the disco ball, I feel it: the birth of the new me. I dance like the old Clare, yet — unlike the old Clare — I don't care who's watching. Maybe it's more fun dancing as a guy, or maybe it's being with Taylor, because I don't feel any pressure to be good at it or look sexy.

At first we just goof around, taking turns doing corny moves like the sprinkler and the running man to make each other laugh. We dance until I'm sweaty and I wish I could pull the beanie off. Taylor is a wicked dancer — it doesn't seem to matter what type of song comes on, they have all the right moves.

"Watch this." Taylor plants a hand down on the floor, kicks their legs into the air, and places their second hand on top of the first as they spin upside down like a top. The other five dancers join in as I cheer and clap.

"That was insane! A breakdancing move?"

"Yeah. It's called the two thousand."

"So you're a legit dancer."

They laugh. "Since I was a kid. I took gymnastics, too."

Out of nowhere, they do a backwards handspring. Then they take both of my hands in theirs, chest heaving, eyes bright. "Having fun?"

"Yeah." I'm hyperaware of the warmth emanating from Taylor's hands. Crazy, but I almost feel like I could do a handspring too.

Taylor sighs. "I wish we didn't have to go to school on Monday."

The moment I hear those words, the spell breaks. I flinch and take a step back, breaking our connection. "You . . ." I can't get the words out. Tears of humiliation burn my eyes. "You knew who I was the entire time but you didn't say anything?"

Taylor frowns as if confused.

"Why didn't you say something when I told you my name was Clay?"

"Because I thought you were telling me the name you want to be called. You weren't?"

"No! I thought you didn't recognize me because you didn't say anything." How naïve, like putting on an eye mask and believing you're in disguise. "I'm just trying something out. It was stupid."

"I don't think it's stupid. I wanted to hang out with you." They take a tentative step forward, but I take a step back.

"Except the *me* you thought you were spending time with is someone else."

"Is it? Or do you feel like this is the real you? Because that's what I thought when I watched you walk in and out of the bathroom at Tim Horton's."

I take a second to process this. "So it wasn't chance that you ran into me here?"

"I've never been here before in my life."

"How did you get in?"

Taylor flashes me a sideways smile. "A fake, of course. ID from the UK. Works every time."

I need to sit down.

It's busier now and the booths are full, so I walk a few steps away and lean up against the wall, yank the beanie off. Taylor stands beside me.

"I have no idea what I'm doing."

"You're doing exactly what you're supposed to be doing. You're figuring it out."

I pull the beanie back on and look them straight in the eye. "What about you? I mean, what are you?"

At this Taylor's eyes seem to cloud over entirely. "I'm me."

"I meant what you call yourself. You know what I mean."

"I'm nonbinary. My whole life, people have wanted me to 'decide' whether I'm a boy or a girl, but I can't because I'm both. I've always been both."

I nod, taking this all in. "Sometimes I feel like a girl and sometimes I feel like a boy. I don't know what to call myself yet."

"And that's okay. Dress to show your unique personality. Wake up every morning and wear what you feel like wearing that day."

"It's not that simple," I insist. "People want to know."

Taylor raises an eyebrow. "You think I don't know that?"

I feel my face heat. What a stupid thing to say.

Taylor chuckles, letting me know they were teasing. "What I'm trying to say is that it doesn't matter what other people think; it matters what Clare thinks. It's not up to anyone else to tell you how to see yourself."

I look down at my Converses. I wish I could be as self-assured as

Taylor. I wish I didn't care what other people think, but I do. The DJ starts playing Lady Gaga and there is a loud cheer of approval followed by a large group evacuating their booth for the dance floor.

"Here's a question for you," Taylor says. "Do you think there are only two genders, or more than that?"

"More, I guess."

"Me too. I think people are born with all kinds of traits and society teaches them which to keep and which to ditch based on one gender. But people are starting to see through the bullshit."

The passion in their voice makes the hairs on my arms prickle in response. "Why did you follow me tonight?"

Taylor shrugs and offers me an almost-shy smile. "I guess when I saw you come out of the bathroom, I thought you might be a kindred spirit. That sounds lame, I know." Taylor laughs and their cheeks flush even in the low light. "You kind of intrigue me, and I thought maybe you could use a friend."

I could. My life has pretty much derailed since Adam's death, and it sometimes feels I'm losing it. Taylor is a complete mystery, an outsider and a rebel — at least that is what Sharon would have everyone believe — and maybe that's exactly the kind of friend I need.

I look down at my hands and thread my fingers together the way I did that day Taylor gave their presentation. How much has changed in a week. "You're the only one who knows. This is the first time I've ever tried something like this."

"I think it's brill."

I peek up, a smile tugging at my lips. "'Brill'?"

"Brilliant." Taylor grins and holds out their hand. "How about we go back and dance?"

So that's what we do, and it's the most fun I've had in a really, really long time. It makes me realize how long I've been pretending with

Sharon & Co. Pretending to care about who's cool and who isn't, pretending to care about the boring boys in our class, pretending to care about celebrities and gossip and all the other stuff that seemed shallow in the face of Adam's death. Taylor is the first genuine person I've met in years.

At the end of the night I don't want to go home, but I know I'll get in trouble if Mom catches me breaking curfew again. Taylor lives in a luxury condo downtown, close enough to walk home, but waits at my bus stop with me. There are so many things I want to ask, but the bus appears too quickly, barreling toward us in the dark. I don't want to leave. I climb on and walk to the very back, like I'm trying to return to Taylor even as the bus pulls me away.

Once home, I slump against the wall in the front entrance and hug Adam's beanie to my chest.

Audrey

Marianne actually does buy a new pad of gold stars. She tells me this as she's doing her morning greeting.

Happy Monday, Audrey! You've inspired the other students. Look at all the gold stars across the board!

She's right. There is a column of gold stars, each one standing on another's shoulders. Gold stars galore.

I'm proud of you, Marianne says. I knew you could do it.

Thank you.

Are you sure you don't want extra time in the art studio?

Peak has an art studio half the size of the school gym. I only get to use it two days a week because we have to rotate with the other students and work on our other subjects. What a waste. So this time I say yes.

I'm waiting for the clock to read 2:30 when Kira appears at my desk. I look up and jump. Kira doesn't make any sound when she walks. She wears long dresses and skirts so it's impossible to tell if she touches the ground. I think she floats.

Today she's wearing a long white dress. Her black hair is halfway down her back. Her eyes are just as dark.

Is it true you want to leave Peak?

She looks sad. Her eyes are upside-down crescent moons.

I heard you talking to Monsieur Martin, she says. Do you not like it here?

Beside me George pulls his finger from his nose. Marianne cleaned his drawer so he's starting a fresh ridge.

No, I don't. I want to go back to school with my twin. We used to go to school together.

Kira drifts even closer. So it's not because you think we're all freaks?

The room goes quiet. I look at the clock but the hand hasn't moved. It still reads 2:12. I look at the front of the room but Monsieur Martin and Marianne are at the back. Then I have to look at Kira again because there's nowhere else to look.

There's a weird feeling in my stomach. I know some people would lie now. They would do it to make her feel better. Mom says it's called a "white lie."

I don't even know why you're here, I say.

I have severe dyslexia.

That doesn't make you a freak. It's a reading difference.

That's my point. My parents thought it would be easier for me to focus in a smaller class. That's why most of us are here.

I just nod.

We're not freaks. Say it.

I was right about the audience. They're holding their pencils and watching. All I can think about is the post Sharon tagged me in.

So FREAKING excited!

I open my mouth but nothing comes out. Kira's waiting with moons for eyes and I just sit there.

She waits.

I sit.

Say it, Audrey. Say it.

I don't think you're *all* freaks, I say. Then I realize my mistake. It's called *inflection*.

Someone gasps. At first I don't realize Kira's crying. At first she's just standing there. Then her eyes fill with tears. But her eyes can't hold all the tears so they overflow down her face.

I grab my books and leave.

Ms. Nguyen's art room is on the other side of the school. I used to be afraid of Ms. Nguyen. Her face is cut in half diagonally with a scar and she sounds angry when she talks. Only she isn't angry. That's just how she talks. Her hair is always up in a tight bun. She wears a smock stained with paint and makes us put on one too.

Being free to get dirty is liberating, she tell us. You won't worry about anything except your art.

Ms. Nguyen taught us how to use pastels and charcoals instead of boring pencil crayons. We've tried pointillism, pottery, and papier-mâché. But I'm kind of nervous to see her alone. The door to the studio is closed so I knock. Then I knock again louder.

Come in, Audrey!

I enter.

Ms. Nguyen is wiping down one of the long tables. She smiles and places something rectangular down on its surface. I assume you want to finish this?

She is referring to the half-finished portrait of Sirius I abandoned a few weeks ago.

I'm no longer drawing or painting Sirius, I tell her.

Oh. For some reason she looks sad about that. She puts the canvas away in a rack with a bunch of other paintings. And why is that?

Her back is to me so I can't see her face. I don't like when people do that because it makes it harder to understand them.

Because Sirius doesn't exist, I say.

Ms. Nguyen turns back around and this time puts a blank canvas and palette on the table. I watch as she fills an old jam jar with water and places a paintbrush in it. She lines five acrylic paint tubes across the top of the palette. Three primary colors plus white and black.

So you don't think you should paint things that don't exist? she asks.

I think people want me to stop. For some reason I'm being very honest with Ms. Nguyen.

She nods as she considers this. You're probably right, Audrey. She pats the chair. I'm ready for you. Sit down.

I do and she brings me a smock. I feel like I'm about to get my hair cut because she doesn't walk away. I can feel her hovering behind me.

Can I ask, is Sirius a dog you used to have?

I shake my head. I pick up the brush and paint a line of water on the palm of my left hand. It feels nice. Soothing.

I've never had a dog, I tell her. But I really wanted one. I asked my parents and promised to take care of it all by myself. Walk it and feed it and bathe it. They always said no. (If Clare had wanted a dog, we would have gotten one. But I don't say that.)

I pick up the black tube. Squeeze a large dollop onto the palette and dip my brush in it. I love the first dip of the brush. It's a controlled mess.

I started drawing Sirius after my brother and I watched *Clifford the Big Red Dog* on TV. It was a Saturday morning and Clare was still at a sleepover with her friend Sharon. I called the show stupid. Red dogs don't exist and no one would want a dog that big. Adam said it didn't matter that he couldn't exist; that's what people like about it.

Your brother was right, Ms. Nguyen says. The author of those books asks his readers to suspend their disbelief in a red dog the size of a house for the sake of entertainment. Do you understand what I'm saying?

I think so.

We use art as a way to escape the everyday. It allows us to explore our inner worlds, and to share our ideas and truths with other people. That is why humans create and enjoy art. In my opinion, that is the entire *point* of art.

I blink and sit back in my chair to see the choice has been made. The canvas has been painted entirely black. The perfect background for Sirius.

Art can also be therapeutic, Ms. Nguyen continues. She moves around the table to face me. Perhaps you want to paint Sirius because that's what you need right now: a friend.

My hand is starting to shake. People think it's weird. I don't want to be weird.

You're an artist, Audrey. Remember that. Artists see the world differently than other people. No artist should ever be ashamed of that because it's what makes their work so emotional and so unique.

Unique as in . . . special?

Exactly! Miss Nguyen beams.

I put the brush back into the jar. Black fog swirls around it like a hex.

I'm tired of painting. I push the canvas away.

Her face falls. For some reason it reminds me of Kira.

No problem, she says. Feel free to try something else. Then her smile is back but it doesn't look like how it did before. It's crooked. She waves an arm toward the back of the room. The art supplies are at your disposal!

I stand and pull off my smock. I think I'll go to the library, I tell her. Then I grab my backpack off the floor and leave.

ClaRe

Monday morning I go to school, but I'm only there in body. I'm not listening — I'm not even pretending to listen. What I'm actually doing is reliving Friday night at the bar with Taylor over and over again in my mind. For the first time in my life, I wish I had bio today. Just so we could see each other.

When the classroom goes quiet, I realize our English teacher has stopped lecturing and we're supposed to be working on our essay outlines. I've zoned out Audrey-style. There's a knock on the door and our teacher goes to answer it and then steps out into the hall for a moment. The class instantly erupts.

Billy turns around in his desk and his mouth pulls into a sneer. I know it's going to be bad before he even says, "What happened to you?"

Everyone stops talking. They look over at us but pretend to be working. I've been one of them. I've seen Billy in action from the other side, making fun of the losers, but this is the first time he's turned on me. I can feel my face heat but I roll my pen along the top of my notebook like I'm cool and casual and ready for anything he throws at me.

I'm wearing another one of Adam's band hoodies, this one Metallica. Sure, I've seen some girls wear them, but they're the girls people refer to as skids or stoners. Plus it's the last week of May and sunny and I used to wear skirts and shorts at this time of year. So of course I know what he's referring to when I ask, "What do you mean?"

"I mean you used to be hot." His smile widens like he's giving me a compliment rather than being a complete douche. His friends laugh; so do some of the girls. My stomach drops at the sound, and my hand falters with the pen. If Billy looks down, he'll be able to see.

He's waiting, daring me to respond, and I don't know what to say. Part of me wonders if I should be upset that he no longer thinks I'm attractive. Another part of me wants to prevent the situation from getting worse by pretending he's giving me friendly advice — maybe if I don't retaliate, he'll take pity on me and turn back around. But a third, stronger part, is itching to tell him that the last thing I'm thinking about these days is how to be hot for *him*.

That part wins.

"It's not my job to look hot for you, Billy," I tell him.

He laughs and it sounds like a real laugh, like we're friends joking around. Then he shrugs, his eyes flicking down to the pen shaking in my hand. I'm so busted.

"I just think it's a shame, that's all," he says in that deceptively casual voice. "You have a nice body, but now you hide it under all those baggy clothes. What a waste."

More laughter from the guys. I glance over at Sharon, looking for help, but she's looking back at me like she's mortified for me. With a bit of *I told you so* mixed in. My face is hot now, so hot I know they can see I'm embarrassed, and that just makes it worse.

Under my breath I say, "Screw you, Billy."

He's still smiling, but I can tell from the slight twitch in his lips that he knows he went too far. He puts his hands up in a *just saying* gesture and turns back around in his seat. I stare at the notebook, trying to ignore the sensation of my cheeks flaring, Billy's words running through my mind.

You have a nice body, but now you hide it.

Nice body. *My* body. So when Billy said that, why did I feel like my body belonged more to Billy than to me?

+ ✳ +

At noon I go to Sharon's locker, the place we always meet for lunch, but no one shows. I send a group text asking where they are, but no one responds, so I go back down to the wrestling mats and look at my phone. Between classes I see Sharon in the halls and pull aside to ask her what happened.

"I got caught up in class and you'd already left by the time I got there," she tells me. Of course this lie doesn't explain Charlotte's or Rhiannon's absence.

"But I texted."

"We got it too late, sorry." She flashes an apologetic pout before continuing down the hall.

At the bar with Taylor I felt high, but now I feel like I'm crashing. For the first time in as long as I can remember, I feel lonely. My friends are making it very clear they're not interested in the new me — whoever that is. If I continue to try to find out, I know I'm probably going to lose them.

After school I tell Mom I'm still working on a school project, and then I go to the library and find the research station in the farthest corner where there is less chance of someone seeing what I'm doing. I'm too nervous to do this kind of research on my phone, and the library is surprisingly empty after school hours, which is perfect for what I want to do.

After a quick glance over my shoulder, I open Google and type *How to tell if "someone" is a girl or a guy* because I don't want to make it about me. Google gives me the following list:

1. Ask for their name
2. Observe their outfit and hairstyle
3. Know that bathrooms aren't always a reliable indicator
4. Know that hobbies don't always line up with gender norms
5. Realize that their anatomy might not match their gender
6. Politely ask them which pronouns you should use

It reminds me of Taylor and my discussion at the bar about how people seem to need to know if someone is a boy or girl, like they can't stand the idea of not being able to categorize other people.

I close the list and search for LGBTQ forums. I don't join or make a username on any of them, I just want to lurk and read other people's experiences. One FTM post has a link to a trans guy's blog called *The Real Sam the Man*. Sam created this blog back in 2012, writing his story anonymously. It wasn't until he was fully out and his blog had blown up with a huge following that he added pictures and videos he'd been recording over the years.

He tells the story of how his family used to be composed of three boys until his mother had the girl of her dreams. Only Sam didn't feel like a girl — Sam felt like a boy like his brothers. Sam spent his childhood being called a tomboy and felt like a phony when his mother made him wear dresses to special occasions, but he was too scared of disappointing her to tell her how he felt. He also struggled with feelings of guilt when he didn't want to participate in "feminine" activities, like getting manicures together. The moment that pushed him over the precipice and decide to transition was the moment he realized a simple truth: by keeping his mother's dream alive, he was destroying his own.

Whoa. I sit back in my chair and wipe my brow with my sleeve. I'm sweaty. I have chills. There are definitely parts of Sam's story that resonate. Like Sam's mom, my mom always wanted girls. Would she be disappointed to learn how I feel? When I think about telling the world I'm different, it's not my friends I'm most afraid of.

It's my family.

+ ❋ +

The next morning, I make sure I'm one of the first people to arrive in bio so I can leave a note on Taylor's chair. So that they won't knock it onto the floor thinking its garbage, I write a large *T* on the folded front. At the end of my message, I sign it *Clay*. Our private joke.

As everyone enters the room, I sit there pretending to read my textbook like a nervous wreck and try not to glance in Taylor's direction. My breath catches when I see them pick it up out of the corner of my eye.

Class drags and then I have another before lunch. It feels like days have gone by before I can finally make my way to the wrestling mats, where I pace back and forth, obsessing over whether or not Taylor will actually show up. Will they think it's weird I left them a note instead of just asking them to their face?

"A secret rendezvous. What kind of trouble are we planning here?"

I stop pacing and glance over my shoulder. Taylor is standing halfway down the steps, looking amused. I feel myself blush with embarrassment. "I don't have your number."

"Well, I prefer an old-fashioned note anyway." Taylor swings off the railing and onto the ground like a gymnast. "I like it here. Nice and private."

"Yeah. That's what I like about it too."

They climb onto the pile of mats and sit with their back against the wall, knees bent, cool as ever. I climb up too, and the moment I do, I feel calm. We're alone here, tucked away in a private alcove under the stairs. No one can see us from the floors above. Adopting the same pose as Taylor, I lean against the opposite wall.

"That was fun the other night," I say. "We should do it again."

The side of their mouth lifts. "I'm down for dancing any time."

"Sweet." The word comes out a little too high. This is the first time I've tried to make a new friend in years.

"So no one comes down here at lunch?" Taylor asks, looking around.

"Only on Fridays for wrestling practice. Otherwise it's pretty quiet. The only quiet spot in the entire school, I think. I've been hanging out here a lot lately."

They smile knowingly. "I get it. Some days going to school feels like being forced into everything. Forced into spending time with people we don't want to spend time with and learning about subjects we aren't interested in. I tell myself it's only three more years, I can get through it."

"And then what will you do?"

"Probably dance on a cruise ship." I laugh and Taylor continues, "No, I want to be a dance therapist. They're not very common here, but there were a lot of dance therapists back home in London."

"What does a dance therapist do exactly?"

"They help people like other therapists, but through dance. It's good for physical health, but also mental and emotional health, because it gives people a way to express themselves. Music is so powerful. When you hear a song, it can bring you back to a certain memory or experience, right?"

"Totally."

"I dance to have a good time, but I also dance to work through my problems. The moment I heard of dance therapy, I knew that was what I wanted to do. I love to dance and I like to help people. Especially other people like me who have always felt like outsiders."

"Wow, that's so cool." I wrap my arms around my legs, hug them to my chest. "I never think about my life that far in the future. I'm still figuring out who I am and what I want to do, but I think I'm also afraid to assume a future even exists. My brother . . . He died so young."

"I heard something about your brother. I'm sorry. Adam, right? He passed away recently?"

"Yeah. I miss him. Like, all the time."

Taylor moves to my side and puts an arm around me. "What was he like?"

"Kind." That's the first word that comes to mind when I think of my brother. The second is *protective*. I think of all the ways he protected Audrey. The ways he protected me. I think of the diner, but not one of our usual Sunday brunches. There was one time when Adam took Audrey and me there, just the three of us.

Adam lied to our parents, saying he was taking us to the park but instead spending a good portion of his first paycheck on getting us all the bad food Mom and Dad never let us order anymore. We were eating in our usual corner booth, the one the restaurant always saved for our family, when Lars and Seamus, two guys in Adam's grade, walked in with their identical haircuts.

"Look at this," Lars said. "Adam spending Saturday morning with his baby sisters. How sweet." He and his friend with an identical haircut knocked fists.

"What do you want, Lars?" Adam sighed.

"We didn't see you at Stacy's wicked party last night. Did you spend the night in playing Barbies?"

Laughter followed by another fist bump.

"I already told you, I got a job."

"He's working at IKEA!" Audrey said, not looking up from her coloring.

The guys hooted. "Well, that's embarrassing. What, your parents lose all their money or something?"

"Yeah, Lars, you got me." Adam winked at me and made a motion that meant, *Can you believe this guy?* I laughed.

Lars grunted. "I've heard your dad is looking around, that he's not billing enough hours. Too bad. I'm sure it's affecting your allowance."

Adam flashed him a smile. "Actually, I'm working so I can take Dahlia out for dinners. We're doing that tonight, in fact."

Lars's smile completely disappeared. That was when I remembered that Lars and Dahlia used to date. Adam told me Dahlia had left Lars for him and now Lars hated him.

As quick as it left, Lars's smile returned, this time turning salacious as he elbowed Seamus. "One time I took that whore for dinner, and afterward she —"

Adam was up in a second. He reached across the table and grabbed the front of Lars's shirt, yanked him forward. "Don't say another word."

"Whoa, man," Lars's buddy said, glancing left and right with his hands up like he wasn't sure if he should get involved. "This is a family restaurant. Simmer down."

Adam glanced down at us and then released Lars, shoving him away. "Move on, Lars."

For a moment I thought Lars was going to retaliate. His face was bright red, his hands were balled into fists, and his chest was heaving up and down. He looked freaky with his military haircut, broad chest, and murderous expression. Unhinged. If he and Adam got into a fight, my bet wouldn't be on Adam.

But then our server came along and Lars luckily decided against it.

"Have a lame-ass breakfast," he muttered under his breath before walking away.

Audrey swiveled in her seat and yelled after them: "You're a lame-ass breakfast!"

We all burst into laughter.

Adam reached forward, patted her affectionately on the head. "I love you, Audrey."

✦ ✳ ✦

"Sounds like Adam was a good guy," Taylor says now. "I wish I could have met him."

"He was. He was the best big brother in the world. He didn't care about being cool; he was just a good person."

"Is Audrey your little sister?"

"No, my twin. Nonidentical."

"I wasn't aware you have a twin! Does she go here?"

"Not anymore. She moved to a different school this year. She goes to Peak now."

"Never heard of it. So do you have one of those telepathic twin bonds?"

"When we were little we used to be able to look at each other and know exactly what the other person was thinking." I can still read Audrey better than anyone else, but it's getting harder, as if the distance growing between us has caused an interference in our connection. I tell myself that it doesn't matter, that I no longer care, but I know that's a lie. If I didn't care, my heart wouldn't have clenched when Taylor asked me that question just now.

"I always wanted a twin," they continue. "I'm an only child and thought it would be awesome to have someone your exact same age to share things with, like the first day of school. Not having to worry about whether or not the other kids like you because you already have your best friend."

Taylor's words strike a chord within me and my eyes suddenly fill with tears. I'm helpless to stop them because I know Audrey felt the same way. She didn't want to worry about what anyone else thought of her because all that mattered to her was me. I wipe the tears away with the back of my hand. "Audrey and I kind of grew apart. Adam's death cemented it, but it had already started happening before that. Adam was always trying to make us close again. I think he thought I was being mean to her."

"Why do you think that?"

I struggle to find the words to explain my relationship with Audrey without making me sound like a complete jerk. "I guess it started after I became friends with Sharon. Sharon thought Audrey was weird. She *is* weird, but Sharon made sure everyone thought that was a bad thing."

Taylor frowns. "So why be friends with her?"

I shrug helplessly, feeling like I'm talking to Adam again. "I don't know, because I wanted to be friends with her? I was growing apart from Audrey because she was still playing with toys in her bedroom, and Sharon seemed so grown-up and knew what was cool. It's hard to believe, but Sharon used to be fun. And I used to care what she thinks."

"I think you still care what she thinks," Taylor says softly.

"Sharon is my friend. She just doesn't want the other kids to make fun of me."

Taylor cocks an eyebrow. "That sounds a lot like when parents say they hope their child isn't gay so that they don't have a tough life, when the toughest life is living a lie. The people who truly love you for you will know that and just want you to be happy."

I bite my lip and consider this. "I just think maybe it's important to fit in sometimes so that we're not alone. I mean, don't we all have to adjust the things we say and do sometimes to make people around us feel comfortable?"

"Sure, sometimes we need to play the part to fit in, but we're not talking about swearing in front of Grandma. We're talking about your *identity*. And we both know Sharon is plain cruel. It sounds like she's been cruel to your sister, and she's been cruel to me ever since I came here."

"There's more to the Audrey thing." I can hear how defensive I sound. I haven't explained myself well, but I'm too raw to get into the story of how Adam died. "It's complicated."

"More complicated than you should have told that twat where to go?"

It's true, so I don't bother to argue. I just sit there feeling like the worst twin in the world.

"Sorry, I shouldn't have said that," Taylor says eventually. "I don't know everything."

"No, it's true. I should have stuck up for her back then. *Adam* would have. And now . . . Well, Audrey did something that hurt me. She didn't mean to, it wasn't her fault, but it hurt me more than anything has ever hurt me in my life."

"You don't have to tell me about it." Taylor hesitates for a moment and then adds, "Just remember you can still make up with Audrey, if you want. There's still time."

I set my jaw before all my mixed emotions surrounding Audrey come bursting forth. Before I tell Taylor that deep down I know I'm being unfair blaming Audrey, but I can't seem to stop.

Taylor rotates to face me, legs crossed. "I didn't know Adam, but from what you've told me, I think he would have been supportive of what you're going through. That you're discovering yourself, I mean. I think he would be proud."

I've never considered that before, but it's probably true. Just like when I wanted to skateboard, Adam would tell me to go for it. Go all the way and never look back.

"Too bad the rest of my family isn't like Adam." Before Taylor can ask me to expand, I toss the question at them. "What are your parents like?"

"My parents were high school sweethearts who considered themselves punks, so I don't think they ever expected their kid to be like everyone else." Taylor laughs. "They're cool parents. They wanted me to experience London life, and, let's be honest, they didn't want to miss out on their own lives after having a baby, so they took me to a lot of concerts, festivals, and theater performances. After they had me, we moved to Belsize Park because it's a short ride from Central London, which they couldn't bear to leave, but at the same time it's sort of suburban. It's calmer and greener. I loved growing up there." Here Taylor pauses and laughs. "If you haven't been to London, you probably have no idea what I'm talking about."

I laugh too. "All I know about London is red double-decker buses and telephone booths, Harry Potter, the Tower, and fish and chips."

"Oh, we used to get chicken and chips takeaway after school!" Taylor actually licks their lips. "I miss that."

"Do you miss living in London?" I immediately regret asking the question because now I'm scared to hear the answer. What if Taylor wants to move back? Would their parents do it?

"Sometimes. There's a lot to do in London, and it's a central hub so you can quickly travel anywhere from there. But to be honest, there are downsides to living in London too. Everyone is always in a hurry, and they think nothing of commuting for an hour on the tube to get anywhere. I was actually kind of glad when my mum told me she was getting transferred to Canada. Moving to a new country was a chance to transform into the person I wanted to be without all the baggage of my childhood."

Baggage of their childhood? That sounds completely opposite to the childhood Taylor just described. I want to ask about it, but that feels rude and intrusive, and then the chance is gone as they continue.

"I was a bit nervous about meeting new friends, but it wasn't as hard as I thought it would be because of the gay-straight alliance. Have you heard of that group? I can tell you where the next meeting will be, if you want."

I just nod because I'm not sure I want to attend. I feel comfortable on the forums, where I can observe other people from the safety of my phone or computer.

Taylor tilts their head to the side. "So what are your parents like?"

"They're good people; they just really worry about what people think of them. Also what people think about us: Audrey and me." I pause, realizing this is an epiphany I never would have come to if I weren't having this exact conversation at this exact moment. "I think that might actually be part of the reason I thought it was so important to fit in. Growing up, my teachers and parents were always so concerned about Audrey being an outsider. Around the time Sharon came to our school, Audrey was starting to get in trouble with the teachers, but Sharon was popular and smart and the teachers loved her." I can barely get the words out —I'm breathless with awareness. All these things I'm realizing about myself, about Audrey, about the people who helped shape who we are today. "I think I saw the way people treated Audrey and the way people treated Sharon, and I made the decision to be like Sharon."

Taylor nods. "I can understand that."

"I've watched my parents do everything they can to help Audrey. They so badly want to be able to help her, but they don't know how. Now they're starting to worry about me."

"Your parents love you and Audrey, no matter what."

"I know that. And I know that my parents only want what's best for us." I inhale a deep, ragged breath. "I want the same for them."

Sam the Man wrote that by keeping his mother's dream alive, he was destroying his own. And Taylor just told me that the toughest life is living a lie. The problem is, neither of them comes from the same background as me, so I can't just blindly follow their advice. Neither of their parents were already suffering following the death of a child. Neither of their parents *paid* to have a child of the gender they wanted. I wish I could explain that to Taylor, but just like I'm not ready to explain Audrey's accidental role in Adam's death, I'm not ready to reveal that my mom wanted daughters. That my relationship with her is already strained and I don't want to make it worse.

I stand up to leave. "You were right about what you said, that we only have three more years of high school. Why make things harder? I can get through three years."

Taylor looks up at me with wide eyes. "What are you saying, Clare?"

I shrug as if it's no big deal, as if I actually believe my own words. "I just have to fit in and survive, right? No one likes high school."

"But Clare ..." Taylor breaks eye contact and looks away. "Never mind."

"I'm not ready!" I snap. I'm not mad at Taylor — Taylor is being incredibly supportive — I'm mad at the situation. Mad at the world. Mad at myself.

There are still ten minutes left in the lunch hour, but I claim I don't want to be late for class and dart back up the stairwell.

Audrey

On Tuesday night, dinner starts at six. Clare is not present. Mom tells Dad Clare is working on a project with Charlotte in the school library. Then Mom tells Dad she doesn't believe that.

Why not? Dad asks.

I don't think she's spending time with her friends anymore. I think she's made some new friends.

I see. Dad frowns even though it's good news.

If Clare and Sharon stop being friends, Clare might be my best friend again. If Clare and Sharon stop being friends, Clare might forgive me for Adam.

Isn't making new friends a good thing? I ask.

You want the right type of friend, Dad tells me.

Anyone would be better than Sharon, I respond.

My parents look at each other. Their faces turn redder and redder until they both start laughing.

What? It's the truth.

Mom nods, still chuckling. I'm not saying it isn't.

The clock changes to 6:45. I stand up and take my empty plate to the dishwasher.

Going somewhere in a hurry? Dad asks.

Yes, I need a ride to the Starbucks in Britannia. I'm meeting Calvin.

Mom and Dad blink in unison. Tonight?

Yes, at 7:00. So I need to get ready now. I go upstairs to put my wallet in my purse. Mom appears in the doorway.

You didn't tell me you have a date tonight.

I did just now. We're going for coffee like you suggested.

Mom smiles. That will be nice.

Both Mom and Dad get into the car to drive me. Neither of them speaks the entire drive. When we park outside the Starbucks, Dad turns to face me.

We'll be here to pick you up at 7:30.

Stewart! Mom knocks him on the shoulder and turns back to me. You remembered your phone, right? Call us when you're ready to be picked up.

I'm going on my first coffee date. It's really happening! I get out of the car but they don't drive away. They sit there and wave at me until I go into the Starbucks.

Calvin is leaning against a wall reading his phone. He smiles and puts his phone in his pocket.

Audrey! You came.

So did you.

Yes, that's a very good sign.

I've never been in a Starbucks before. There is a lot of green and cursive writing on the walls. It's noisy. The tables are really small and only fit two people. Some of them have a checkered pattern on them. I wonder if they can be used to play checkers.

There is no line at the cash register. What would you like? Calvin asks and pulls out his wallet.

Tea.

What kind? The woman behind the register motions to a tower of teas. I point randomly at one.

Calvin goes for the Frappuccino. When I see it, I wish I did too.

He asks me where I want to sit. I choose the table in the corner by the window. It's the farthest away from most people but it's still noisy. I try not to listen to the people around us. Calvin takes a sip of his drink so I take a sip of my tea. I wish I didn't because it burns.

Here, Calvin says. He takes the lid off my cup. Let it cool down for a minute.

Peppermint steam spirals into the air. I don't know what to talk about. I wish I'd written a list of conversation points like I did before I called him.

Calvin looks out the window. He pulls out his phone and looks at the time. We have to have a quick coffee, he says.

Oh. Okay.

Not because I'm not having fun. Because I want to take you somewhere at seven thirty.

Where?

To the park. To the LARPing event I told you about. He leans forward to whisper across the table. I registered us both as NPCs.

What are NPCs?

Non-player characters. Basically scenery or human props. But the nice thing about playing as an NPC the first time is that you don't have to make a character or bring props or anything. The game masters supply you with everything. It's a good way to try it out the first time. So do you want to try?

I do!

Sweet. That leaves us exactly fifteen minutes to get to know each other better. Let's start with something easy. I'm an only child. Do you have any siblings?

I think of Adam in the basement.

I had an older brother named Adam. But he died.

Oh, I'm so sorry.

And I have a twin named Clare.

Twin! Are you identical?

No, we're nothing alike.

He takes another sip of his Frappuccino. His whole face disappears except for his eyes. How so?

Every way.

Calvin blinks and I know I haven't said enough. You need to tell people about yourself to make friends, Dr. Jackson once told me. If you don't share anything personal, you can't bond with someone.

We weren't even born on the same day, I tell Calvin. Clare is Taurus and I'm Gemini. On a family vacation my dad found a mug in the airport gift shop that separated astrology signs into three groups: Different, Difficult, and Perfect. Gemini was listed under Different and Taurus was listed under Difficult. After that, Dad called us Different and Difficult.

Calvin smiles with one side of his mouth. Is that how you see yourself? Different?

I nod.

And what about Clare? Is she difficult?

Lately. Before I always thought she was perfect.

Calvin leans forward so that his elbows rest on the table. The table is small and he's the closest he's ever been to me. His eyes are only a shade lighter than his pupils. That's why they look so big.

No one is perfect, he says. Why do I get the feeling you compare yourself to Clare and always come out on the losing end?

Because people like her better than me.

Well, just so you know, being different is what I like about you. You know why? Because I'm different too.

The stupid smile is back. I pick up my tea and can finally take a sip. Calvin smiles and sits back in his chair.

You are? I say when I can talk again.

Oh yeah, and proud of it. I know some people would make fun of me for wanting to LARP. Some people think we're a bunch of weirdos who can't tell the difference between reality and fantasy, but that's not true. We're just having fun.

The back of my scalp goes tingly and my heart leaps.

That's exactly how I feel, I tell him. I do something similar. I act out scenes with figurines.

That's very creative of you.

Calvin is the only person who has ever said that to me. When he smiles at me, my entire belly goes warm. And it has nothing to do with the tea.

At 7:30 we walk to the park where we first met. I hear the grunts and the clashing of swords before I see the fighters. Everyone is in fantasy attire. There are soldiers, elves, witches, and other characters I don't recognize. A man who resembles the Mad Hatter. A woman wearing a white tennis band on her head.

Calvin! A man with a thick dark beard slaps Calvin on the shoulder. Is this your lady?

This is Audrey. Audrey, this is Frank. He's the one who told me about this event.

Frank holds out his hand. I look at it. His fingernails are very dirty.

Frank coughs and bends down to pick a sword off the ground. It looks like a pool noodle with a duct-tape handle. Everyone's swords are made out of foam. How do they not flop around?

Did you catch up on the story? Frank asks Calvin.

I did. I'll fill Audrey in.

Good. See that lady over there wearing the tennis band? That's Jeannie. She's the game master and will tell you what role you're playing.

Calvin turns to me. So they're only on the second chapter — we haven't missed much. The heroes have been summoned by the king of Elderbrook because the princess drank a potion that turned her evil. The heroes have to find the reversal potion and have her drink it before the full moon, or else she will remain evil for good. Rumor has it she is currently working with the neighboring realm to usurp her father's throne.

I wear purple and fight for the king of Elderbrook, says Frank. But those soldiers over there wearing red, they fight for the blood king.

We meet Jeannie and she takes us into a tent to tell us our roles and show us our costumes.

As NPCs, you'll be playing villains, she tells us. Today the heroes must travel through the dark forest and find the hidden scroll amongst the branches. The scroll will provide them with further direction on their quest. But before they find it, the goblins will attack. You'll play a few different roles today, starting with the goblins. Then, after the heroes find the scroll and the first battle between Elderbrook and Ollendale begins, you'll play tree fairies who are angry their home is being invaded and attack all players besides other fairies. As goblins, you'll attack with clubs. Do you two know the combat rules?

Calvin looks at me and grins. I'll teach her.

Like karate, LARPing is different than I expected. But in a good way.

It's not actually about hitting, Calvin says. It's about touching. Like this. He gently taps my arm.

I give him a look: This means war.

He grins. You've lost your arm. You have to put it behind your back.

I stick my tongue out at him but do what he said.

If you take a leg hit, you lose the leg and must lift it up. But even with no legs you can still walk on your knees.

Calvin falls to his knees and walks around in a circle to demonstrate. I laugh.

If you take a body hit, you're dead. Assume the death position. Calvin squats on the ground with his weapon held horizontally across his shoulders and behind his head.

There are a lot of rules. But I like rules, so they're easy to remember. Calvin explains them all and I commit them to memory.

Then the game begins. The heroes enter the forest in search of the scroll, and Calvin slips a goblin mask over his head. I do the same. There are five of us goblins waiting for the game master's signal. When it comes, Calvin holds out a fist for a bump.

And then we attack.

With a terrible roar, we leap out from behind the trees. An elf is so surprised, she backs up and trips over a rock. A soldier brandishes his sword and shield. The five goblins circle with our clubs raised and ready for battle.

A witch appears in front of me. She has hair whiter than snow and eyes like a snake. When our swords clash, I think of Adam.

Sword fights with brooms in the basement.

Mom calling down to say someone was going to lose an eye.

I blink and the witch cuts off my leg. I raise it to show I've taken the hit. I'm wobbly, close to death.

Are you afraid, little goblin? the witch asks. Then she whispers so no one else can hear her. I'm only pretending to be a hero. I'm going to betray the king of Elderbrook in the end.

I slice off her arm and she laughs.

Good one, little goblin.

Then she chops off my other leg. I'm on my knees. The witch is looming above me. She grins with bloodred lips.

Her sword comes down to stab my torso and complete the kill. Only I somersault away. Reach up and tap her lightly on the back. Body hit.

Adam would have loved this.

I've finally found my extracurricular activity.

+ ✳ +

At 8:30, I apologize to Calvin.

I can't stay to be a forest fairy. My parents will wonder where I am.

That's okay, Calvin says. He watches me call them. I tell them I'll be waiting outside Starbucks. It's not a lie.

I'm going to Toronto to visit my dad for a few weeks, Calvin tells me. But I'll call you when I'm back.

Okay.

I had fun tonight, Audrey.

I did too, Calvin.

I can't believe you killed a witch.

Until her friend resurrected her with that spell.

Calvin laughs. Those pesky resurrection spells.

Yeah, I say. If only they existed in real life.

Then I turn and run back to Starbucks.

Clare

When I get home from working on a school project, aka lurking on Internet forums and avoiding going home for dinner, I find a note on the counter: Driving Audrey to Starbucks and running errands. Saved you some chicken in the fridge. Mom even signed it, as if anyone else could have left it for me.

As I pull the Tupperware out of the fridge, I realize what the note means. Audrey must be on a date! Why else would she be at Starbucks, unless she made a new friend at Peak? I guess that's also a possibility. It's not like either of us knows what's going on in the other's life anymore.

I zap my dinner in the microwave and then head to the basement to eat while watching Netflix. The new season of *Stranger Things* is out, apparently. That's something Adam would have known.

I swallow hard and press play.

It feels wrong watching without him. Whenever something scary happens or I want to comment on something, like Joyce and Hopper's constant bickering, which is getting annoying, I glance toward Adam's side of the couch. And each and every time I do, the pain of his absence pierces my chest. That's the thing about losing someone: there's one major death followed by a million little deaths.

I *can't* watch this show without Adam, so I stop looking and just talk as if he's right there beside me, and a kind of peace I haven't felt in months settles over me. It feels good to talk to him again.

When the show ends, I turn off the TV, and as the screen turns black, I close my eyes and allow the darkness to surround me too. I stay perfectly still and try to feel for Adam. Could his soul still reside in this basement, like the ghost bride's soul that's trapped in the Fairmont Banff Springs Hotel? The folklore goes that as she descended the staircase toward her lover, her wedding gown brushed up against a flickering candle flame and caught fire, and she tumbled down the stairs. Ever since guests and hotel staff of the famous hotel swear they've seen her floating up and down the staircase or dancing alone in the ballroom, pining for the first dance denied her by her death. The one and only time we stayed there, Adam dared us to sneak out of our room in the middle of the night to see if we could catch a glimpse of her. We didn't, but I'll never forget sneaking through eerie hotel hallways behind my big brother, my entire body buzzing with expectation and fear.

"Hi, Adam," I say now with my eyes still closed. Addressing him directly is harder than making comments about a show. I have so much I want to say to him, so much I want to tell him about my life. "I made a new friend. Taylor. I think you'd really like them. They're like you, Adam: independent and kind." My voice quivers on the last word, and I have to take a deep breath before continuing. "I miss you. I just want you to know that. I wish I could talk to you about everything that's going on right now."

The only response is the air spilling from the vent and the fluttering of the curtain, but I keep talking.

"I think I might have messed it up with Taylor today. I hope I didn't. I really hope I didn't."

I open my eyes and my gaze lands on the cabinet against the wall, the one that used to hold all our toys when we were little, before it got populated with video games, craft supplies, and board games. I look inside and feel a jolt of excitement. It's still there! The lid of the box is faded, the bottom of the box broken at the corners because Audrey sat on it one Halloween — she didn't notice it under all the candy wrappers littering my bed. We'd snuck treats into our room and stayed up way too late, riding a sugar high and hoping to conjure some spirits.

I rest my fingers lightly on the planchette and close my eyes again. I'm not playing anymore.

"Adam, are you here?" I hold my breath and wait, praying that the planchette will inch toward the top left corner of the board, the *yes*. But it stays frozen in place, lifeless. Maybe it needs more energy. Maybe it doesn't work without our twin connection. That Halloween night, I was certain Audrey was nudging the planchette along, but now I want to believe.

I try again. "Adam, if you're here, please give me a sign."

A door slams upstairs and my eyes pop open. Was that someone coming home, or was someone already in the house? Directly above me, the ceiling creaks as they move down the hall toward the kitchen.

Audrey's voice. Not her regular voice, though, her old voice, the one I haven't heard in years. She's talking excitedly, the way she used to when we were kids and she could tell the 'rents full stories of our adventures without even taking a breath.

I move to the bottom of the stairs, but it's not good enough. Audrey is walking around above me, her words bouncing off walls and disappearing around corners. I still can't hear anything, so I ascend higher, step by quiet step, straining to hear . . .

Suddenly Mom yanks open the basement door, and I cry out in

surprise. I also grab on to the bannister, which is briefly strong enough to prevent me from tumbling backwards, but not strong enough to save itself — it falls right off the wall.

"Clare! Oh my gosh, are you okay?"

"I'm fine."

"That bannister is a death trap!" She bends down to inspect it. "Was it even screwed into the wall?"

Good question. My breathing is ragged, my body still vibrating from the shock.

Moms straightens. "Are you sure you're okay? I was just checking if you were home. Did you eat your chicken? How's your project coming along?"

"Yeah. I did." I purposefully don't respond to the project part of the question, but of course she pries anyway.

"What's your project on?"

"I just did homework, actually."

"For what class?"

"Uh, bio." Why is she so interested in me all of a sudden? It's Audrey she's supposed to be worried about. "Bio reading, I mean. Lots of memorization."

Mom nods, but she doesn't look convinced. "That bannister. Thank goodness you didn't fall! Were you coming up?"

I look over my shoulder at the empty basement, the silent TV, and the still curtains of Adam's room. I'm very much alone down here, I realize, and suddenly I want to be anywhere else.

"Yeah, I think I will."

Upstairs, Audrey is already in her bedroom, and the house is quiet again.

✦ ✳ ✦

Even though I read for an hour before turning off the light, I toss and turn for hours and sleep doesn't come. Instead I lie in bed in the darkness, staring at the light fixture Audrey and I used to call our boob light. It's one of the many old fixtures in the house my parents never updated, and now there's an orangish tint to the inside of the glass.

It's 2:15 a.m., but I need to get out of here. Out of this room I shared with Audrey, out of this house full of old memories too painful to face. I want to ride. I want to glide as fast as I can under the stars.

So that the 'rents won't hear my bedroom door click, I twist the knob as far as I can and hold it that way as I close the door behind me, then carefully release. I've only taken a step away from my bedroom when I hear it: a strange noise, kind of like a hiccup or a whimper. A line of light crisscrosses the hallway, shining up the stairs from the hallway below. Someone is downstairs.

I don't want to deal with it, but somehow I find myself at the top of the staircase anyway. I creep down slowly, already knowing what I'll find, and peek through the railing.

Mom is on the couch, clutching a photograph to her chest, her knees drawn up. She looks young like that. Like a child mourning a child. Adam's photograph is missing from its place on the mantel.

"I'm sorry," I hear her say. "It didn't mean I wasn't happy with you. I was disappointed when I had the ultrasound ... I admit that." She chokes on a sob.

I feel frozen to the spot. My hand is wrapped tightly around the bannister, and my mouth is drier than sand. I don't know what to do. I want to say something to let her know I'm here, but I don't know if she'll be upset with me, like I've walked in on her secret.

Mom drags in a ragged breath. "I'm so ashamed, Adam. I'm so ashamed that I wasn't a better mother, that I wasn't the type of mother who was just so happy to have a healthy baby." She pauses to glance up at the ceiling. When she closes her eyes, fat tears slip down her cheeks. "But you have to believe me that I loved you. I shouldn't have favored the girls, and for that I will never forgive myself."

At her last sentence, I pull back in shock, and the stair I was standing on creaks. Mom freezes and then glances up.

"Clare."

"Hi." My tone is colder than I intended.

Mom wipes away the tears with the back of her hand. "What are you doing up? Did I wake you?"

"No. I was on the way to the bathroom." *And I heard you.*

"I'm sorry, sweetie."

"I said you didn't wake me up."

She stands, turns away from me to wipe the remaining tears from her face, and replaces Adam's photo on the mantel. Her hand shakes a little bit, and for a moment I think the photograph might fall and my heart does this awful leap, but she catches it just in time.

"Did you hear what I said?" she asks me without turning around.

"No," I lie, but the anger is boiling within me again. Anger for Adam. Anger for Sam, who was worried about telling his mother his secret. Anger for me, who is terrified my mother won't love me as much if I tell her I don't always feel like a girl.

Mom returns to the couch and pats the spot beside her. "Come talk to me."

I want to run back upstairs. I want to hide under my blankets with a flashlight and read Adam's Harry Potter books knowing he's sleeping peacefully in the room across the hall. I don't want to have this new information, don't want to have to ask the question that's burning its way up my throat.

"Would you not love me as much if I were a boy?"

Mom's hands fly to her mouth. "You did hear me. Oh, Clare, of course I would love you. I loved all of you the exact same."

"But you just said you favored Audrey and me. The girls."

"I think maybe I did. I know I did more things with you growing up, which I regret. But it wasn't that I didn't love Adam as much as you; it was that your dad and I naturally fell into a pattern of him doing things with Adam, like taking him to baseball practice, and me doing things with the two of you girls. I wish we'd taken turns so that I was just as involved as he was with Adam."

"Okay," I say, but I still don't move from my place on the stairs. I'm still processing everything I've heard.

"Come talk to me." Mom pats the spot beside her.

"I'm really tired."

"Of course you are." Mom scrubs her face with her hands. "I should get to bed too."

I turn and quickly go back up the stairs. At the top of the landing I go into the bathroom and sit on the closed lid of the toilet. I dig the heels of my palms into my eyes, but I still can't block out the image of Mom crying on the couch alone. I can't stop remembering what she said about feeling ashamed and how she'll never forgive herself.

This whole time I've been so worried my mom might judge me, when really she's been judging herself.

+ ✳ +

I wait until I hear Mom pass the bathroom and close the door to her and Dad's room. Then I hold my breath, open the bathroom door slowly so it doesn't make a squeak, and sneak back downstairs.

Using my phone as a flashlight, I lift Adam's photograph off the mantel.

His hair is sandy blond, his eyes blue. He has started spiking his hair with gel because it's the cool thing to do. His smile is relaxed, calm. He gazes out at me from behind the wall of glass and I wish I could reach out and, like Alice with the looking glass, my hand would go through and I could touch his face.

I didn't feel like that at the funeral. The same photograph sat at the front of the church, blown up so that people could see it all the way at the back, and when I looked at it I felt nothing. Maybe it was because there was no glass. *He's waiting behind it in another dimension,* I tell myself now. *He's in the upside-down, if only I can find a way to get there.*

My entire family cried at the funeral, except for me. I just felt angry. I wanted to run to the front of the church and kick over that huge photograph. I wanted to yell at everyone to go away because they didn't understand, they could never understand. They dabbed at their eyes with tissues, but once they left the church, they would be on the way with the rest of their day.

Our family will feel that pain forever.

Audrey

Clare is holding the photograph of Adam.

She's frowning at it and doesn't know I'm standing there. Until I say, Hi.

Then she jumps and blinds me with her flashlight. Audrey! What are you doing up?

I had a bad dream. About Adam.

Oh. Clare puts the photograph back. Straightens it on the mantel. You're still having a lot of those?

I nod. Why are you up?

Clare looks at me. It feels like a long time that she looks at me.

I couldn't sleep, she says. I miss him too.

I can't look at her after that, so I look at the photograph. It's his grade-eleven photo, the one we used at the funeral. In it he's smiling like he had no idea. And the photographer taking the photograph had no idea. And Mom and Dad put it in a frame having no idea.

No one had any idea it would be his last school photo taken ever.

Adam's in the basement, I tell Clare.

Yeah, I go down there sometimes to feel closer to him.

You do? Now I'm excited. I mean, you've seen him too?

Seen . . . ?

Adam's ghost!

Clare's mouth falls open. She goes really pale. What are you talking about, Audrey?

Adam's ghost. It's in the basement.

Clare suddenly grabs the sides of her head with both hands. Then she starts shaking her head back and forth. Faster and faster. Covering her ears.

This isn't a game, Audrey. This isn't a stupid ghost story. It's *Adam*.

It isn't a story! He's down there, I swear. I've talked to him!

I'm not going to stick around and listen to this crap, Clare says. I can't believe you don't get that Adam's gone — *all* of Adam — and there's nothing we can do to bring him back. I can't believe I actually *missed* you.

She shoves me aside and walks back upstairs. I stand at the bottom and watch her go.

One sibling above me and the other below me. Never to be together again.

+ ✳ +

The next day is a Wednesday, but I don't go to my special art period. When Marianne tells me it's 2:30, I go to the library and draw in my sketchbook instead. Neither Monsieur Martin nor Marianne says anything about it, so I assume that it's settled.

But then on Friday at 2:30 p.m. on the dot, Ms. Nguyen appears at the door to my classroom.

I'd like to walk Audrey today, she tells Marianne.

Ms. Nguyen isn't wearing her smock. It's the first time I've seen her in normal clothes. She's wearing a sleeveless white top with a colorful glass beaded necklace that's wrapped around her neck twice, and cropped jeans. Her hair is down and wavy instead of up in a tight bun.

We walk to the studio together in silence. She tells me to sit down at the table and sits down across from me.

I think we got off on the wrong foot the other day, she says. I think I might have hurt your feelings. Did I hurt your feelings, Audrey?

I realize that in the pause she was waiting for me to respond. Only my brother ever asked me that, I tell her. Then I blush because it was a weird thing to say.

That's too bad. You're allowed to have hurt feelings. But you haven't answered my question.

I look off at where she stores the paint canvases. I wonder if my most recent Sirius has been stored away there too.

No, that wasn't it, I tell her.

Then what was it?

My fingers are in knots under the table. I take a deep breath.

You said I'm special. I don't want to be special.

I thought as much. Ms. Nguyen sighs. I'm sorry, Audrey. I didn't mean it as a bad thing. I was trying to make you embrace and be proud of who you are. You don't have to stop painting Sirius just because other people want you to. Who cares what other people want? It's your life.

My heart starts beating faster. Almost as fast as it did that time Sharon caught me talking to the flowers.

People make fun of me, I say.

Kids make fun of other kids, she says. It's part of growing up. Why do you have to change who you are to please other people?

Because I want people to like me.

Okay, but can I tell you a secret?

I nod.

It's okay if people don't like you.

I feel my mouth fall open, and Ms. Nguyen chuckles.

I know, I felt the exact same way when a friend said that to me. But don't you think it's better to enjoy your life than spend your time trying to make people like you? If you're worried painting Sirius makes you a target for bullying, then do it in private. Just don't ever stop doing something you love because someone else tells you not to do it. Okay?

Okay, I say. Then I look down because my eyes have filled with tears and I don't want her to see.

She clasps her hands on the table in front of her and leans forward. Now that's settled, one question remains: Would you still like to be in my art class, Audrey? I haven't told your teachers about your absence the other day, and I still won't even if you tell me you're no longer interested. I only want you here if you want to be here.

I am interested. I do want to be here.

Great. So what would you like to focus on during our time together?

I don't know.

I was hoping you'd say that. Ms. Nguyen smiles. I thought we could try something different. Something I wouldn't try with all my students.

She walks over to a cupboard against the wall. She turns around with a dark block on her palm. Do you know what this is?

I shake my head.

Soapstone. Have you heard of soapstone?

In grade six we carved a bar of soap.

Ms. Nguyen throws her head back and laughs. I love it! Did you carve it with a butter knife?

I consider that for a moment. I think so.

She laughs again. We won't be using a butter knife this time, Audrey. This is the real deal. We'll be carving real soapstone using handsaws and files. That is why I wouldn't let other students try it. Using handsaws and files can be dangerous. But I think you're ready.

I smile. Maybe I don't need Monsieur Martin. I already have an ally.

You can make anything you like. A bear. A cat. A boat. Of course I'll have to get your parents' permission before we can actually start cutting. What do you think? Would you be interested in trying your hand out at sculpture, Audrey?

My heart is beating so loudly, her voice is a hum in the background. Ms. Nguyen repeats the question.

Would you be interested in carving soapstone, Audrey?

Yes! I jump up and sit down. Jump up again. I don't know what to do. I'm so excited. Sculpture!

I thought you might be. I think you're a very talented artist and I've told Monsieur Martin as much. I would love to see what you could do with sculpture.

What should I make? All the different ideas run through my head. All my usual sketches. I can make a physical representation of them. Of Sirius. Then it might really feel like he's real. Isn't that what I've always wanted?

I'll prepare a permission form for you to take home this evening, Ms. Nguyen says. But for now you can sketch your ideas.

I don't need to sketch Sirius because I have a million drawings of him already. Ms. Nguyen goes to the other side of the room and organizes the closet. I start to draw. I don't think about what I'm drawing. It starts out as an oval and then I draw two smaller ovals inside it. Add a circle to each oval for the heads. Arms reaching out. Legs entwined.

I've seen it in my head but never drawn it. The page goes dark. I look up and Ms. Nguyen is looking over my shoulder.

Two babies in a womb. Twins. Is this what you want to carve?

Yes.

She takes the pencil from my hands and shades the area behind the babies. You would have to carve this area out, she says. You could add a base here so it stands on its side rather than lies flat like a plate. What do you think?

I like that.

The babies are small and intricate. It will be difficult. Much more difficult than a bear or a cat.

Or Sirius.

She nods. Yes, or Sirius. Are you sure you don't want to carve him?

I can give the carving to Clare, I realize. The carving will say all the things I cannot say to her.

That makes my decision.

+ ✳ +

The first thing I do when I get into the car is show Mom the permission slip from Ms. Nguyen.

You get to carve soapstone! What are you going to carve? She seems really interested. She's an artist too.

I'm going to carve Clare and me in the womb, I tell her. It's going to be a present for Clare.

Oh. Mom smiles but it looks wrong. That's really nice, sweetie. What made you decide to do that?

I take the permission slip back from her so she can start driving. Because I want things to go back to the way they were.

And you think giving her a present that shows how much you care is the way to do it.

I nod.

She sighs. Audrey, Clare is in a difficult place right now. I just want you to be prepared that she might not react the way you want. I don't want you to get your feelings hurt.

I do up my seat belt. You can drive now.

I'm just trying to help.

You can drive now.

Mom shifts and pulls away from the curb.

Clare thinks Mom and I are closer than her and Mom, but sometimes it feels like Mom lives on a different planet than me, too. That's
because no one lives on the same planet as me.

At home Mom signs the form. Her signature is perfect and always
looks the same. That's why it takes her forever to sign things.

The door slams and Clare walks in. It's the earliest she's come home
in a really long time.

Not working on that school project today? Mom asks.

Nope. The word comes out like a pop.

Mom finishes signing and I snatch it away before Clare can see it. I
want it to be a surprise. But I'm too late.

Clare gestures at the paper I'm stuffing in my pocket. What's that?

Audrey is doing so well in school that they enrolled her in a special
art period just for her. She's carving soapstone.

Clare's eyebrows rise. As in actual soapstone? Using a saw?

Yes, using a saw! Mom snaps.

Clare's face turns Clifford red. I wasn't criticizing, just asking, she
snaps back. Maybe I actually think it's cool. *God!* She stomps out of the
kitchen and up the stairs.

Mom turns to me. She's wringing her hands and looks like she wants
to say something but isn't sure what. So I speak first.

Don't tell Clare what my carving is going to be, okay? I want it to be
a surprise.

Mom nods.

I go upstairs to my room. I'm working in my sketchbook when there's
a light knock on my door and then it opens immediately. I never know
which one to expect when that happens: Mom or Clare.

It's Clare.

She steps in slowly. Cautiously. Her eyes skitter across the room like they always do when she comes in here, which is almost never. She looks around like she stills sees Adam's things.

I turn back to my sketch because I'm not drawing Sirius so I don't have to be embarrassed. It's a drawing of Lake Louise. I'm using a photo I took when we stayed at the chateau. It was just after Adam died and they wanted us to spend family time together. Only that was the trip when I realized Clare hated me.

She's right behind me now. I can feel her breath on my neck. The back of my neck gets all tingly.

Now who's in whose space?

I want to say it but I just keep drawing. I wish I were using pastels instead of charcoal because Lake Louise needs blue. No, teal. The teal is what makes it so famous. I once saw a joke online of a man painting the bottom and then refilling it. What do they call those? A meme.

That's really good, Clare says.

Then she walks away. What does she want? My hand shakes but I keep drawing. Through my armpit I see her sit on the bed.

I get it if you're mad at me, she says. I've been kind of a jerk.

My hand stops. I let out the breath I was holding. Okay. This is new. I turn to face her, gripping the charcoal tightly. I still haven't spoken a word and I'm too afraid to. What if I mess it up?

She trails a finger as thin as a spider leg along my bedspread and shrugs. I guess I just don't understand.

I watch as she pushes the blue streak behind her ear with the opposite hand. Her middle finger has a thick ring on it. Adam's ring. She's wearing Adam's sweatshirt again too. She wears one of his sweatshirts almost every day now.

She looks up at me. *Look*, I just don't get why you even want to come back. You weren't happy. You hated school.

No I didn't.

Audrey, everyone was mean to you. Don't you remember? Clare kind of cringes like she doesn't want to be the one to remind me.

As if I could forget.

I need to go back! I shout and then tell myself to calm down. Otherwise I just prove Clare right that I'm not ready.

Maybe if I go back now and I'm older, I can show them . . .

That you've changed? Clare asks quietly.

No. My voice is very quiet. I can barely hear myself speak. I take a deep breath. That I'm who I used to be.

Oh. Clare goes totally still. Then her hands find each other like two spiders entwined in her lap.

The thing about teenagers, she says, is that they're mean. High school is worse than middle school. Kids are meaner. They pick on each other so people are too afraid to pick on them.

My hand tightens on the back of my chair as I wait for her to finish.

Do you remember Billy?

I nod.

He snaps all the girls' bras. Like *all the time*. A bunch of them have told him to stop doing it, and told the teachers on him too, but it doesn't make a difference. He keeps doing it.

Why?

She throws her hands up. Because that's what guys do! And then there's Sharon. Remember what a bitch Sharon was to you all the time? Well, I told her you might be coming back, and she was like *Oh my God, please tell me you're joking!* She is totally going to pick on you, Audrey.

I think of the picture Sharon posted of me on Facebook and the back of my neck turns hot. Soon the heat will move to the front and then climb up to my face and Clare will see it. I grip the chair harder. Clare doesn't notice. She keeps talking.

Do you remember that time Rhiannon made you cry in the bathroom all afternoon? She made fun of your drawings and you ran out of the room and never came back. The teacher sent me looking for you. It was awful.

Now I can't even look at her. My face is so hot it burns. I know she can see it and that makes it burn hotter. Clare is embarrassed of me. I hate that she's embarrassed of me.

Look, you don't have to prove anything to anyone. If that's what you're trying to do. You don't need to do whatever I do.

I'm not trying to copy you, Clare.

Do your own thing. Be yourself.

There it is again: Be yourself. Be yourself be yourself be yourself. Except no one likes it when I'm myself.

I realize I've said it aloud when Clare stands abruptly. I blink once and she's beside my chair.

I'm trying to protect you, Audrey. I'm your twin and I love you. My school sucks. Trust me, you're better off at Peak.

With people like me, right? Well shows what you know because those people are nothing like me either.

Clare's eyebrows knit together. Her hand reaches out like she's going to touch me, but she doesn't. She's nodding.

Sometimes I feel like that too, she says. Sometimes it doesn't matter where you are. You can still feel like no one else in the entire world is like you.

What do you mean?

She looks down at the floor. I'm saying I feel different from everyone else too. So I get what you're going through.

You do not know what I'm going through. I ball my hands into fists in my lap. You have no idea. You have everything, Clare. You have friends and a normal life. What more do you want?

Get it together, I tell myself. Don't get emotional in front of Clare. But I know it's futile. I'm breathing faster now. The tears are imminent.

Do you know what it's like to have everyone think you're a freak?

Then I start to yell.

You're popular! People *like* you. So don't pretend I'll be happier at Peak when you know you'd hate it yourself, Clare. Don't come in here and *lie* to me.

Clare's eyes widen. Her mouth falls open. It's the first time she's ever looked afraid of me.

Get out of my room! I scream.

She turns and runs.

CLARE

Audrey's words ring through my head as I pull her door closed behind me.

You're popular!

People like you.

Don't you dare come in here and lie to me.

Still grasping the doorknob, I suck in large breaths of air. I can hear Mom and Dad talking downstairs, oblivious to what just happened up here. All the times I ignored Audrey or treated her badly, I never considered she might actually stop liking me. If only she knew everyone else has stopped liking me too.

Lately it feels like my world is shifting. Being popular was part of my identity. Audrey was the beautiful but weird twin, and Clare was the popular twin, the socialite who could morph her personality to make anyone like her. Now I'm finally trying to embrace the real me, and Audrey's trying to prove she can be someone else. Worse, she's trying to be someone else because of me.

I wonder what Adam would say if he could see us switching places. Maybe one of us has to fail for the other one to succeed. Maybe that keeps the balance in the universe.

In the bathroom I stare at my reflection, at my blah blond hair that's grown too long, well past my shoulders, and the makeup that no longer feels like a war mask. Whereas a few weeks ago I thought I looked badass, now I just look like a strung-out girl. And I don't want to look like a girl.

What has my hair ever done for me? It's annoying to have to take care of it. Most importantly, my hair is my strongest feminine characteristic. My hair is a crutch. I hate my hair.

Before I can think twice about it, I yank open a drawer and root around in it for the first-aid kit. Mom keeps scissors in there to cut gauze and stuff. They're small and shitty but my hair is thin, so it won't take me too long. After a quick glance at the door to make sure it's locked, I grab the streak of blue hair and lean over the sink, chopping it off at the halfway mark. When I step back, I have a blue chunk of hair hanging at my chin.

Not good enough.

I repeat the step, but this time I chop even higher. Then I move all around my head hacking and sawing off as much hair as I can until I'm left with a really messy version of a pixie cut. I dump half a bottle of eye makeup remover onto a cotton pad and rub it across my eyes, removing makeup that has probably been layered on top of makeup for weeks.

Now when I step back, a new person is staring back at me. Raw and uncomplicated and real. The true me.

I kind of wish I'd made a YouTube video.

The sink is full of hair. I'm going to need a real haircut to even all this out, and fix the blue spot on the side, but for now I gather handfuls and drop them into the wastebasket. Then I tie the bag and remove it, rinse whatever remnants are left down the sink. Not like the 'rents aren't going to find out what I did, but at least they can't get on my case about leaving a mess.

My heart is racing — partly excitement and partly fear. What are my parents going to do to me? What are kids at school going to say tomorrow? Will they think I'm going crazy?

I can hear Mom and Dad in the kitchen making dinner when I leave the bathroom. Audrey's door is closed. I rush into my own bedroom and toss the bag of hair, etc., into the trash under my desk. Then I turn on my laptop and open tabs to my favorite forums, the ones I've been looking at compulsively for two weeks. It's time to finally join. I want to be a part of the conversation. I need to tell someone what I just did because it's the first major step I've taken in becoming my true self.

I direct-message Sam the Man and tell him how much his story inspired me. Then I introduce myself to the group under the username Skatergirl/boy and open up to them about how I shift between feeling like a girl and feeling like a boy and that I literally just cut off my hair. My hands are shaking, and I feel high from the rush. I create the same username on the next forum and copy the message introducing myself and announcing that I did it. I cut off my hair.

Someone responds to my first announcement while I'm still working on the fourth.

You're so brave! It takes a lot of courage to do that.

Other messages start pouring in and it's like being hugged by a warm blanket. Online I'm already the person I want to be.

Way to go! You should be proud of yourself.

Congratulations!!! How amazing did it feel? You're freeeeeee!

And a response to the one above: When I cut off my hair was one of the best days of my life. It was like two feet long and I sent it to charity.

Sitting back in my chair, I read the messages as they come in from people all around the world, people I genuinely consider friends of mine now. These people and their stories have made me realize I'm going to be okay, that there are seven billion people in the world and some of them are like me.

I haven't shown my family yet, **I write.** I'm only fifteen and have to go downstairs for dinner soon.

Maybe you should wear a hat ;).

No way! Go down there with pride. It's your f@$#ing hair. You do what you want!

I laugh and type back, My mom is going to Freak. Out.

My mom did the same thing. But she got over it because what can she do? It's not like I can glue it back on.

I bet she forces me to wear a wig.

Lol. Take it off the second you're out the door.

The conversation makes me feel better at first, but then I realize that even if I have online support, I'm still going to have to face the flesh-and-blood people in my life at some point, and suddenly I feel back where I was before: alone. Adrenaline from my bold move is dissipating and it's starting to feel less revolutionary and more reckless. Maybe I really should go out and get a wig.

As if on cue, Dad calls up the stairs, "Dinner's ready!"

Dad and his family dinners. Now I'm really regretting having used up all my sick excuses.

Sweat breaks out under my arms and I pace the end of the bed, desperately trying to come up with a plan. Wear a hat? Too obvious. Wear a hoodie and pull the hood up, maybe slap on a pair of headphones while I'm at it? Totally unacceptable dinner-table behavior, they'll say.

Well then, I guess it's now or never.

Taking a deep breath, I open the door a crack. Audrey's door is wide open now. She probably went downstairs the second Dad called. I step out onto the landing where I can hear them chatting downstairs. Mom and Dad both laugh, and it feels like a knife in my back.

I wish they understood who I was and didn't think I was a bad person all the time. Yeah, I kind of deserve some of it because of how I've been acting lately, but why can't they see all the ways I've been an awesome twin as well? All the times I've walked Audrey to school, looked out for her, stressed when people were mean to her . . . Sometimes at school it felt like I had to be her mom because Mom wasn't around.

None of this matters right now! a voice yells inside my head. *You're just trying to distract yourself from the very real present problem.*

Then there's Dad. He comes home for dinner at six after working a ten-hour day and has no idea what is actually going on here, so he just listens to Mom. I've seen him in Audrey's room having a heart-to-heart, but he hasn't once stopped by to see how I'm doing. Not even about Adam.

Earth to Dad: Clare isn't doing so stellar.

You don't have to ask permission to cut your own hair, I tell myself as I take the first step. *Don't be such a wimp. It's your f@$#ing hair.*

Holding my head high, I descend the stairs, walk down the hall, and enter the kitchen.

Audrey notices me first. Her mouth falls open and she drops her fork onto the plate with a plop. What a drama queen. Dad and Mom twist around in their seats to see whatever has set Audrey off. Mom's hand flies to her mouth and she makes an old-lady cry, a mix between shock and dismay, before exclaiming, "Oh, Clare!"

Dad just tilts his head to the side and then nods like this isn't something completely unexpected. "Is there something you want to tell us?"

"I cut my hair."

"We can see that." Dad's voice is creepy calm. "Why don't you come sit down?"

An uneasy feeling settles over me. I sit down beside Audrey, who is still looking at me with wide eyes. In my mind I snap my jaws at her and she wipes that look right off her face.

"You cut your hair," Dad repeats in the same eerily calm voice. "Just now. Upstairs."

I nod.

"What made you do that?" He sounds casual enough, but I wonder if in a moment he's going to pull out his own hair.

I shrug. "I wanted to."

"You just had the urge to chop off all your hair." Mom isn't coming off quite as self-contained. In fact, she keeps blinking at me like she thinks it's an illusion. Dad puts a hand on her leg.

"I've been thinking about it for a while," I tell them. "Then I decided, why not just do it now?"

"Why not?" Mom repeats like a robot.

Dad glances at her and I can tell he wishes she weren't in the room. I wish she weren't in the room too. Since Adam died I always feel guilty for upsetting her, and I don't want to have to feel like that right now.

"We'll discuss it more after dinner," Dad says, and his meaning is clear: Audrey is still eating her dinner and they don't want her to hear whatever they have to say to me.

"There really isn't anything to discuss." I sit back in my chair and cross my arms. "You know, since it's done."

Now Dad actually glances at Audrey.

"Stop treating her like a baby!" I snap. "She's fifteen like me. She isn't some naïve idiot you need to coddle, and you shouldn't treat her like one."

There's a stunned silence. Then Mom shakes her head, snapping out of her daze. She looks thoroughly shocked. Dad's cheeks are a bit pink and he's looking at his lap. Good.

I sneak a glance at Audrey and I'm surprised to see her give me a small smile. It makes me feel strangely nostalgic, like tears might pop into my eyes or something. I'm almost tempted to reach out and take her hand under the table like when we were kids.

With a sigh, Dad raises his head and looks me right in the eye. "All right, Clare. We'll have an adult conversation. Your mother and I have been concerned about you recently, and we've actually been thinking about talking to you about it." Here he looks at Mom, who manages to nod even though it looks like her neck can't bend that way. I've never seen her sit so straight. "We understand adolescence is a time of exploration and discovering who you are. We remember what it was like — rebelling against our parents and testing limits."

"That's not what I'm doing," I jump in. "This has nothing to do with you. Either of you."

"Well, that's good to know," Dad says. "Because we've been noticing you're acting differently lately, most noticeably wearing different clothes. A lot of Adam's old clothes. So we wanted to ask if you're depressed about Adam? By wearing his clothes do you feel closer to him?"

I laugh-snort. "Of course I'm depressed about him. Aren't we all depressed about him?"

I glance around at everyone and see Audrey's head fall. She does that whenever she's hiding her tears.

"Yes, we're all very sad, and the grieving process is going to take a long time. In fact, it will never end. Grief becomes a part of us and something we learn to manage, not forget. Does that make sense?"

"Not really," I mutter.

"Do you understand the difference between being sad and being depressed?" Dad presses on. "Depression can follow a loss of a loved one, and it's much more serious than feeling sad sometimes. It's a pervasive feeling that life is hopeless and a feeling of being lost. Do you feel that way?"

I take a moment to respond. "I don't feel like life is hopeless, no."

"But you feel lost?"

I shift uncomfortably in my chair, arms still crossed. "Aren't I supposed to talk to Kyle about this stuff?"

"Yes. Do you?"

"Not really. But I'm not depressed," I rush to add. "I just like wearing his clothes more than my own."

"Okay . . ." Dad draws the word out. "So my next question is: Why? I mean, you used to like dressing more . . . feminine." Now he looks crazy awkward. "What I'm trying to say is, well, is this some kind of fashion fad or does it mean something more and that's why you cut your hair?"

"What your father is trying to say is that he will understand if you want to confide in us. We are completely open and accepting."

Oh. Wow. This conversation has taken a drastic turn. Beats the sex talk in elementary hands down.

My parents are sitting there waiting for me to tell them I'm a lesbian. Isn't it supposed to be the other way around? Aren't parents supposed to try to avoid bringing up these kinds of conversations however possible and kids are supposed to work up the nerve to 'come out'? Here my parents are telling me they're completely cool with my being gay, and I still can't feel relieved because there is so much more I would need to explain. I don't think they even understand the concept of sexuality being separate from gender.

So I tell them, "I'm figuring things out."

"Okay," Dad says, like we've made progress. "Now it all makes sense."

"What makes sense? 'Clare cut her hair; she must be gay'?"

Now Dad's face turns bright red.

"Clare," Mom chastises me. "He's just trying to understand."

My wrath snaps to her. "Is that what you both want? To *make sense* of me?"

"We're your parents. We love you. We just want to know you."

I pick up my fork and take a bite of the shepherd's pie so I don't have to talk to them anymore. From the corner of my eye I see Audrey pick up her fork as well. Everyone is so quiet, the screech of cutlery scraping china practically echoes off the walls.

As I continue to eat, I start to feel better. Maybe it's a good thing. If they think they have some sort of answer, they can stop fussing over what I wear or wondering if I'm depressed. They can relax a bit. My shoulders relax too and I realize a weight has been lifted off me.

At least it's a step in the right direction.

+ ✳ +

All good feelings vanish on Monday morning when I think about facing my classmates. I spent the weekend chatting on the forums, reading books, and playing video games, but I was awake all last night imagining the various ways Sharon, Billy, and the rest of them are going to tear me apart. It's going to be like diving into a shark pit with a gushing wound.

Mom's surprisingly gentle when she opens the door to tell me I'm going to be late for school. She sits at the end of my bed the way she used to when I was a kid.

"How are you feeling?"

"Terrified."

She nods and glances away, but not before I catch her pained expression. When she looks back at me again, she manages a small smile. "It's going to be hard. It's going to be really hard. But it's going to be worth it."

My head snaps up in surprise and Mom doesn't miss it. She reaches out and takes my hand, gives it a little squeeze. The contact is both foreign and comforting. When was the last time we touched each other like this? I remember when Audrey and I were little and we used to fight over who got to cuddle her in bed. In the middle of our wrestling match, Mom would laugh and catch us, one in each arm.

"If you want your life to change," she continues, "you have to be the change. And you have to be prepared for people not to like it."

I nod and return the squeeze, feeling my eyes flood with tears. It's in this moment that I consider going a step further and telling her the complete, unabridged version of my messed-up life, but that's impossible. I mean, it all started by finding Adam's sexy videos. No mom wants to hear that story.

"You can do this." Then she perks up with an idea. "Hey, maybe you should get one of those rainbow bracelets I've seen kids wear. Then people will have the answer and won't need to ask questions."

I laugh. "I've thought about it."

"I can weave something for you quickly if you want."

"Sure," I say because her tone sounds so hopeful. She wants to do something to help me any way she can, and I appreciate that.

Clapping her hands, she leaves the room. Through my open door I see her feet disappearing up the ladder. By the time I'm slipping past it into the bathroom to shower, she's whistling.

My hair doesn't look too bad soaking wet — it kind of looks like it's supposed to be messy — but I know after it dries it will be a different story. I can't find any gel in the bathroom, so I use hairspray in an attempt to force it into submission.

Back in my room I take a little longer than usual picking out what to wear. It's a big day. I don't want to wear one of my usual hoodies because that might make it harder, but I also don't want to dress up too much either. In the end I choose a low-key gray sweater that doesn't scream girl or guy and a pair of jeans.

Audrey's in the kitchen eating eggs when I come down. "Hey," I say, and offer her a smile. She actually looks surprised. I don't blame her.

"Hey."

I scoop some eggs onto my plate. "How was your sleep?"

"Good. Yours?"

"Not so good."

She doesn't say anything to that. I pull out a chair and sit down beside her to eat. When was the last time we ate breakfast together like this?

"How's school going?" I ask Audrey. "I heard you're doing awesome."

Her eyebrows shoot up and she almost chokes on her food. "Yeah. I'm, um, it's going . . . awesome."

"Good."

Mom comes downstairs and presents me with the bracelet. "Ta-da!"

It's pretty cool. I've never seen that design before and have no idea how she did it. It's a loom cuff with a rainbow pattern that looks like multiple arrows fading into the next color.

"You made this just now?" I ask in disbelief.

"Yeah," she says proudly. "Do you like it?"

"I love it."

"Good." She beams as I pull it on.

My stomach is queasy as I force-feed myself eggs, knowing I'll feel worse if I don't. I don't think I've ever been this nervous about anything in my life. Okay, besides the talent show Mom made Audrey and me enter in grade four. We were wearing matching dresses and singing "Every Breath You Take." When I watched the videos years later, I was eerily reminded of the little girls from *The Shining*.

"We need to do something about your hair," Mom says, snapping me out of my thoughts. "It's completely uneven."

Guess the hairspray was a bust.

"And there's that blue spot . . ."

"Can't do anything about that."

"No." She pulls scissors out from the penholder on the counter. "How about I try giving you a haircut?"

I know I must be desperate when I hear myself agree. She slings a hand towel across my shoulders and tells me to bend over the sink so she can wet my hair before cutting it. When she turns the water off, I stand back up, reaching behind my head with both hands to keep my hair from falling in my face, but there's nothing there. With a laugh, I give my head a shake. Water flies everywhere.

"Hey!" Mom cries out. "Watch it!"

"Sorry." I'm grinning. *Sorry not sorry.*

After guiding me to a chair, Mom stands in front of me with a finger on her chin like I'm a messy canvas and she's trying to figure out if a stroke here and there will be enough to fix me. "It's the blue spot," she says finally. "It's just so . . . there."

"Maybe we should add more blue spots," Audrey pipes up. Images of Dr. Seuss characters waltz in front of my eyes.

"I know what to do." Mom goes to clap her hands together and then remembers the scissors. "I'm just going to even everything out and then I'll grab the hair dye."

"Hair dye?" I squeak.

"Yeah. You're going brunette. I have some upstairs for when I cover my grays."

Brunette. I guess that could be good. Projects more of an I-planned-to-do-this rather than an I-completely-went-off-the-handle vibe.

We only leave the dye in for twenty minutes rather than the recommended thirty. First of all I have to get to school, and second of all my hair is so light, it dyes easily. Afterward I jump back in the shower to rinse it out, bend over, and rub my head with a towel. It's so short now that it dries in less than five minutes. Sweet.

When I step in front of the mirror, the breath squeezes out of my lungs. I look like a completely different person. I also look a million times better.

In the car Audrey sits in the front like usual and I sit in the back, but I don't put in my earphones. Instead I watch out the window, my foot tapping the floor in a frantic beat.

Mom pulls up at the usual curb where she drops me off, and Audrey whips around to face me, eyes wide with excitement like a typical annoying little sister. Sitting on the railing laughing at something on Sharon's phone are Sharon, Rhiannon, and Charlotte.

My foot starts tapping double pace. I'm choking on my own heart and can't get enough air. Mom and Audrey are twisted in their seats, their mouths moving, but it's like looking at them through a kaleidoscope: they seem so far away and warped like they're in a house of mirrors.

"Clare, are you okay?" It's Mom. She passes me a bottle of water from the console. "Drink this."

I chug it back, wipe my mouth with the back of my hand. *I can do this. I can do this.* Too afraid to look at them again in case I lose my nerve, I push open the door of the car and step out. A wind gust blows up all around me, bringing with it the smells of spring, but my hair doesn't whip my face. *This is worth it already. You can do this.*

Sharon & Co. are completely wrapped up in conversation as I walk up the path, holding on to the strap of my bag tightly. The outside world is so loud. Laughter rings through my ears. Someone shouts and I jump a little, look over my shoulder. No one's looking at me. I keep walking. They're less than ten feet away from me now. I take a deep breath and plaster on a smile and keep my eyes on them, prepared to catch their eyes and act like everything is completely, boringly normal.

It's Rhiannon who sees me first. She's talking to Sharon, who has her back to me. She must feel my eyes on her because her gaze shifts away from Sharon's face to land on me, and as if on instinct, she gives me a flirtatious smile . . . and then goes completely pale. I hurry past.

Things are about to get complicated.

As I walk through the front door, the sky cracks open and begins to pour.

+ ✳ +

My first period is graphic design and media, so it's full of students from all over the school, not just my grade. People don't know me as well here, so it's a good start. Mom's rainbow bracelet is like this giant flashing arrow pointing at me. Even as I try to focus on my work, I can't help but notice out of the corner of my eye the students nudging each other and whispering, and some of them seriously need to work on controlling the volume of their voices.

Most people are friendlier, though. Way friendlier. Kids who used to pass me without a glance actually smile and nod, and others make excuses to come over and talk to me, asking questions about how to use certain tools in Photoshop.

English is another story. This is the class I've been dreading the most all night and morning because it's the class I have with both Sharon and Billy the Bully. I'm practically shaking as I pass people in the hallway on my way to class. I sit down at my desk and twist around to pull my books out of my bag, and that's when I meet Sharon's eye. She has one thin eyebrow arched and is looking at me with complete disdain. As I watch, she turns to Rhiannon sitting beside her and says something behind her hand. Rhiannon keeps her eyes down like she doesn't want to look at me.

I quickly turn around in my chair, but that's a mistake because Billy has turned around as well and is watching me. He smiles like a cat that has just cornered a mouse.

"What's that bracelet you're wearing there, Clare?" he asks loudly.

My first instinct is to lower my wrist below my desk as everyone turns to look at me. But I can't move even if I want to. I'm frozen in place, and there's a twitching in my throat that makes it impossible to talk.

Billy tilts his head to the side, his cruel smile inching up a notch. "I guess that explains why you were such a shitty kisser."

I try to laugh it off but it comes out like an awkward bark. I feel myself redden, from my neck all the way up to my scalp, and the knowledge that I'm nervous and that Billy can tell I'm nervous makes me even more nervous.

"You're the shitty kisser," I retort, and it sounds super lame.

Billy's full-on grinning now, relishing my discomfort the way he relished taunting Taylor during their presentation. "Good one. So what does your family think about you being a dyke? I bet that's exactly the news they want to receive right now."

"My parents don't care."

"That's so much better."

Everyone laughs at that. When they do, I take the chance to swallow. I want to say that there's nothing wrong with me, that he's just a hater and that I hate him back, but the twitch in my throat has turned into a lump and my heart is beating too fast — I know if I try to speak again I'll sound afraid for sure. And I don't want him to know I'm afraid.

So instead I look back down at my books. The laughter rings in my ears. Of course Sharon isn't saying anything in my defense. For all I know, she's one of the people laughing along.

"I warned all the guys to stay away from you," Billy continues. "I told them they'd be better off kissing a horse. I mean, those *teeth*."

Someone else says something, and it's followed by more laughter, but I force myself to stop listening. I'm shaking, I'm trying not to cry, and this time I know for sure no one is going to come to my rescue. All those times I was on the other side watching the kids torment Audrey, I was only sharing a portion of her pain. The worst part is praying for the people you care about to stick up for you and knowing it won't happen.

The teacher walks in, but that doesn't matter because Billy isn't afraid of the teachers, they're afraid of him. Before the taunting can continue, I take the chance to ask for a bathroom pass, stride through the hallways, and shove through the stall door so that it bounces off the concrete wall. Now I'm hiding like Audrey too.

Is this worth it? Is allowing myself to go down this road worth all the bullying and bullshit? Losing my friends, living life afraid of the other kids and feeling like an outsider?

Rubbing my face with both hands so I don't cry, I look up at the ceiling vent. Without my popularity, what's left? I'm turning into someone completely opposite of the person I thought I would be. Or maybe I never knew myself until now.

When I come out of the bathroom, Taylor's leaning against the wall by the water fountains.

"Hey," I say, surprised. The hallway is completely empty. Everyone else is in class. "What are you doing here?"

"Waiting for you."

"How'd you know I'd be here?"

They push off the wall, arms still crossed. Looking casual and cool, today's outfit is black parachute jogger pants, a hooded gray sleeveless top and black canvas sneakers. "Tamra from the gay-straight alliance is in your class."

"So she told you what happened?"

"She sent me a text and said I'd probably find you here. I'm in art class." Taylor makes a motion — thumb over shoulder — at the door ten feet away. "I came to make sure you're okay, but also to tell you not to let that crap get inside your head. You can't worry about arsemongers."

As if on cue, the door to the boys' bathroom swings open and out walks Smith, a senior on the football team. He takes one look at us and his eyebrows shoot halfway up his forehead before a sneer mangles his already-ugly mug.

"Well, well, well. Does this finally answer what you've got in there, Freak?" On the last word, Smith grabs his crotch and air-humps in Taylor's direction.

They just laugh. "Wouldn't you like to know."

"I would. How 'bout you pull down those *knickers* and show me?"

Taylor gives him the finger.

Still laughing, Smith continues down the hall toward his classroom. Before I can register what I'm doing, or if I even have a plan, I run after him. With a surprising amount of strength, I grab his shoulder and force him to turn around and face me.

"Don't talk to my friend like that."

Smith blinks down at me and laughs. "Oh, I get it. You think I won't hit you because you're a girl. Well, guess what? You don't look like a girl to me."

"I mean it, Smith." I take a step closer and narrow my eyes threateningly. "Remember how I used to go to parties with you? Well, I've seen you drunk and stoned, and my friends have told me more secrets about you than you know."

Smith tries not to react, but the tick in his jaw gives him away. He's thinking of the thing he doesn't want anyone to know.

"So be careful what you say and do, because I'm not afraid to tell."

Smith's mouth forms a straight line. He stares me down for a few seconds as if considering whether or not to retaliate, but then he sidesteps me and disappears into a classroom.

Taylor appears beside me. "That was kind of badass. Do you really have something on Smith?"

"Other than seeing him drunk and stoned? Nothing. But nobody is perfect, right? I figured it was safe to bluff."

Taylor laughs, and the sound makes me feel warm inside. I no longer feel like that person in the bathroom: scared and full of doubt. Maybe I'm stronger than I think.

"Will you come to the alliance meeting tomorrow with me?" Taylor asks. "I want to introduce you to my friends."

This time I don't hesitate. Online friends are great, but I could really use some new friends at school. Mostly I want to get closer to Taylor. "Yeah. For sure."

"Brilliant." They grin and the warm feeling intensifies. I feel it travel up from my belly, over my chest, and into my cheeks.

"I, uh, better get back to class." I reach to tuck my hair behind my ear, a nervous habit, and then laugh awkwardly when I remember I hacked it all off. Of course Taylor notices the gesture.

"Loving the hair, by the way."

"Thanks." If possible, I blush even harder. "I'd better get back to class."

Their lip twitches into a smirk. "You said that already."

"I sure did." I back away step by step and give a little wave. "So here I go. Heading back to class."

With a laugh, Taylor mimics my movements, backing toward the art room. "See you tomorrow."

Audrey

Today Mom doesn't drive away when we drop Clare off. We watch her walk right by her friends and into the school. Then it begins to rain. It's an imminent thunderstorm but Mom just turns on the wipers and we still don't leave.

I'm worried about her, Mom says.

Aren't you happy the blue streak is gone?

Mom puts a hand on my knee. At least things are going well with you.

I think things are going better with Clare, too, I say. She's changing for the better.

Mom's eyes fill with tears. I think so too.

The storm makes it hard for Mom to drive. She turns the wipers on quadruple speed and leans over the steering wheel like an old lady. I run as fast as I can into Peak and still get soaked.

In class Marianne writes the date on the blackboard: June 3. Mom said three days is a long time to wait for someone to call you, but I've been waiting twice as long. Calvin said he was going to visit his Dad and that he would call when he got back. But when did he say he would get back again? I realize I forgot to ask Calvin's birthday. I also forgot to ask him his favorite color. I mark down fuchsia for now because it's mine but add that question to my new list of conversation topics.

I think about Calvin on the swing during lunch hour.

I think about Calvin as I work on my math questions.

I think about Calvin while Marianne shows us a map of the United States of America. Why do they need fifty states? Canada is bigger and only has ten provinces and three territories.

I think about Calvin until Monsieur Martin says, Audrey, you've been staring at the wall for five minutes.

I wonder if we can call ourselves boyfriend and girlfriend now that we've been on a date. Will Calvin and I fall in love?

No, that is silly. That is childish. Teenagers only fall in love and get married in the movies.

If he hasn't called me yet, he probably isn't going to call me at all.

At the end of the day, Marianne doesn't give me a gold star to put on my chart. I'm really sorry, she says. Then she draws a frownie-face with permanent marker.

I don't tell Mom on the drive home. I don't tell Dad at dinner, either.

When we're finished eating Dad says, Get your coat. Time to go.

Go where?

To see Dr. Jackson. It's the first Monday of the month.

I've been focusing so hard on school and Calvin, I forgot. I'm very tired. Focusing on focusing all day is very exhausting. One can only be on for so long. Going to Dr. Jackson today is risking slipping. Up.

I'm not feeling well, I say.

Dad looks at Mom. Mom avoids looking at Dad.

It's too late to cancel, Dad says. Get your coat.

He means raincoat. Everyone keeps saying, I've never seen so much rain. It reminds me of that *Winnie the Pooh* episode.

Tut-tut, it looks like rain. Tut-tut, it looks like rain.

Water flies off the sides of the car like giant swan wings.

I remembered to make a plan for Monsieur Martin, but I forgot to make a plan for Dr. Jackson.

Do it now. Do it right. Do it before it's too late.

But it's already too late. The ride is rumbly and the car is warm. "Imagine" is playing on the radio.

Dad gently shakes my shoulder. Honey, we're here.

I sleepwalk my way into the appointment.

+ ✳ +

Seven things that are impossible not to notice in Doctor Jackson's office:

1. *It takes six steps to get from the office door to the patient chair.*
2. *Dr. Jackson has bits of whatever he had for dinner in his beard.* (Tonight: pastrami sandwich.)
3. *The room smells like meat.*
4. *There is no window. Only an air vent in the ceiling.*
5. *The plant beside the patient chair has a bite in it.*
6. *The motivational posters rotate.* (This week: *Walk the Talk* written above penguins walking on a sandy beach.)
7. *The clock on his desk ticks loudly when no one is talking. At the end of the session an alarm goes off.* (This terrified me on our first day.)

Dr. Jackson opens his top-secret notebook and crosses one leg over another as he skims it. Right, I remember, he says. Interesting. Very interesting.

What is so interesting? My legs start to bounce. They're moving on their own. They're going to leap across the coffee table. Next my arms are going to grab the notepad. Disarm him.

I clasp my hands in my lap. Imagine myself behind a brick wall. Try to contain myself.

As Clare used to say, Try to contain the weird.

Dr. Jackson glances up. Are you okay, Audrey?

No. There are cracks in my bricks.

He frowns and jots something down in his notebook.

The best thing to do in a situation like this is to avoid talking. That way, you can't reveal anything at all. If only I'd claimed laryngitis. I could have written it on his pad and caught a glimpse at the same time.

Can't talk today. Laryngitis. Reschedule?

Your father called me the other day and said you would like to return to your old school. Let's explore that. How do you feel you are progressing at Peak?

My chart is full of gold stars.

That's marvelous news. And have you made many new friends?

No.

Are you finding it hard to talk to the other kids?

I haven't tried.

Dr. Jackson frowns. Why not?

Because I don't plan to stay. I want to return to my old school with Clare.

Yes, but why is that?

I think the answer is obvious. Yet I don't know how to answer.

Dr. Jackson crosses one leg over the other and leans closer. You once told me you didn't feel like you had a lot of friends at your old school, so what makes you think you'll be happier there? Clare has friends she wants to spend time with as well, and you should too. You've been trying to fit in with your twin for so long that you haven't tried making your own friends. Perhaps if you give the kids at Peak a chance, you'll discover that some of them share your interests and have more in common with you. Maybe you'll even like them.

I think about Calvin and how we both like playing pretend. Then I think about Kira and how I made her cry last week. I wish that hadn't happened. I should probably apologize for hurting her feelings. The truth is I actually do like Kira. Maybe we could be friends.

I would like you to try talking to one new person a day. Can you do that, Audrey?

Yes. I will.

Good. Dr. Jackson sits back in his chair again and props the notebook up on his leg. Now, a few weeks ago we talked about that game you play in your mind, the one with the letters. Do you still play it?

Sometimes.

I'd like to discuss that game in further detail.

Why, are you writing a rule book?

Don't be rude, Audrey.

I'm not. I want to know.

He considers this. I can tell because he taps his pen against his lips.

No, I'm not writing a rule book, he says. It's your game. I would like you to tell me more about it. The truth, please.

And then I have to tell him.

Sometimes I dissect sentences, I tell him. Like Hello, how are you? would be split into four groups of four. The question mark is worth two because it's broken into two pieces.

He blinks at me.

(Hell)(ohow)(arey)(ou?)

I see.

You could do two groups of eight, but I like to break it down into as many groups as possible. I used to count spaces but I don't anymore.

How often do you do this? he asks.

Sometimes when I read a sign. Sometimes when someone speaks to me. I'm very good at it now. I can do it in seconds.

Dr. Jackson sits back. He puts the tips of his fingers together like he's making a tent. And when did you start doing this?

Shoot, that's twenty-nine. I guess I can change it to a period instead of a question mark to make it work. Seven groups of four.

Audrey, please answer the question.

I don't know. Probably since I started to read. At school I do it in French.

Do you play any other counting games?

Whenever I drive somewhere, I count the number of green and red lights on the trip. Whenever I take a stairwell, I count the number of stairs and memorize it. So that I won't trip during an emergency.

An emergency?

A blackout.

Ah, I see. What about walking on flat ground? Do you count steps then?

Only in places that make me nervous.

Does my office make you nervous?

Yes.

He doesn't answer but writes something in his notebook again.

It's unfair. Counselors take notes about you, but you never get to see them. Even though you're paying them to do it.

What did you write? I ask.

He glances up and smiles. You'll have to change that question mark to a period.

I smile too. I know, I say. I hate seventeen for that reason. I hate most prime numbers for that reason.

His smile grows larger. I have a question that will stump you. You said you count question marks as two points, so would an exclamation point count for two as well?

Of course.

Okay, then why not a lowercase *i*?

That's a very good question. Thank you, Dr. Jackson.

You're welcome, Audrey.

I think this is going very well.

+ ✳ +

Dad seems tense when he drives me home. His hands are doing the white-knuckle thing on the wheel.

How did the appointment go? he asks.

Je ne sais pas. He never lets me read the notes.

He told me about your game. Dad's voice sounds funny. Like he's trying to speak but there's an orange peel across his teeth.

Oui. He gave me some pointers.

At this Dad looks surprised. Yeah? Like what?

Like that the *i* should count as two points as well. Like the question mark and exclamation point.

Dad frowns. I don't know why he would do that.

Do what?

Dad glances over at me. Smiles the way that doesn't reach his eyes. Are you sure you want to switch schools, honey?

Sure. Certain. Positive.

It's just . . . Dr. Jackson is a bit concerned.

Concerned? When did he express this concern? I want to ask. When I went to the bathroom? I clench my fists. After-session bathroom sabotage!

He doesn't think you're ready, honey.

Why not?

He says he's observed some changes in you. He's concerned you seem more anxious since Adam passed. He's worried you'll spend time playing games in your head and fall behind in a large classroom.

I won't. This whole drive I only counted three red lights. I'm too busy talking to you.

Dad rubs his chin and looks out the window.

At home he and Mom retreat to the attic. They always talk in the attic when they don't want us to hear. When it's an especially private conversation, they pull up the ladder. But you can still hear them through the vent in the bathroom. I lock the door like I'm using the toilet and then sit on the lid and listen.

Dr. Jackson said psychological disorders don't always work in isolation, I hear Dad tell Mom. They can feed off one another. What is the word he used? Comorbidity.

That's convenient. He still can't settle on a diagnosis so he's put together a bag of tricks.

That's what I thought. What exactly are we paying him for? We could have just surfed WebMD.

Silence while they consider this. Maybe Mom is booting up her laptop.

So what does he recommend? she asks.

He said that he would like to keep using the broad term *neurodivergent* at this time. He wants to keep focusing on treatments and strategies that work for Audrey as she continues to develop.

Maybe we should get a second opinion?

Do we really want to put Audrey through that? I think she has a level of trust with Dr. Jackson now, and you know how much she hates change.

The ceiling creaks as someone paces around. Probably Mom. She's the pacer.

Maybe we're thinking about this the wrong way, Mom says. Maybe it's better that he wants to keep working with her rather than give her a quick fix. Maybe we're causing her more heartache by trying to fit her into one box.

Maybe. Dad sighs. You should have seen her face when I said she might not be able to go back with Clare. I suppose sometimes being a parent is making the tough calls.

And sometimes being a parent isn't doing what the books or anyone else says. It's making decisions based on our gut feelings. What do we think is right, Stewart? In our hearts?

I don't know. I promised her I would really consider it, but the classes will be bigger: thirty kids instead of the fifteen Audrey is used to now.

More pacing by Mom. Then: She won't be thrown to the wolves. They'll help us create an individualized education plan, and they have a private study room where she can work with other students with learning differences. We can get her a tutor if need be.

Marianne emailed us that Audrey spaced out all day.

Yes, but we're seeing improvement. It's clear she can succeed when she has a goal, right?

Silence. Maybe Dad is nodding. I wouldn't know.

Then he says, But things are already difficult with Clare. You told me you were terrified to drop her off at school today, that you watched her walk all the way in, worried some kid was going to pick on her.

I was, but we have to let her live her own life, right? We can't protect her all the time.

I know.

So shouldn't we give Audrey the same chance?

It's not the same. What if it just doesn't work? What if it ends up being a disaster and she feels even worse?

Isn't it better to take that risk? To do everything we can to help her succeed and be there to support her if she fails? Isn't that our *job* as parents, to give her every opportunity we can?

I don't want to be the bad guy here, Margaret.

There's a long silence and then Mom's sewing machine starts up. I hear her pumping the pedal while Dad puts down the ladder. It squeaks as he descends. Louder and louder until he's right outside the bathroom door.

I hold my breath for ten seconds and then step into the hallway. Empty ladder. Dad downstairs. Mom in the attic. I dash to my room.

My eyes are burning. They're not going to let me change schools. I know it. I can feel it.

+ ✳ +

Ms. Nguyen is pleased when she receives my permission slip on Wednesday. Wonderful! she says. Have you decided on a subject?

The twins, I tell her. The GMO twins.

Okay. I have a thinner piece of stone I think we can work with. It will be hard work, but I have faith in you, Audrey. And I can help.

No! I want to do this on my own.

She jumps a little at the tone of my voice. Okay, Audrey, whatever you want. Just remember I'll be here to support you.

I feel a bit bad about yelling. Ms. Nguyen is so nice. But she's on the other side of the room at the cabinet already so I don't say sorry. She comes back with a large green rectangular block, a pair of goggles, and a bundle of canvas wrapped around what looks like a set of dentist tools for a giant. Including a hammer.

We'll be using chisels and files. She picks one up. It's the smallest tool in the set. We'll start with the file first to create the outside shape of the womb and base. The important thing to remember is to file away from you. Slide it forward and lift it off the stone. Then return to the starting position until you've filed away the amount you want.

Next she picks up the tool with the wider end. We'll use the chisel to cut away the portion that needs to be removed. We'll save this part for last. When we're more confident. The key with the chisel is to tap it lightly with the hammer. Let the tools do the work for you and don't worry about hitting air.

I'll go over this again when it's time. After the general shape is formed, we'll smooth down the sculpture with sandpaper. I'll help you apply wax to keep moisture out.

I'm so excited. This will be the best thing I've ever made. Better than the K'Nex towers. Better than all my drawings and comic strips combined.

It will fix me and Clare. When she sees it she will remember that we are twins and what we used to be like. Everything will go back to normal. She will forgive me.

I reach for the file but Ms. Nguyen plucks it from my fingers. She lays it back down on the table. My apologies. The very first step is to trace the outline of your design onto the stone with pencil. Then you can see where to file and there is less chance of making a mistake. Remember to trace the design on the side of the block as well.

I pick up my pencil and pull the stone toward me. Glance up. Ms. Nguyen is hovering. She gets the hint.

Don't start filing without putting on the goggles. The dust can be very harmful to your eyes. I'll come back in a half hour.

Alone in the studio, I begin.

If Clare had been born thirteen minutes later, she would have been a Gemini like me. Geminis are always searching for their other half. The person who will understand them. For most of my life that person was Clare. But Clare didn't need me.

When we were in grade one, our teacher asked us to write about our first memory. She said it's hard for some people to pinpoint their very first, but I didn't have any trouble.

Mine was Clare. We were lying side by side in a crib. I remember turning my head to look at her.

Our teacher didn't believe me. People don't start retaining memories until they're at least two years old, she said. I must have used my imagination to come up with that memory.

It's different working with sculpture. Like drawing in 3D. On the side of the block the sculpture starts out thin (side of the womb) and gets wider (base of sculpture).

Clare's first memory was playing with Adam in the backyard. He was teaching her soccer. She told the teacher we were probably about two. The teacher believed her.

I've finished tracing the design now. I put on the goggles, which make it very hard to see, and pick up the file. After standing the block on its side, I follow Ms. Nguyen's advice and slide the file away from me. I'm surprised to discover that the sandstone strips away almost as easily as the bar of soap. Only it doesn't smell as good. It feels kind of like skinning a rectangular apple.

I remember Clare's first memory too. It was a sunny day. Adam was running around the backyard kicking a ball. Mom asked if we could kick it too. Before that he'd never really played with us.

After that he played with us all the time.

We were lucky. Adam was a really good big brother.

A week after the funeral, Clare and I got in a fight. She was angry that I was in the basement. She thought it was his area and that no one should go there.

He wouldn't like you better than me if he knew it was your fault, she yelled.

He didn't like me better, I told her. He liked us the same.

No he didn't. He always took your side, but he wouldn't anymore.

Tears streaked her face. I picked up the remote and threw it at her. Then I stomped on a Nintendo controller and ran upstairs.

A tear hits the soapstone and I wipe it away.

Eleven months. Eleven months Adam's been gone but it feels like yesterday. What would he be doing if he were still alive?

Another tear hits the sculpture. And then another. I file faster like I'm racing the tears.

There was an accident.

Adam was driving to pick up Audrey.

Adam will never come back.

I wish I'd never been born. If I'd never been born, Adam would still be here. Why do I even exist? The extra baby no one wanted. It was only supposed to be Clare.

I ditch the file and pick up the chisel I'm not supposed to use yet. Filing will take forever. I lay the block on its side and line up the chisel, lightly hit it with the hammer. Then harder. A chunk of rock falls away.

Sometimes I wish I could find a time machine. I wish I could tell my parents I don't want to take karate. If they made me anyway, I would sit on the bench outside and not call home. I'd just wait for Mom and Dad to pick me up. I would do anything to have a second chance.

Lining the chisel up on the opposite side of the stone, I take off the entire corner. Dust flies up into my face and I'm glad I'm wearing the goggles. It lands on my lips and my tongue instinctively darts out. Takes it in.

There is no time machine and there are no second chances. There is only regret.

I'm hitting harder now. I forget to let the tools do the work. Hit and miss. Hit and miss. I file a stubborn chunk of rock off but accidentally nick a finger, put it in my mouth and taste blood.

I'm not done. I have hours to go. But I flip the block over. Scratch the words I cannot say into the base.

Please forgive me, Clare and Adam.

Clare

For the first time in three weeks, I wake up feeling very feminine.

When I look in the bathroom mirror, I no longer feel free with my short hair — I feel plain. I dig around in the vanity drawers until I find a headband. Much better. Next I apply lipstick and eyeliner the way I used to and put on my black sweater and black-and-red plaid skirt.

Mom almost drops the coffeepot when she sees me. "Clare! Hi. Are you okay? I mean, you look . . ." Her mouth continues to open and close but she doesn't finish her sentence.

I glance around. "Where's Audrey?"

"She's not down yet."

"What? Why?"

"You're up early."

I look at the clock. So I am. Mom hasn't even started making breakfast. She sits down at the counter, coffeepot still in hand, and motions for me to do the same.

"Clare, did school go okay yesterday? I know you said it did, but we didn't have much time to talk about it. And now you're dressed like this, and I can't help but wonder . . ."

"Wonder what?"

Mom shifts on the stool. "Well, you were so brave cutting your hair like that, and wearing the bracelet. I know kids can be mean. Were they mean to you?"

Now it's me who shifts uncomfortably. Maybe it's pride, maybe I'm embarrassed; I don't know. "Some of them. But I'm making new friends too."

"Okay, that's good. But just to check because I'm your mom and that's what moms do, you're not changing how you're dressed today because you got bullied yesterday?"

Oh. Now I get it. I'm not going to explain to Mom, just like I'm not going to explain to the other kids who will assume the exact same thing as her, so I go back upstairs and change into jeans and a black T-shirt, take off the headband, and wipe off the makeup. It feels wrong, I feel itchy, so I slip a toe ring on under my sock and an anklet on under my jeans where no one else can see them. I still don't feel as confident as I did five minutes ago, but it's worth it today. I can't let people like Billy think they're scaring me into dressing differently. Mom and Audrey are already in the car when I go back downstairs. Mom doesn't say anything, but she smiles at me in the rearview mirror. I smile back awkwardly. I'm still not used to this new supportive version of my mother, but I like her.

After they drop me off, I walk into school and practically smack into Kyle. "You've been missing our weekly appointments."

"Sorry, I've been busy working on a project."

Kyle smiles tightly. "Now, we both know that's not true. Come on, let's have a quick chat." A casual suggestion, but I wouldn't put it past him to have been waiting at the front entrance for me.

"I'll be late for class."

"I'll give you a note."

Great. I sink down into the chair. Kyle squeezes through the sliver of space between his desk and the wall to get to his own chair, and it's not as uncomfortable to watch as I thought it would be. Today is full of surprises.

With everything I've been going through, all the time spent browsing forums instead of working on a school project, or any school project for that matter, my marks have plummeted further than they did last semester. I failed an English exam because I didn't read the book. I didn't even read the Internet synopsis of the book because I entirely forgot about the exam. I also skipped a science lab because I couldn't summon the urge to care.

Apparently Kyle heard about both incidents. Worse, he called Sharon in one day to find out how I was doing.

"You talked to Sharon about me?"

"When you failed to show up — again — for our meeting, yes, I did. She says you're not acting like yourself." He gives me a once-over. "You cut off all your hair."

"Is it a crime to get a haircut?"

"She's concerned about you."

"If she's so concerned, she would talk to me instead of you. Instead of avoiding me. What Sharon is actually upset about is the way I've been dressing. Weeks ago she told me I'm starting to look emo, because it embarrasses her to be my friend. It's all about image for her."

"Ah, I see." Kyle sits back in his chair. "You're in the process of reinventing yourself. Trying the *emo* label on for a bit."

"There's no label. I'm not labeling myself."

"I understand. Teenagers feel like they have to belong to a group. It makes you feel safe during times of uncertainty and change."

Here I assume he's referring to my brother's death.

"It's great to reinvent yourself," he continues. "Do you know the average person reinvents themselves multiple times over their lifespan? I once read that to not reinvent yourself is like being resistant to life itself. Don't you think that's true?"

"Well, yeah."

"There's a quote by Ralph Waldo Emerson that I like to share in times like this. I'm sure you've heard it before. 'To be yourself in a world that is constantly trying to make you something else is the greatest accomplishment.' I'm proud of you, Clare."

"Thanks?"

"However, I don't want all this self-discovery to get in the way of your schoolwork. It's not like you to fail exams. Next week is the last day of classes, and grade nine achievement exams are coming up the week after that. They're worth twenty percent of your grade. Normally students complain about how unfair that is, but I'm sure you'll be jumping at the chance to improve your marks, am I right?" He laughs and I smile back weakly. "I've spoken with Ms. Dunphy, and she'll give you an extension on the bio lab. I'll try to organize a rewrite for the exam as well. Everyone understands you've had a tough year, but this will be the only special treatment you get. Understood?"

"Okay. Thank you," I say because it's what I'm expected to say. I'm about to leave, but instead I decide to try something. Kyle is old, so he must have some answers. Maybe he can help me.

"Clothing doesn't have to be gender-specific, right?" I ask him.

"I agree clothing isn't inherently gendered."

"Okay, well, what if I told you that some days I feel more like a guy?"

"Are you saying you'd rather be male, Clare?"

"Sometimes, maybe. Not all the time." Here it comes. "Maybe I'm a girl and a guy and it changes with the day."

"Changes with the day?" Kyle's eyebrows shoot up and he actually strokes his beard. For a few moments we're just looking at each other, and then he says, "That must be very confusing."

I get up to leave.

"Clare, wait." Kyle stands. He's stroking his beard with such intensity now, I'm worried he'll pull it off. "I didn't mean it that way. I'm just trying to learn all the new lingo. This new trend with you young people, it's all new to —"

"It's not a trend. We've always been here. We just finally feel safe enough to make that known."

"Right. You're right, I'm sorry. I've been trying to educate myself and the other teachers as well. I think the best thing I can do is tell you about the gay-straight alliance we have here at school. Have you heard of it?"

I feel myself smile. "I have. I'm actually going to the meeting at lunch today."

"Good." Kyle nods and then repeats himself. "Good."

"So . . . I guess this is our last meeting before summer."

"Last official meeting, but my door is always open."

As I walk back to class, I realize I kind of like Kyle. Unlike some of the teachers who only use Taylor's pronouns because they have to, Kyle is an adult who actually cares.

I spend my morning classes thinking about the alliance meeting. This week it's going to be at a coffee shop a few blocks from school. Tamra knows the owner and she lets them use the upstairs area where it's a bit more private. The group is larger than I expected it would be, with students from all the grades. Most people I recognize but don't know by name, but I'm surprised to see a guy from my grade named Stefan. He gives me a friendly wave, which I return.

As the leader of the alliance, Tamra welcomes everyone and then introduces me, asks if I have anything I want to say. This makes me even more uncomfortable. I stutter out a no and turn bright red. She explains that they usually go around the circle and give everyone the opportunity to share their experiences, but I don't have to share if I'm not comfortable, so I just nod.

Tamra begins by telling us that her grandmother is coming to visit and that she's nervous for the visit. "Grandma no longer pretends Abigail and I are just really good friends, but she doesn't want to meet her just yet. Maybe on her next trip." Tamra pauses and then adds, "But to tell you the truth, I don't know how much longer she'll live, and it makes me really sad to think she'll never get to know Abby."

"You can't change other people," Stefan responds. "All you can do is hope they accept you, and be ready to accept that they might not."

Tamra's story makes me think of everything I've been through to get to this point, how nervous I was, and still am, to confide in my parents, and the conversation we had after I cut my hair. I'm lucky to have the family I have. So when it's my turn to speak, I square my shoulders and tell myself I can do this. I can open up to people at school about who I am.

"Hi, my name is Clare. I'm Taylor's friend." Taylor gives me a reassuring smile and I continue. "I'm not really sure how to explain what I've been going through, but I want to."

"There's no pressure," Tamra tells me, and everyone nods. "Say as much or as little as you'd like. We're glad you're here."

"Okay. Well, I actually woke up feeling like a girl today." The words slip out of my mouth and I let them. "That's kind of weird for me because for the last few weeks, I've been feeling like a guy. I know I don't have to choose, and for the moment at least I'd like to keep using she/her pronouns. I've been doing a lot of research online and joined some chat groups and stuff, and there are people who feel the same way I do." So that I won't panic and stop talking, I look at my fingers in my lap, but I can feel Taylor's eyes on me. "I'm terrified of labels. I'm scared of hurting other people by trying to label them, and I'm scared of using the wrong label on others or myself. The other night I watched a YouTube video about someone who is gender-fluid but who used to tag Tumblr photos as both 'gender-fluid' and 'trans' and got comments from people who didn't think they should use both labels, or that they don't mean the same thing. Sometimes it feels like you can't make any mistakes."

"I know what you mean," a girl I don't know says. "That kind of thing happened to me too. I didn't mean to offend anyone else; I was just trying to define my own experience." There are murmurs of agreement, and then everyone goes silent again as they wait for me to continue.

"I do think labels can be helpful sometimes. Until I heard that term, I didn't feel like I could even describe what I was going through. Learning about other people who are gender-fluid helped me finally understand myself." I still haven't looked up. I'm afraid that if I do, I won't finish my story, and it's something that needs to be said. "I wanted to dress how I feel today, but I was worried that if I did, the kids who have been making fun of the way I've been dressing would think I changed because of them. So in order to not give them that idea, I dressed like this, and now it feels like I'm living in somebody else's body. I just want to go home. I thought I was taking some sort of stand today, but I guess I'm still living my life for other people and worrying about what other people think." I finally risk a glance up to see Taylor looking at me the way we looked at each other during their bio presentation, like for the first time we're truly being seen.

"So, going forward I'm going to try to stop doing that. I'm going to make an effort to like myself for who I am and to be a better person to others." I take a deep, steadying breath, still looking at Taylor. "That's it, I guess. Thanks for listening."

When everyone starts clapping, I finally break eye contact with

Taylor and feel the heat rise into my cheeks. Just like the other day when we were on the wrestling mats, all my secrets spilled out of me, but I'm okay with that.

On the walk back to school, Taylor slings a casual arm around my shoulders as we joke around with their friends, and I feel something inside me change. I feel lighter. Spending time with Taylor feels like spending time with Adam, learning to skateboard or playing Nintendo. Like we've been doing this for years rather than days. As Taylor lets out a loud laugh, I risk a glance at them, trying to decipher what they're thinking. Was putting their arm around me a friendly maneuver, or are they trying to tell me how they feel?

When we enter the school, their arm slips off my shoulders, and I feel an urge to pull it back around me again.

"I've got maths now." Taylor sticks their tongue out in disgust.

I laugh. "I love that you call it *maths*."

"That's what it's supposed to be called." With a wink, they head away down the hall.

I realize I'm watching them like a weirdo and quickly dart into the stairwell. Maybe I'm completely misinterpreting things, but it seems like Taylor's and my friendship is shifting. I think I might really like them — scratch that, I *know* I do — but I'm not sure they feel the same way. How am I supposed to figure that out without scaring them? I've never been through this before.

I'm completely in my head as I make my way to the second floor to grab my books and almost trip over my own feet when I see Sharon & Co. waiting for me beside my locker.

"Hey," I say warily as I approach. What are they doing here?

"Where have you been?" Sharon asks.

"Uh, do you mean just now, or since you stopped hanging out with me or texting me?" I move to open my locker and Sharon takes the hint, steps aside to lean against the next locker.

"So I'm dating Billy now." I'm focusing on my combination instead of looking at her, but I can hear the smug tone, which implies I'm supposed to be jealous at this news.

I yank my locker open. "What happened to Jeff?"

"He was boring." She laughs. "In bed, if that's not clear. Then Billy asked me out. I guess all it took was for him to see I was single. Or maybe he was just majorly turned off by all of *that*." Here she waves her hand in a circle, encompassing my wardrobe.

"Oh shit!" Charlotte and Rhiannon bust out a laugh.

I grab my books and shove them into my bag, wanting to get out of there as fast as possible, but then I think better of it. Time to finish this for good. I face them again.

"Why do you care so much what I wear?"

"I just think it's really *weird* you're wearing all of Adam's clothes."

"Holy hell." I roll my eyes. "Do you use that word for everything?"

"You know," Sharon ignores me and continues, "now that I think about it, it's almost like you're trying to become him or something. Like you're trying to *turn into your brother*."

"Don't talk about my brother."

"Why not? I knew him too."

"I mean it, Sharon." I'm seething now, but behind all the anger is the hurt. Sharon is my best friend, *was* my best friend, and the person who was there for me after he died. To think I once thought she understood me better than anyone else.

"I'm just saying that's a really messed-up way to mourn someone, Clare."

"You don't care about how I mourn Adam. You didn't even care about Adam. I don't think you really cared about me either, only about having a best friend who did whatever you wanted. And you know what? I think you were mean to Audrey because you were jealous of her."

Sharon snorts. "Yeah right. I was jealous of *Audrey*." She rolls her eyes at Charlotte and Rhiannon.

"Stop acting like there is something wrong with Audrey. You were jealous of her because she and I were so close. And you know what? I think you're jealous that I'm doing what I want to do, regardless of what you think about it."

Sharon glares back at me, her eyes shiny, but she doesn't deny it.

"Look, I still care about you, Sharon, but I'm not going to hang out with someone who is cruel to my twin or my other friends, including Taylor. I saw that post you put on Audrey's wall, I've heard the way you talk about Taylor, and I'm no longer going to put up with it. So if you ever valued our friendship, stop."

Charlotte and Rhiannon glance nervously at Sharon, who purses her lips together tightly. Before she can retaliate with something nasty and ruin things between us forever, I sling my bag over my shoulder and walk away.

Audrey

It takes me over a week to finish the carving. I work on it nonstop during my art period and at lunch. I work on it even when my hands start to curl and I can barely hold the chisel.

It developed a different shape than I originally planned. I didn't even know my idea until the carving was complete.

You look happy, Audrey.

Ms. Nguyen is standing behind me. I didn't even hear her approach.

I feel happy. Like a weight has been lifted off me.

Ms. Nguyen touches the symbols and asks me what they stand for. I tell her and her eyes fill with tears.

That's very touching, Audrey. Clare will love it.

I hope so.

It's heavy. Almost as large as a bowling ball. The top of the womb is like a handle but you shouldn't carry it that way. It might break. So I cradle it against my chest as I get up to wrap it in paper to take home.

Ms. Nguyen sits on the table. Audrey, I talked to Monsieur Martin about your desire to change schools.

I freeze and almost knock over the carving.

I'm going to give my support to your parents, she says. Monsieur Martin will too.

You will? I pinch myself but I'm not dreaming.

Ms. Nguyen nods. She's smiling.

Thank you, I say. Then I give her a hug. It surprises both of us because I don't usually give hugs.

After Mom drives me home, I wait in my room for Clare to come home. I don't even know she's downstairs until the phone rings. Then I hear her in the kitchen talking to someone, most likely Sharon. The old feeling of being replaced returns, but I pick up the carving anyway. It's time to make up.

When I enter the kitchen with my carving still wrapped in paper, Clare gives me a weird smile. At first I think I was right and she is talking to Sharon. But then Clare makes a motion with her hand for me to come closer like when she talks to Grandma and wants me to talk next. I stop dead in my tracks. I hate talking on the phone.

Then Clare says, Oh, I thought you two met at Peak.

Understanding dawns.

No! NO! I run forward and whisper-yell at Clare. Take it back! Pretend you were joking!

What? Clare frowns. Joking about what?

I can't breathe and I know it's coming. A panic attack. It feels like the world is crashing. Like that time we went to the go-karts and Clare cut me off. I ran into a large stack of rubber tires.

BAM.

Clare's mouth pulls funny so I can see her bottom teeth. Um, just a second, she says to Calvin. Then she holds the phone out to me. Do you want to talk to him?

What do you think? This time I yell it at her. No! *Hang up now!*

Clare's eyes go big. She quickly puts the receiver down. What the hell, Audrey? He heard that, you know.

Why would you tell him that about me? Why would you tell him I go there?

Clare blinks at me. Doesn't he go to Peak too?

No! And he doesn't know that I do.

How was I supposed to know that? You never lie, Audrey.

I didn't lie to him. I just never told him.

That is a lie, Audrey. It's called a "lie of omission." Why didn't you just talk to him? Now he knows you go to Peak AND you insulted him. I doubt he'll ever call back now.

Now he'll never want to be my boyfriend!

He won't want to be your boyfriend because you hung up on him! she yells back.

You told him on purpose.

Why would I do that?

Because you hate me. I say the words and know they're true.

Clare's mouth falls open. I think she might try to deny it. I wait.

And wait.

I turn and run from the kitchen.

My legs shake as I climb the stairs. I hold tight to the bannister as I carry the carving back to my room. I find Calvin's phone number in my sketchbook and rip it into tiny little pieces. They flutter to the floor like snowflakes.

It's over. It's done.

None of my stupid fantasies will come true. That's just what they were: stupid fantasies. Like Sirius.

I know I shouldn't, but no one will know. I open the chest under the window and pick up where I left off. I play a scene.

Iron Man has a minion hostage on top of the K'Nex roller coaster.

Elsa could normally make an ice staircase and save him. But Iron Man's goon is holding her hostage: a troll doll with a pink diamond embedded in its stomach.

Elsa yells up to Iron Man. Why are you doing this? Because I broke your heart?

And he says, You're so conceited.

Elsa keeps him distracted while the monkeys slip out of their barrel and inch toward the roller coaster.

Maybe I just like to be bad, Iron Man says. Maybe I'm not really the good guy. Maybe all the battles alongside the Avengers made me realize what I want.

The monkeys are at the back of the roller coaster where Iron Man can't see them. They begin to climb in a chain. High, higher, highest.

You could join me, Elsa. With your powers, we would be unstoppable.

I want to use my powers for good. I just got my sister back.

For good? That is so *boring*. Only the good die young.

Billy Joel's song begins to play.

Nice touch, Elsa mutters. Very theatrical.

The song echoes through the abandoned theme park. The other rides are half-broken. Empty. Soulless.

Iron Man flies closer to the minion tied to the roller coaster. You would risk it all for your sister, but would she do the same for you?

No, but I don't care. She means everything to me.

More than a life?

Everything.

That's the answer I was hoping for. With an evil smile, Iron Man cuts the ropes, releasing the minion.

He falls to his death.

CLARE

Gasping for air, my eyes fly open and I roll to the left, reaching out like I did as a child. But Audrey's no longer there. Instead of a twin bed, I'm sleeping in a queen bed in the middle of the room, and my heart is still racing from the nightmare.

It was as if I were a ghost, floating above Calgary's river valley. At first it was peaceful — the sun was shining, people were tubing down the Elbow River and having a good time. Then the sky grew dark and full of clouds and rain began to fall, harder and faster, until the roads were slick. I heard a screech and looked down Elbow Drive to see a TJ swerve to miss an oncoming car, roll down the bank, and into the turbulent river. Adam's TJ.

Adam! I screamed. *Adam, I'm coming! I'll save you!*

The TJ was upside down in the water. The fog was thick and the wind kept pushing me backwards, but at last I reached the car, grasped the edge of the broken passenger window, and ducked my head inside.

Only it wasn't just Adam inside. He'd made it in time to pick up Audrey before the accident. Both of them were covered in ice.

Still reeling from the nightmare, I draw my knees up to my chest and press my forehead against them, panting hard. Outside, rain hammers my bedroom windows.

That wasn't how it happened. On the night of The Accident, it hadn't been storming like it is now. The roads weren't even slick. Adam had swerved to avoid a car whose driver was texting and drifted into the opposite lane.

And thankfully Audrey hadn't died too. Audrey was still here.

I hug my knees until the remnants of the dream finally fade away. My skin is covered in a thin layer of sweat, and I'm staring at the space where Audrey's bed used to be. It's been almost two years since we shared a room. Back when one of us had a nightmare, we would climb into the other's bed. We didn't have to say anything — we knew what had happened. That was because it was usually me crawling in with her.

I should have said something to her after our fight. I should have told her that I didn't tell Calvin on purpose and that I don't hate her. Audrey never asked for any of this. She never asked to be different, and that's something we have in common. I really hope I haven't wrecked things with Calvin because he's the first real friend she's had in years. Kind of like Taylor is to me, I realize, and feel extra bad.

I have to see Audrey.

I throw my blankets off, tiptoe to my door, and open it as quietly as possible. Audrey's room is across the hall, the door closed. I grasp her doorknob to open it but then pause. What if she refuses to talk to me, the way I've refused to talk to her in the past? What if she yells at me again like she did before I cut my hair?

Her words from our fight earlier come flooding back: *You told him on purpose. Because you hate me.* Is that what she really thinks?

Of course it is.

A month after Adam's death I had Sharon & Co. over, and Audrey came into the TV room where we were watching a movie and just kind of leaned against the door, waiting to be asked to join. I knew what she wanted but I didn't invite her. Everyone else ignored her too. So eventually she pretended that she was getting construction paper out of the cupboard and went back to her room.

I knew I was punishing her and she knew she was being punished. Now I can barely remember a time when I wasn't punishing her.

I let go of the doorknob and slip back into my room.

+ ✳ +

It's been a week since my standoff with Sharon. She's ignored me since, indicating she's made her choice, but I'm okay with that part of my life being over. I've been dressing how I feel every morning, and to my surprise, none of the kids have made any comments. So maybe we've struck a truce.

Since the GSA meeting, I've been getting together with Taylor and the other kids from the alliance to eat lunch in the park, or grab a slice of pizza or a smoothie down the street from school. On Friday, the last day of classes, everyone is giddy and excited for summer, and the juniors and seniors have an epic water fight in the courtyard before a bunch of teachers rush out of the school to break it up. As we're heading to Pizza Palace, Taylor grabs my hand and pulls me off the sidewalk and behind a tree in Tomkins Park.

"You okay?" I ask as they release my hand and pace back and forth, back and forth.

"Yes. No. I'm nervous." They stop pacing and take a deep breath. "Okay, I'm just going to come right out and say it. I don't know how you see me. I mean, we've just started hanging out, but we have a connection. Do you feel it?"

"Yeah." I look into those beautiful storm-gray eyes and know this is serious. This is one of the most serious moments of my life. "I do."

"At first I thought maybe we were just intrigued by each other, you know?" Taylor begins pacing again, talking fast. "But I think it's more than that. At least for me. I wasn't sure for you."

I step forward to close the gap between us and take both of their hands in my own. I look at their lips, at the subtle shape of them, so naturally red. I get it now: the sweaty palms, the racing heartbeat, the adrenaline that courses through my veins whenever Taylor touches me. "Don't worry, I feel the exact same way. It's more than that for me, too."

"Thank goodness." Taylor sags into me with relief. "I've been trying to fight it because I wanted to be a friend to you. A real friend."

"You are my friend. Probably the first real friend I've had in years."

"Same. That's why I'm terrified of messing it up."

"It would be worth it. Even if it completely ruins our friendship, which it won't, it would be completely worth it to have you as my . . ."

"Datemate," Taylor offers with a smile.

"Datemate," I finish.

"All right, then how about we go for dinner tonight to celebrate?"

So when I get home I tell the 'rents that some kids from class are going for burgers and ice cream to celebrate the start of summer. I pull almost everything out of my closet before deciding on a ripped jean skirt and a black backless sweater. It's my sexiest sweater, the one that used to make guys throw themselves at me. I hope it does the same for Taylor. Maybe it's the idea of going on a date, but I feel extra feminine today. In addition to the dark liner I used to wear, I apply bright red lipstick.

The 'rents are playing Scrabble in the living room when I leave, and they do a really bad job of hiding their shock when they see me. Dad even scratches his head like he's confused.

I shrug so they know it's not a big deal. "I just felt like wearing this."

"You look good," Mom says and then adds, "But sweetie, don't feel like you have to act a certain way just to fit in with the girls."

This time I say, "Don't worry, Mom. This has nothing to do with them. It's all me."

Outside, Taylor is idling in the rain in a little black hatchback. I'm super nervous as I run down the walk with my umbrella and almost wish I could hide behind it in the car. Instead I fumble with it outside the passenger door before sliding into the car.

"Dressing for my personality," I explain. "Date night."

"Love it."

And then we're off. Across the console Taylor reaches out and takes my hand as we drive, gives me a reassuring squeeze.

"You look beautiful."

"You like this look?" Even though I no longer feel the need to label Taylor, I still can't help but wonder if they prefer me dressed as a guy or girl.

"I'd like you in a paper bag." That suggestive smile is back. "Actually, we should try that."

"Mmm, paper bags. So sexy," I joke.

"*You're* sexy."

Reddening, I try to pull my hand away, but Taylor holds tight and I don't really want to stop. There's no room to park in front of the restaurant, so we have to run through the rain, huddled under my umbrella. It's exciting and I'm not even afraid of who might see us. It's been a long time since I've felt this confident. As we walk up, I see couples sitting at small tables with white tablecloths, flickering candles warming shy smiles. Taylor gives my hand a reassuring squeeze.

We shake off the umbrella and dart inside.

It's a little French restaurant, dimly lit and romantic, with gold-framed mirrors and paintings of French bistros, rivers, and gardens on the walls. I'm glad I dressed up — I feel pretty and confident, even though I have to keep reminding myself to take deep breaths. It feels so grown-up to be here, smiling at each other over the flickering flame as we butter our bread and swap plates to try each other's meals. I ordered macaroni au gratin, and Taylor ordered a savory crepe filled with bacon, potato, onions, mushrooms, and parsley. The server knows Taylor and brings us free mochas with whipped cream for dessert. We sit by the rain-soaked windowpane holding our steaming cups, our legs entwined under the table. I like how the rain obscures the view of outside and makes it feel like we're in a different world.

"Have you been here a lot?"

"It's my parents' favorite restaurant." Taylor laughs. "They love crepes. When we lived in London, it was easy to take the train to Paris for a weekend. They miss that, so we started coming here."

"A train from London to Paris? Isn't there an ocean between them?"

"The English Channel, yes. You can ferry across too but it's longer and more expensive than the Chunnel. It's a train that goes underwater."

My mouth falls open. "Underwater? That's so scary. How deep does it go?"

"Seventy-ish meters? About two hundred fifty feet," Taylor clarifies.

"And you've been on it?"

They laugh. "Of course. The whole ride takes two and a half hours, but you're only underwater for maybe twenty minutes. It just feels like going through a really long tunnel."

"I would probably pay more for the ferry."

Taylor laughs again. "Maybe one day we can go on it together."

It's a nice dream, especially in this setting. "Where else would we go?"

"Anywhere you want."

"We could travel through France and then go to Italy."

"Yes, let's go to Venice! We can take a gondola ride and drink cappuccinos. It's very touristy, though. There are a lot of shops and stands selling glass jewelry and masquerade masks."

"Where else have you traveled?"

"Oh, all over. Ireland, Spain, Croatia, Austria, Germany, Poland . . . Do you want me to keep going?"

I laugh. "Tell me your favorite place."

"That's impossible! All right, I suppose I would say Italy because of the sculpture and art. Oh, and the fountains and the food and the cappuccinos. I know, that's what everybody says. Croatia reminded me of a smaller and less-busy Italy, which I liked. On that trip we rented a car and drove to the little towns along the coast. You could pull over practically anywhere and take a dip in the ocean. Then we hopped on a train to Vienna. I spent most of my time at the MuseumsQuartier."

"Wow. It must be amazing to be able to travel to another country so quickly. Canada is so big."

"I like that about it. I like the space, that you aren't crowded by other people like you are in London. I love the big sky and the mountains and the wilderness. I want to try skiing in the winter, and in the summer we're going on holiday to Vancouver Island. We'll drive through British Columbia and visit beaches, try surfing in Tofino, and look for whales. Have you been?"

"I have." I remember Adam, Audrey, and me searching for crabs in the tide pools on Rathtrevor Beach. Adam telling us, *Be careful not to step on them; we don't want to hurt them.* The memory is sweet but painful.

"I love traveling. It's good to see other places and people and be pulled out of your own little bubble. When I felt sad as a child, my parents used to take us away for a weekend and we'd have so much fun as a family, I'd forget everything that was happening at school."

I remember what Taylor said that day in the stairwell about the baggage of their childhood, and this time I can't help but ask what they meant.

They shift in their chair before responding. "I guess by *baggage* I meant the reputation I had and the way I felt about myself when I was younger. Growing up, the other kids didn't exactly like me. In primary school boys and girls all played together, but in lower secondary school it was as if a line was drawn and I was supposed to pick a side, only no one wanted me. The girls ran away from me when I tried to join them and whispered about me in class, and the boys didn't let me play football with them. I read a lot of books and watched a lot of TV."

I don't know what to say. My heart aches, thinking of Taylor as a tiny kid alone on the playground.

"My parents were worried about me being lonely, so they suggested I register in something after school, and I chose dance. I'm so glad I did. I discovered I'm really good at it, and I met friends who weren't afraid of being different or weird. My dance friends actually *wanted* to stand out and be noticed. They were loud and silly and fun. Going to the studio after school felt like ... like being a turtle and finally reaching the sea."

Wow. Goose bumps break out all over my body, and tears prick my eyes. I cradle my mocha with both hands as Taylor looks out the window, a smile playing on their lips.

"My dance friends made me realize you can choose who you want to spend time with and how you want to live your life, you know? Some people go through their whole lives feeling afraid. When I'm a dance therapist, I hope to help people rediscover what it felt like to be a kid, before we started worrying about what everyone thought about us. We'll move however our bodies feel like moving and let the rest of our lives just . . . disappear."

That's exactly how I felt when Taylor and I danced at the club that night. It felt like going back in time to the person I used to be, back when I was close with Audrey.

"Was it hard to leave your dance friends and move to Calgary?"

"It was. But for the first time, I'm glad I did."

"Because of all the rain, right?" I joke. "You finally feel at home?"

"No, because of you." Taylor gives me a look that makes my entire body flush.

The question I've been wanting to ask them since we decided to go on a date is on the tip of my tongue, and I'm terrified to ask in case it's somehow insulting, but at the same time I really want to know. "Can I ask you a question that might sound stupid?"

"Shoot."

I shift in my chair. Take a sip of my mocha and quickly put it back down. Better to just get it out. "Are you attracted to me more as a girl or a guy?"

"I'm attracted to Clare the person. I'm attracted to your soul."

I'm attracted to your soul. That's the perfect way to describe it — like falling in love with the person and their individual energy.

"I feel the same way about you. It's almost a magnet drawing me to you." My cheeks heat at how lame that sounds, but Taylor doesn't laugh at me. "I felt it for the first time during your bio presentation, when we made eye contact across the room. There was a connection between us."

"Perhaps the gods tied red strings around our ankles. Have you heard of the red thread of fate? We're destined to be in each other's lives because the gods tied us together."

"I like that idea."

Taylor leans forward across the table, close enough to kiss. "Want to know why I like you? Because I see the real you, Clare. I see the kind, protective, and sensitive soul that you are, and it makes me want to be a better person too."

I look down at the white tablecloth. "No one would ever call me kind."

"I just did. I know that's why you struggle with Audrey. An unkind person wouldn't care so strongly."

I nod because I can't speak. I'm afraid if I do much more, I might cry.

"Whatever happened between the two of you, you'll find your way back to each other."

"I hope so," I say, and mean it.

The rain has stopped and the sun is setting, painting orange, pink, purple across the sky. The stars will be out soon.

Taylor takes a final sip of their mocha and places their mug to the side. "Can I tell you a secret?"

"Of course."

"You're my first datemate. Ever."

"You're my first datemate too. I've only ever been attracted to two people: you and someone else I shouldn't have been attracted to." The moment the words are out of my mouth, my cheeks flush with embarrassment. I can't believe I just said that.

"Why shouldn't you have been attracted to them?"

I squirm in my chair nervously, but Taylor just waits, giving nothing away. I have to look down at my mocha as I begin my confession.

"Because she was dating someone else. Someone close to me." My face and ears suddenly turn hot as the hurtful things Sharon said to me about wanting to be my brother pop into my mind, and I know I won't be able to follow through — I won't be able to tell the whole story. "Do you think that makes me a bad person?"

"That you realized you were attracted to someone else's girlfriend? No. People often want someone they can't have, and you never acted on it, right?"

"No."

Taylor reaches out and takes both my hands so we're now entwined above and below the table. "I'm really glad I met you. I'm glad the gods didn't tie the red string around some other fool's ankle."

I laugh. "Me too."

It's a perfect night, a perfect *first date,* and I wonder how I ever felt jealous of Audrey when Calvin called. That lonely person doesn't exist anymore. What exists is here and now, safely tucked away at a cozy table with Taylor while the rest of the world speeds by.

✦ ✳ ✦

Saturday afternoon, I receive a Facebook notification letting me know I was tagged in a poll created by Megan, a girl in my grade I'm not really friends with but whose friend request I accepted years ago. When I click on the notification, my heart literally stops.

Attached to the poll are two pictures: Taylor and me at the Italian restaurant holding hands across the table, and a side-by-side comparison of me dressed in my old clothes and Adam's clothes. I have to read the words over and over again until I can process that they're really there and this is actually happening.

Vote, people! Will Clare return to school next fall as a girl or a guy?

Guy is winning by a landslide.

My hand shakes as I scroll through the voters. Billy, no surprise, voted *guy.* I feel my gut clench every time I see someone I used to think liked me voting "against" me — people from my grade but also the grades above and below. Then there are a bunch of fake accounts with only one or two friends, usually each other. People hate me enough to make fake accounts just to bash me.

Sharon & Co. haven't voted, even though I'm sure they saw it. But even if they did vote *girl*, it wouldn't make me feel better. There are a few votes "for" me, but I know they're supporting the old me, the popular Clare, and that girl doesn't exist anymore.

I report the poll to Facebook and delete Megan, but one of her friends tags me again. I repeat the process and it happens again so that I'm deleting "friends" every few hours. My stomach is in knots. Every time I receive a Facebook notification, I open it up and try to mitigate the damage. Then I run to the bathroom and either puke or dry heave.

The 'rents are surprised to find out I'm not going out on a Saturday night and ask if I want to go for dinner with them and Audrey. I tell them I'm not feeling well. After they leave, Taylor calls, but I don't answer. Not because I'm ashamed of the picture of us together, but because I'm ashamed of how I'm reacting to the bullying.

I thought I was doing okay. I have new friends. Only Billy and Sharon and their friends taunted me at school, but now, behind the safety of their computers and phones, the rest of the kids have an outlet to say what they're too afraid to say to my face ... and it's completely overwhelming. I can't read all their hatred without feeling like I want to run away and hide forever.

Eventually Taylor messages me and tells me to stop deleting the post. They're Internet trolls who feel better about themselves when they bash other people online. The more you fight them, the more you fuel them.

I message back that I'm going off Facebook for a while. With my headphones on, I crank up my music to block out the rest of the world, and write myself a letter while I release all the tears and stress. Then I read and reread my words until I finally believe them.

You'll get through this. People making fun of you
doesn't change who you are.
It doesn't make you worthless.
Not everyone will like you. It's just not possible.
You're never going to make everyone happy and
you don't have to argue or convince anyone else of
anything. You know who you are and who you want
to be. In the end that's all that matters.

Audrey

It's spring and thunderstorms are rolling over the prairies. I like to fall asleep counting the seconds between the lightning flashes and the clashes of thunder. When they are on top of each other, the storm is on top of me.

I've been counting every night for two weeks.

Water is backing up out of the drains and into the street. On the news a bunch of cars got stuck in an underpass and couldn't drive out. Their cars started to float away. The people had to be rescued by firemen. Too bad they haven't invented a car that turns into a boat.

If the rain continues like this, the dam is going to breach again, Mom says.

When did the dam breach? I ask.

In 2005. The reservoir got so full that the dam couldn't contain it and water went over the dam. A lot of streets and houses flooded along the river.

That sounds like a natural disaster, I say.

Mom's mouth goes really thin.

Did people have to canoe in the streets?

No. People weren't allowed on the streets. The streets were closed.

So another natural disaster might happen in Calgary, I say. I think we'll be prepared. But maybe we should move the water and food upstairs.

Mom throws her hands up. We won't get flooded, Audrey! We didn't in 2005 and we won't now. We're blocks away from the river and far down from the dam.

The people who got flooded had houses right on the river, Dad says. You know the Andersons? Their entire basement was flooded. They had just built a new house the year before, too. Such a shame. They had to take a chainsaw to their brand-new pool table just to get it out of there.

You're scaring her. Mom gives him a look. Let's stop talking about the dam.

Yeah, damn the dam! I say.

Dad laughs. Don't worry about it, honey. We'll be fine.

But things don't seem fine. Mom and Dad keep the news on all the time, showing footage of flooded streets and riverbanks all over the city. More cars have gotten stuck.

The mayor's Twitter feed flashes across the bottom of the screen: I can't believe I actually have to say this, but the rivers are closed. I have strong words for the people I saw rafting on the Bow today, none of which I'm allowed to tweet.

Everyone at school is talking about it.

I thought our French exam would be canceled, Kira says. We never get snow days so we should get rain days.

Everyone laughs at the idea. Then on Thursday night it happens.

The doorbell rings, followed by three hard knocks. Whoever it is, they want to be heard.

I open the door. It's a police officer. Across the street there is also a fire truck.

My heart goes into overdrive, but then I remember that everyone's home. Mom and Dad are in the kitchen. Clare's upstairs studying for her biology exam tomorrow. There's not going to be another accident.

But a police officer at the door is not a good thing. Do police officers ever knock on the door to tell you good news? This one was the youngest officer I'd ever seen. He looked tired.

Are your mom or dad — er, parents home? He turns bright red. Sorry kid, long day.

I call over my shoulder to Mom. I don't want to miss what he has to say.

Mom looks just as scared as me when she sees him. Is everything okay? she asks.

Good afternoon, ma'am. We're going door-to-door this afternoon letting people know there's been a mandatory evacuation. The dam is set to breach this evening. I'm going to have to ask you to leave the premises. Do you have family or friends you can stay with?

You're *evacuating* us?

That's right, ma'am. We're suggesting you stay with family and friends until it is safe to return to your home.

Isn't that a bit much? We're three blocks from the river. We didn't get flooded in 2005.

I'm sorry, but this is a mandatory evacuation. We're not only concerned about flooding, but also power outages. Some areas like Mission have already lost power. So we're evacuating neighboring areas, including yours. Downtown has been evacuated as well and schools are closed for the summer.

What about exams? Mom asks.

I believe they've been canceled. I'll be back to check that you have vacated.

Then he leaves, presumably to go to the next house.

Mom closes the door angrily and marches off to find Dad. He's still in the kitchen.

What was that about?

They're evacuating us! An officer was at the door and said we have to go stay with someone.

That's ridiculous!

I know, but he said it's mandatory. We have to leave. Sounds like they're more concerned about power outages than anything.

Dad stalks to the front door as if the officer will still be there. I hear him open and close it and then he returns. He rubs a hand on his jaw. There are army, police, and fire outside.

Should we go stay with your mother? Mom asks.

Dad sighs. I guess so . . .

Yay! I cheer. I love Grandma. She's the funnest person in the world.

Funnest isn't a word, Mom tells me.

I don't think she should be worrying about grammar at a time like this.

Dad opens the fridge. If we lose power our food will rot.

Grab what you want and we'll take it with us. Mom turns to me. Go upstairs and tell Clare to pack.

I'm scared to talk to Clare. We haven't really talked since our fight about Calvin. But when I tell her the news, she hugs me.

Are you saying I don't have to go back to school this year?

Nope.

So I can stop studying?

Yes. Exams are canceled.

She hoots and slams her book closed. Tosses it across the room. My grades are already terrible, she says. As long as I pass, I don't care what I get.

Are you worried about getting in trouble with Mom and Dad?

Nah. What will they do, ground me? I don't want to see anyone all summer anyway.

So no Sharon for the entire summer? I hoot too and Clare hoots for a second time. Then we're standing on Clare's bed like we used to as kids, jumping and hooting. Reaching up to touch the ceiling. It's easier now. But I lose my balance and almost knock off the boob light. When did it turn orange?

Stop jumping on the bed!

We both go still as statues. Mom is in the doorway looking furious. Are you trying to destroy the house? Drywall is practically raining down into the kitchen!

Clare wipes a hand through her hair even though there's none left. Sorry, Mom. But aren't you glad we're getting along?

The moment Mom leaves, we burst into laughter.

The car is packed so full, Dad can't even see out the back window as we drive. I'm kind of excited even though it's an emergency. Grandma lives on a farm with horses and barn cats.

Only no one wants to ride the horses or pet the cats with me because they're too worried. We try to play Monopoly, but the game goes on for hours until no one cares anymore. Then they tell me I won and we all go to bed.

In the morning the TV wakes me because Grandma is almost deaf and listens to it at max volume. I hear the words: the largest flood since 2005.

Mom, Dad, Grandma, and Clare are already crowded around the television. We see houses with a river raging past them. Except the river shouldn't be there. It's a street.

Calgary has turned into Venice, I say.

We are still in a state of emergency, the mayor says. Because the water is contaminated, we want to wait until it recedes before we allow residents to return to their homes. We understand that everyone is anxious to assess the damage but we are urging people to stay safe for now.

They can't keep people out of their own homes! Grandma looks like she might cry.

They don't want people killing themselves to get their belongings. Dad puts a hand on her arm. We have to wait.

Clare is biting her nails and staring at the TV screen. Our house can't flood, she says. We're not even close to the river and the dam is so far away. There wouldn't be enough water to reach us.

Flooding by sewer backup, Dad says. The sewers can't contain the runoff water so it's overflowing into the alleys and streets.

In the afternoon, our neighbor Bruce who didn't evacuate sends Dad a picture of our house. There is a foot of water surrounding it.

No one talks after that.

That night I can't sleep. I'm on the top bunk and Clare is on the bottom. In the middle of the night she says, Audrey?

I think it must be a dream, but I still respond. Yes?

I'm scared for our house.

Me too, I say and wish I could see her.

If it did flood, it will only be a few feet, she says. Not high enough to reach the stuff on the shelves.

I don't know what to say so I don't say anything at all.

We've lived there our entire lives, she whispers. I don't know how to live anywhere else.

+ ✳ +

In the morning a newscaster says, Seventy-five thousand Calgarians can now return to their homes. The mandatory evacuation has been lifted.

Then the mayor comes on. He looks like he has been up all night too.

We've turned a corner, the water is receding, but we're still in a state of emergency. We're also heading into tough times. As people return to their homes to find them damaged, some people might feel despair. As a city, we must lift them up with kindness and support.

On the way home, we stop at Walmart and buy the only rubber boots left.

Hasn't the water receded? Clare holds up a pair of Hello Kitty boots and frowns.

You have no idea what we're in for, Mom tells her.

The first thing I notice is the mud. The water is gone, and mud coats the grass, and the bottom of every tree and house. There's a fog in the air and a humming that sounds like it's coming from more than one house. Not sure what it is. The streetlights flicker above me.

It looks like a war zone. I think it and then an army convoy roars by on Elbow Drive.

My boots sink into the path as we walk up to the front door. It's like walking through melted chocolate.

The windows to the basement have a line of mud. That's where the water touched them.

Dad's hand shakes as he tries to put the keys in the lock. He's probably worried water will rush out when he opens the door. I'm worried about that too. He puts the key in the lock and looks over his shoulder. Mom nods and he turns the key, opens the front door.

Nothing happens.

Dad's shoulders visibly relax. No flooding on the main floor, he says.

The front hall is too dark for us to see anything. Dad flips the light switch. Oh right, he says. The power is out.

Clare has her boots off and is already racing down the hall. I know where she's going so I run after her. She yanks open the basement door and screams.

It's not what she expected. Water is lapping the staircase two feet below us.

Dad goes to the kitchen and opens the fridge, pulls out a beer. Twists the top off and takes a sip. A really large sip.

It's warm, he says.

What are we going to do? I ask.

Right now I'm going to have this beer.

I go back outside. Mom is standing on the sidewalk. I join her as Mrs. Hutcheson rushes across the street and pulls Mom into a hug. They both start crying.

Did you just go inside for the first time?

Mom nods and sobs.

How bad is it?

The basement is entirely flooded.

You need a pump. Donald has a pump and is pumping out everyone's basements. You need to talk to him.

Okay. Mom doesn't move.

He's at the McNally house, Mrs. Hutcheson says.

Okay.

Mrs. Hutcheson pulls her into another hug. Oh, honey! They start crying again.

Across the street another neighbor is sitting on his front step, smoking. His shoulders are hunched and he's shaking. Behind him, mud people come out of the house. Drop what they're carrying into a pile on the sidewalk.

My insurance company will only cover sewage backup, Mrs. Hutcheson is saying now. And even then only a portion of it. No overland flooding.

How do they know which one it is?

You need to take a sample of the water in the basement. To qualify as sewage you need to have evidence of feces. That's what I've heard.

I think about all the possible germs in the sample. E. coli, salmonella, norovirus, staphylococcus, shigella, and streptococcus.

They're calling it the hundred-year flood, Mrs. Hutcheson says. None of us knew it would be this bad. It happened to all of us.

I go back inside. Dad is still in the kitchen. There's an empty beer bottle on the counter and Dad is holding another.

I look at Clare. She's staring straight at the wall.

His entire room is underwater, she says.

Dad tilts back the beer and then puts it down. Glass rings against marble. I'm going to go call Bruce, he says. See if he's had any luck with finding a pump.

Donald has a pump, I say. But I don't know if Dad hears me because he doesn't respond as he walks away.

Clare finally blinks and looks at me. I can't believe all of Adam's stuff is gone.

I walk to the basement door and open it again. Adam's stuff is gone and Adam's ghost left with it.

Clare is upset, but I'm happy. If Adam's ghost moved on, maybe he has forgiven me.

CLARE

A superstitious person would say that I wanted this. That I asked for it months ago when I daydreamed about a wrecking ball outside my window. That's all I can think about as I lie awake in my room all night. By midmorning, the basement has been pumped and we have the all clear to enter and check out the damage. After pulling on our rubber boots, we go down the stairs.

The rugs are no longer in a path to the couch. They've migrated across the room and tangled themselves into muddy snakes on the concrete. The couch is now angled in front of the curtain that leads to Adam's room. The curtains are still shut but entirely brown. *Everything* is brown. Every single item is the same awful color, like someone opened a can of shit and tossed it over everything.

I swipe aside the one curtain still remaining and it barely moves, it's so stiff with mud. *And sewage,* I think, and want to gag. Like the main room, nothing is untouched. His comforter, his books, his picture frames . . . his clothes. It feels so messed up to be standing in Adam's room mourning clothes I've worn in secret. I glance at the nightstand, relieved Adam's phone is safely tucked away in my room upstairs.

Dad and Audrey come into the room seconds behind me. Dad's face is a tight drum, stark white against all the brown. He doesn't move from the doorway, but his eyes scan the room, veiny and sad. When he speaks, it's like he has to focus to say the words in their proper order.

"I don't even recognize it. But then, I was never allowed in here anyway."

None of us move. We're just staring at one another across the room, breathing in shit-filled air, and there's nothing we can do. Like when Adam died. We saw his body in that stupid box before they cremated him and he looked so much like Adam but asleep, and I kept wishing that I could just lean down and kiss his forehead and he'd wake up.

"We can save some things," Audrey says in that matter-of-fact way of hers. "The stuff that can't absorb mud or water. That isn't contaminated. We can clean it off with the hose outside. I'll go grab some bags."

Then she disappears and Dad sways on the spot, like the breeze she created is enough to knock him over.

"Are you okay?" I ask him.

The question seems to awaken him. He walks over to a shelf and picks up a baseball trophy. "I remember this. This was the very first trophy he ever got. Baseball. He could hit anything." Dad chuckles. "That was part of the problem. He hit the balls he should have left, too."

"I remember," I say, even though I don't. I remember being told the story.

"Adam was very athletic. He picked up sports right away. But all he cared about was skateboarding." I'm waiting for that edge that always seeps into Dad's tone when he talks about skateboarding, but this time it doesn't. Instead he says, "He was really good at that, too. He just got on it and rode. Never seen anything like it."

"I know. I used to watch him with his friends."

Dad grins over his shoulder as he picks up the next trophy. "Skating at the elementary school, right? It's okay, he never lied to us about it. We never asked."

"Yeah, at the school. He could ride the handrail. It was scary to watch."

"I bet." Dad releases a sob. His drum face crumples and he puts a hand over his eyes. His whole body is shaking. I come up behind him and wrap my arms around him, my cheek against his back. We stay like that until Dad squeezes my arm, letting me know he'll be okay.

It's crazy to think the water was high enough in the basement to touch objects on Adam's shelves, considering we live a few blocks from the river. But from what I've heard on the news, the cause was storm-water backup — because of the excessive rainfall, the rivers rose, and water flowed into the storm-water pipe system and spilled back onto the streets through storm-water drains. I pick up the picture frame I looked at only a month ago, the one that made me want to reach through the glass and touch Adam's face, and wipe the mud off with my sleeve. Water has seeped between the glass and melted our faces.

It's replaceable, I tell myself. Somewhere in storage is an SD card with the original photograph.

In storage. My heart ricochets against my ribs. I drop the picture frame and run.

When Adam was moving to the basement, Mom made us go through our bedrooms and separate items into donations for Goodwill and special keepsakes to box up and store in the furnace room. It was like she suddenly realized the house was too small for all of us. We also boxed up all the toys we'd outgrown and stored them with our baby items.

I thought I was prepared for this, but I'm not. All I keep thinking about are Adam's baby photos and baby blanket, the matching dresses that Audrey liked and I hated, our drawings, the toys I wanted to pass on to my kids, and all the family heirlooms to be saved for the next generation.

As I shove open the door to the furnace room, my heart is in my throat and the tears are already pooling in my eyes. The skis are on their sides instead of leaning against the wall. Ski and snowboard boots have migrated across the room like the couch. Boxes are no longer on shelves — they're everywhere. I blink and the tears hit my cheeks as I run between the boxes, checking for labels, which of course have floated away. The boxes themselves are soggy and most of them are destroyed, their contents strewn across the room. I recognize some shipwrecked items, including Christmas decorations and Dad's tools that didn't fit in the garage.

Releasing a cry of despair, I squat on the concrete floor, both hands grasping what's left of my hair. I'm going to pull the rest of it out in anguish. I can hear myself, low and guttural like an animal, and I know it's happening. My walls are all coming down. Like the water breaching the dam, I'm going to bleed all over this F-ing house because I've finally lost everything.

"What are you doing?"

Audrey's shape appears in my vision, blurry like we're on opposite sides of an aquarium.

"Are you okay?" she asks.

"No." I don't bother to stand up. "I can't find it. Any of it."

"Can't find what?"

"Our memories. The stuff Mom had us pack up to save."

"Do you mean the boxes I took upstairs?"

I blink. Then I'm on my feet. *Oh please, please, please let her be saying what I think she's saying.* My heart is thumping in my chest, but I force myself to speak slowly so I don't freak her out. "Audrey, what boxes did you take upstairs? When did you move them?"

"The important ones." Audrey shrugs. "I took them to my room when they announced the natural disaster. I wanted to be prepared."

With a cheer, I rush her. I pull her into my arms and squeeze her so hard, she actually winces. "Thank you, Audrey. Thank you, thank you, thank you. You don't know how much this means. You've saved us."

Audrey

When I show Mom and Dad the boxes under my bed, Dad cries. Mom pulls me into a gigantic hug and kisses my cheeks over and over again.

Oh, Audrey! You have no idea what you've done for us. We thought we'd lost it all.

When did you do this? Dad asks.

When you told me the dam might breach. I thought if the house flooded, the water bottles should be upstairs so we could drink them. Then I saw the boxes and decided to take them upstairs too. I put everything under my bed for safekeeping.

Now Dad is hugging me too. He lifts me up and spins me around and says my name over and over again.

You are so clever. Cleverer than the rest of us. What would we ever do without you?

Late in the afternoon we take a break from cleaning and sit in the family room to go through the items. First we look at Mom's and Dad's photo albums from their childhoods. They only have a handful of albums each because cameras used film back in the days. It was expensive to take and develop a lot of pictures.

My grandma was a scrapbooker and made albums and albums of

Mom growing up, from baby to university student. Mom and Dad were in high school in the eighties, so Mom's wearing colorful leggings and leg warmers in a lot of photos. In one of Dad's high school photos, he's wearing a tie-dye track coat and pajama pants.

That's hideous, Clare says, and they laugh.

There's also the baby book of Dad that Grandma made. It's full of pictures of Grandpa. I don't remember Grandpa very well because I was only seven when he died. He looks like a stranger in the pictures of him holding Dad as a newborn. He looks too young to have a baby.

Next we move on to our baby items. Our three baby books. Photo albums. Folders of school pictures and artwork. Little dresses, sleepers, and blankets Mom wanted to keep.

She picks up a small blue sleeper with teddy bears on it and presses it to her face. When she pulls it away there are tears in her eyes.

It still smells like him. How can it smell like him after all these years?

I don't even realize I'm doing it. I crawl into her lap like I used to do as a little kid. I'm crying now too. Mom presses my cheek against her chest and kisses the top of my head. Out of the corner of my eye I can see Dad and Clare are hugging too. Dad has pulled her into the crook of his arm and she's burying her face in him.

I want to apologize. I need them to know that every day I wish I could have just stayed in that stupid gym-not-dojo.

The important thing is that we still have each other, Dad says. And our memories.

I feel Mom nodding. A hot tear hits the top of my head.

Adam was always so happy, Clare says. Her voice is muffled because she's talking into Dad's chest. That's what I loved the most about him.

Dad tilts his face to the ceiling like he hopes the tears will slip to the backs of his eyes. I loved that too, he says. Adam was always up for learning new things and doing something. Dad laughs but it sounds like a sob. Even when he was six and we took you all to Mexico. We thought he'd be happy just playing in the pool and swimming in the ocean, but he wanted to go on all the excursions.

He was so sweet and loving, Mom agrees. Her voice breaks on the last word.

It's my turn. Everyone goes quiet.

He was nice to me, I say, and feel Mom's arms tighten around me. I know it was my fault. I say it loudly enough for everyone to hear. Adam would still be alive if not for me.

Oh, sweetheart! Mom turns me around to face her. It wasn't your fault. We've been so worried you felt that way but didn't know how to bring it up with you.

It was just an accident, Dad tells me. A terrible, terrible accident. None of it was your fault. Please don't blame yourself, Audrey.

I glance at Clare. She's staring at the floor. Dad's hand is rubbing her shoulder over and over again. A robot arm.

Sometimes bad things happen in life, Mom says. We can't prevent them. Sometimes we can't even learn from them. Sometimes bad things happen and we wonder why they could possibly happen to us and what we did wrong. But we did nothing wrong. You and Adam did nothing wrong. You're a good kid, Audrey. Do you hear me?

I nod because I don't think I can speak.

It's normal to feel guilty when someone dies, Mom says. It's one of the stages of grief. We all feel guilty about something when it comes to Adam. I feel guilty for things too, but I loved Adam with all my heart.

Dad reaches out and takes Mom's hand. I feel guilty for pushing him to play sports when he wanted to skateboard, he says. I wish I'd told him I thought he was great at it.

Clare finally looks up. He knew, Dad. And Mom, he knew you loved him and he wouldn't want you to feel guilty about anything. I think he'd be happy to see us all getting along. I know that's what he wanted.

Thank you. Mom's voice sounds like a whisper.

Dad glances at Mom. Clears his throat. I think this would be a good time to tell Audrey. Don't you think, Margaret?

I feel Mom nod. She twists so I can see her face. It's wet with tears.

Sweetie, we've made a decision.

We're going to give it a try, Dad tells me. You can go to whichever school you choose.

Really?

Really.

I look at Clare. Mom and Dad look at Clare. I can feel Mom's arms tense around me. When Clare stands, I stop breathing. She's going to get upset. She's going to yell and run out of the room like she always does.

Instead she pulls me to my feet and gives me a hug.

You deserve it, Audrey, she says. I'm glad you're coming back.

CLARE

After I hug Audrey, Mom and Dad join in so we're doing the group-hug thing, all of us laughing and crying at the same time. When the doorbell rings, I tell them I'll get it and wipe my tears away before I open the front door. Volunteers have been stopping by all day. I've seen them walking the streets, knocking on doors and offering to help homeowners carry items out of the basement or shovel the mud. Everyone keeps saying that the one and only good thing about this flood is how our city seems to be coming together.

I pull open the door, prepared to thank the volunteer but let them know we're taking a break. It's Taylor. Standing on my doorstep, holding Safeway bags full of food.

"Hey," I say, surprised.

"Reinforcements." They grin and hold up the bags. "Sandwiches and snacks."

Fresh tears prick my eyes as we embrace. "You're amazing!"

"I figured you'd be too preoccupied to think about dinner." Taylor follows me into kitchen, where we start unpacking the bags. I talk about the flood, about all the things we've lost, and they listen. As usually happens around Taylor, I say stuff I didn't even know I felt. How terrified I was of losing everything until Audrey told me what she did.

Mom comes into the kitchen when she hears us talking. She looks at Taylor and I can see it on her face — she's doing what everyone does when they first meet them. My heart rate increases at the knowledge she is probably trying to figure out how Taylor fits into my new world.

"Mom, this is my friend Taylor."

I don't miss Taylor's sideways glance at the word *friend*.

Mom looks down at the items on the kitchen counter and smiles. "Did you bring all of this, Taylor? How kind!"

We arrange the food on the kitchen counter and then call Dad and Audrey to dig in. Dad has the same reaction as Mom when he sees Taylor, and I see her elbow him and do the thing she does with her eyebrows when she's trying to communicate with him telepathically. As we sit down at the table, Taylor says to Audrey, "It's awesome to finally meet you, Audrey. I've heard so much about you."

"You have?" Audrey sounds worried.

"Of course," Taylor says, as if I've never uttered a bad word about Audrey in my life. "Clare told me about the things you used to do as kids and I was super jealous. I always wanted a twin and instant best friend."

At that Audrey and I make eye contact, and I give her a smile. "Audrey's coming back to our school in the fall."

"That's great!" Taylor looks genuinely happy. "You can hang with me if you want."

"Really?"

"For sure. I know what it's like to be the new kid."

Audrey's answering smile is huge and infectious, and in that moment, I realize how happy it makes me when my friends accept Audrey and how long it's been since that happened. Usually I'm a tense ball of nerves, waiting for someone to call her a nasty name. Apparently the 'rents feel the same way — they grin at Taylor like dopey idiots.

"So, Taylor, where are you from?" Mom asks, leaning in closer. "I detect a British accent."

"You're not wrong." Taylor laughs. "I'm from London. We moved here at Christmas."

"London! I always wanted to live in London."

Dad is equally smitten. He only asks people questions when he actually cares. "We always wanted to travel there with the youth visa, but life got in the way. Worked out, though, because we had incredible kids!" Dad shoots me a killer smile and I return it with a roll of my eyes.

As I listen to everyone talk, I find myself relaxing and take a few bites of my sandwich. It's amazing how Taylor just fits into my life. It feels so natural, so easy. Maybe my parents won't care that I'm gender-fluid. Maybe all they care about is if I'm with someone who is a nice person and that I'm a nice person too.

Everything is going awesome until Dahlia walks into the kitchen.

Dahlia, who we haven't seen since Adam passed away. Dahlia, who used to be over at the house all the time but who disappeared from our lives, leaving only Adam's videos behind.

My sandwich slips from my fingers and plops onto my plate. I stop breathing. She stands there smiling shyly and holding a cardboard coffee carrier in one hand and a large Tim Horton's bag in another.

"Hi," she says, a flush creeping up her beautiful neck. "Sorry to interrupt. The front door was open so I just came in. When I heard this area flooded I thought of you, and I meant to come by earlier. I just thought you probably had enough volunteers and didn't know if you'd want to . . . see me." She glances away briefly as tears fill her eyes. "Anyway,

I wanted to bring some food. I've got coffee, chili, doughnuts, and . . . sandwiches." She frowns with what I assume is disappointment at the sandwiches already sitting on the plate.

Mom is the first to acknowledge her. She stands up and pulls Dahlia in for a hug. "Dahlia! It's so good to see you. We've missed you around here." When she says the words, I know they're true. She didn't particularly care for Dahlia before — not because she didn't like her, but because she was worried about the usual things moms worry about when teenagers disappear into the basement together. But I guess none of that matters anymore.

"Let me take that for you," Dad says, and slips in to relieve Dahlia of the bags. Now her arms are free and she hugs Mom back and they both start crying. An uncomfortable emotion rises in me, like I'm an imposter but worse. More like I'm a total creep.

My own neck flushes with the thought and my palms turn sweaty as the flush rises into my face. Taylor elbows me and raises a questioning eyebrow. All I can do is smile back weakly. I wish there were some way I could get off this stool and slip out of the kitchen without anyone noticing me or calling me out for being rude. I want to lift the bread off my sandwich and crawl inside.

"Sit down," Mom says and offers Dahlia her seat. Dahlia slips into it and clasps her hands in her lap. She's right beside me, so close that when I falter in my seat, our arms brush.

"Hey, Audrey and Clare," she says, as if just noticing us. Her large eyes widen a bit when she sees me. "Clare, you changed your hair! It looks good."

For a moment I can't even speak. Then I garble a thank-you that's practically incomprehensible.

Silence follows.

Dad jumps in and introduces Taylor. Then he starts asking Dahlia questions. What has she been up to lately? How's her family? The usual chitchat people toss around when they had a single link they shared and now that link is irrevocably severed. It's impossible not to think of Adam with Dahlia in the room, and I can see and feel the pain emanating behind the wrinkles around Dad's eyes and Mom's wavering smile.

Dahlia is nervous too. She keeps clasping and unclasping her hands and her cheeks are still that shy shade of pink. When she answers the next question she ducks her head a little bit, and I'm thrown back into the video at the moment when she smiled coyly at Adam and began unbuttoning his shirt . . .

I don't know how it happens, but I end up on my back on the floor. I've tipped my stool over backwards — I must have instinctively shoved away from the counter. There's a commotion of faces above me, and then Taylor reaches down to help me to my feet.

"Are you okay?"

"I don't feel so well." That doesn't even begin to cover it. I'm mortified.

"Are you hurt?" Dahlia puts a hand on my arm and I flinch, pull away.

Taylor's eyes widen and then narrow in understanding. No one needs to know about my obsession with Dahlia's video to know that I have a crush on her. I'm acting like a total basket case.

What would Dahlia think of me if she knew I'd watched private videos between her and Adam, and liked it? What would Taylor think? What would *Adam* think? If Audrey was right and his ghost was in the basement, did he see what I did that night? And the days and nights after that? Was he angry that I trespassed on his privacy?

I wrap my arms around my stomach, afraid I'm going to be sick.

"Did you bump your head when you fell?" Dahlia asks. She and Taylor crowd closer, and I close my eyes against them.

"No, I didn't. I'm fine, I'm fine." They both keep asking me questions until finally I yell, "I said I'm fine! Just leave me alone!"

A heavy silence follows.

"I'm sorry," I mumble as my cheeks burn hotter. I can't bear to look at anyone. "I just want to be alone."

"That's okay, I should get going anyway." It's Taylor, and I can hear the hurt in their voice. They turn to address my parents. "Thank you for having me."

"Thank you for bringing the food," Mom says. "That was very sweet of you."

"See you in September, Audrey." And then Taylor is gone.

"Everything okay?" Mom asks, looking from me to Dad like she's clearly missed something.

Dad shrugs and holds his sandwich up to Dahlia. "I tried one of yours. Delicious."

The front door is already closing by the time I run out of the kitchen, and through the glass I can see Taylor walking toward their black hatchback. I stand frozen in place, watching them leave my life with one hand on the door handle, too afraid to go after them because I know I will have to admit what they already know: Dahlia is the person I told them about, the person I shouldn't have had a crush on.

"Are you fighting?" The voice comes from behind me. I turn to see that Audrey followed me out of the kitchen. "I hope not. I like Taylor."

Tears prick my eyes. "I like them too."

"Then why are you just standing here? Whatever is going on, fix it." She gives me a hug and then practically shoves me out the front door. "Go."

The engine roars to life as I sprint down the walk. "Wait!" I yell. Neighbors and flood volunteers pause in their work to watch me running like a lunatic without shoes, but I don't pay any attention to them — I only care about Taylor. I yank open the door of the car. "Don't leave."

They stare straight forward, both hands on the wheel, and shake their head. "You just told me to leave."

"I didn't mean it."

"Then why did you say it?"

I open my mouth to explain myself, but I don't know how without revealing my history with Dahlia. It doesn't matter what I say, though, because Taylor is already forming their own opinion.

"You fancy her, don't you?"

"No! I mean, not anymore."

"Is she the one you said you shouldn't have been attracted to? Because she seemed a lot like your brother's girlfriend."

I look down at the cement between my toes. I don't want to answer, but I'm on thin ice. I can feel everything that's important to me slipping through my fingers. Everything I thought I'd gained in the last half hour — Taylor liking Audrey and my parents liking Taylor — will be lost if Taylor walks away.

"Yeah," I say and flush with shame. "Dahlia was Adam's girlfriend, but I didn't like her while he was alive; I realized afterward. And I don't like her anymore — I just acted weird in there because I felt guilty about my old feelings, and then the more awkward I acted, the more worried I became that you would think I liked her."

"She's a pretty important person to you." There's more than a trace of insecurity in Taylor's tone. "I mean, she's the person who helped you discover who you are."

"No, that was *you*. I know it sounds messed up, but everything that's

237

happened to me over the past two months ultimately led me to you. It was the reason I was at the club the night we started hanging out. You're the person I want to be with."

"Are you sure?" Taylor finally looks at me, vulnerability reflected in their eyes. "I thought you changed your mind after that whole Facebook thing. You suddenly signed off and stopped talking to me."

My mouth falls open. I had no idea they would take it that way. "You told me to stop deleting the post so I logged off, and also because . . ."

"Because all of that happened after our date so you weren't sure you still wanted to be with me," Taylor finishes. "I know."

"No! Not at all. Is that what you really thought?" I feel awful for letting them feel like that for the past week while I've been busy studying for exams and then dealing with the flood. I run a hand through my hair and then drop it heavily to my side. "I logged off because I didn't know if I could take it. All the bullying. But do you want to know what I did after that? I wrote myself a letter reminding myself how important it is for me to be myself so that I won't chicken out ever again. I couldn't have done that without you, Taylor Matthews. You inspire me."

"Please." They roll their eyes but can't hide their smile. "That's the corniest thing I've ever heard."

"Hey, I'm being serious right now! I definitely want to be with you. Nobody else. Okay?"

Another smile tugs at Taylor's lips, followed by a nod. When they step out of the car, I slip a finger through their belt loop and tug them closer. Then we kiss right there in the middle of the road. Someone whistles and we break the kiss to see Dad, Mom, Audrey, and Dahlia standing on the front step. Mom elbows Dad. They're all grinning like idiots.

"Oh my God, Dad." I laugh and shake my head.

Taylor laughs and opens the car door. "Wanna get out of here?"

"Definitely."

I feel high, better than I have in years, because this is it: the moment I start living. From now on I'm going to follow my heart. I'm going to be good to the people in my life and show them I love them every single day because who knows how much time any of us have left with the people we love. I'm going to make my time count. I'm going to make my life count.

Audrey

When Clare and Taylor drive off, I know what I have to do. I wait until Mom and Dad are busy in the kitchen and then I leave too.

I've never taken a city bus. I have no idea how much it costs but figure bus drivers don't always watch that closely and drop a handful of coins in.

I'm right.

The front half is full and there are stairs up to the back half. The bus starts moving just as I take the first step, and I trip, fall onto my hands.

Careful, dear, says a lady with frizzy red hair. She bites loudly into an apple.

There really isn't enough room back here either, but it's too late now. I plant myself between the lady and a guy knitting a scarf. One of them smells like broccoli. The scarf is so long it touches the floor. As he knits it grazes a dried piece of gum by his feet.

The bus sounds like a plane about to take off. The open window beside me howls. We hit a bump and everyone bounces.

The people on the bus go up and down, up and down . . .

Where are you going? I ask the lady.

I'm going across the country! she responds loudly. Tiny apple bits fly from her lips to rain on my face. You can go all the way across the country on one transfer, did you know that?

I wipe my cheek clean and shake my head.

Yep. Two-fifty will get you right across the country. Right across. Can you believe it? Well, I'll tell you how I found out . . .

It's about then that I realize I don't know where I'm going. It feels like I've been traveling for hours. How do I know I won't go across the country?

I call out to the bus driver, How do you stop this thing?

The lady has been talking the whole time but she pauses to say, Pull the wire, dear, before launching back into it.

I pull.

The bus stops suddenly. I tumble off and it speeds away.

I have no idea where I am. I'm completely lost. I pick up a rock from the sidewalk and throw it. Cars fly by me but I keep moving. If I walk in the opposite direction the bus took me I will eventually make it home. Up ahead a shopping area comes into focus.

Now I know exactly where I'm going.

The park is full of kids because there's no school. I keep walking along the path, disabling gopher traps as I go. Cross the street and climb the steps to the little white house Calvin pointed out to me the day we met. It looks empty but I ring the doorbell.

Inside the house, I hear his mom call for him to get it. Then Calvin pulls open the door. His eyebrows fly up so high they almost touch his hair. He crosses his arms and leans against the door frame.

What are you doing here, Audrey?

I'm here to see you.

Calvin pushes off the door frame. His hair is messy like I remember.

But this time I want to touch it. I wonder what it would feel like to run my fingers through it. Is that normal? Do other girls think about things like that?

I thought you didn't want to talk to me, he says.

Why would you think that?

Um, because you yelled that when I called.

Oh. Oh no.

That isn't why I yelled at her. It wasn't because I didn't want to talk to you.

Well you could have fooled me. First you wanted to go on a date and then you didn't want anything to do with me. Are you embarrassed of me or something?

No! I look down. Take a deep breath and let it out like a whale. Like Monsieur Martin.

I was actually worried you would be embarrassed of me, I tell him.

Why?

Because Clare told you I go to Peak.

Why does that matter?

You know why.

He doesn't say anything. I focus on his socks. They have different colored diamonds on them.

I don't care that you go to Peak.

He's speaking softer than usual. One of his feet steps closer and I look up. Calvin is very close now. His face takes up my entire view. I hold my breath until after he speaks.

Why didn't you tell me?

I let my breath out in a sigh.

Because the other kids have always called me weird. Now that I go there they call me Freak. I didn't want you to think that about me.

First of all, I form my own opinions about people. Second of all, your parents *pay* for you to go to school. Don't you think that's cool? They love you that much, Audrey.

I've never thought of it that way.

I would go to Peak if I could.

You would?

Definitely. And not just because I'm homeschooled and lonely. Because Peak has good teachers and good programs. That's what I've heard.

Oh. That's good to know. I smile up at him.

Calvin smiles back and kicks something out from behind the door. His shoes. One two. He slips his feet into them and then holds out his hand.

Have time for a second date now?

I take it. Of course.

Instead of crossing the street to the park, he turns left. I don't ask him where we're going. I'm not sure if that will ruin the moment. He tells me about a movie he just saw called *This Is the End*, which is hilarious and has the same actors as *Freaks and Geeks*.

What's *Freaks and Geeks*? I ask.

A TV show that came out in 1999 but takes place in 1980. It's about this tomboy Lindsay who starts hanging out with the "freaks," but they're really kind of cool. At least I think they are. Do you know who James Franco is?

I shake my head.

Well he plays Daniel Desario. He's cool and charming but a total burnout.

How can the freaks be cool? I ask.

It's all perspective.

We turn the corner and we're at the shopping area with the Starbucks where we had our date. Only Calvin keeps walking past it and goes into the grocery store instead.

It's finally stopped raining, he says. Let's have a picnic. My treat.

I'm not that hungry after eating one of Taylor's sandwiches, but Calvin grabs a large container of assorted sushi rolls and a pop and I grab a vitamin water. We walk back to the park where we first met and Calvin places his jacket on the ground for me to sit on.

I'm such a gentleman, he says.

I laugh. The summer sun is still high and warm on my shoulders. I pick up a piece of sushi with my chopsticks and Calvin's eyes widen.

Is that blood?

I glance down at my shirt and for a moment I'm worried too. Then I realize.

No, it's paint. It's an old shirt I usually paint in. I was wearing it because we were cleaning out our basement today because of the flood.

Calvin's mouth forms an *O*. Your house was flooded?

I nod.

That's awful. Did you lose a lot of stuff?

I tell him about how I moved our special keepsake boxes a few days before the flood.

You're a superhero! Calvin says and gives me a high five. I would never have thought to do that. He reaches out and touches the large splotch of paint on my shirt. So were you painting your room red or something?

I laugh. No, just painting. I'm an artist.

Really?

Yeah. Calvin is looking at me like he's never met an artist before. Maybe he hasn't. I feel myself sitting up straighter.

In school I carved a soapstone sculpture for Clare, I tell him. I used a saw and everything.

His eyebrows rise halfway up his forehead. Wow, that's so cool. I've never done anything like that before. Was that in art class?

A private art class. Not everyone got to do it, I tell him, and feel proud. I wish I could show him the carving. I wish I had a picture.

I grab my bag and pull out my sketchbook. I'm not even nervous to show him my drawings. I'm excited. I flip through until I find the picture of Lake Louise.

You made that? Calvin knocks over his drink and quickly rights it. He doesn't seem embarrassed at all as he leans over the sketchbook. It's beautiful. How did you do it?

At first I just used charcoal, but then I realized I needed to make the lake teal. The only color in the picture. So I used two shades of blue pastels. They're like crayons but mushier. You can spread the colors on the page with your fingers.

Calvin is about to touch it but pulls back with a grin. You're a very good artist, he tells me and taps his drink lightly against my bottle.

I could help you make a sword, I offer. So you could create a character and play for real.

You'd do that? His whole face splits into a grin. How would you make it?

I've been doing some research. Some people make them with PVC piping, but other people say that snaps easily. I think we should use a fiberglass tent rod and cut it to the right length with a handsaw. Then all we need is PVC insulation foam to wrap around it and duct tape to keep it in place. We could get everything at Home Depot.

That sounds perfect. And would you make a sword for yourself, too?

To LARP with you again?

Yeah, for our third date. He winks. We could help each other create our characters. We can write entire backstories about them. All their likes and dislikes, their hopes and dreams, their fears, their families.

I'd like that, I tell him. Because it's the truth.

I'm really glad I met you, Calvin.

I'm really glad I met you, Audrey.

I stuff a California roll into my mouth to hide my grin.

Calvin isn't just a friend, and he isn't just a boyfriend. He's the first person since Clare to understand me.

ClaRe

It feels good to just drive. I don't ask Taylor where we're going and allow myself to enjoy the feeling of being alone together. It feels like we can go anywhere we want, be anyone we want, do anything we want.

What Taylor apparently wants is a milkshake.

"I know a good place," I tell them. When the neon lights of the diner come into view, my heart squeezes and my eyes sting, but I allow myself to feel sad and breathe through it. I know I'm not ready to go inside just yet, that just being here is enough, so I suggest the drive-through. One day I'll tell Taylor that this is the diner Adam took Audrey and me to that day he stuck up for his siblings and girlfriend, but today I just want to enjoy time with them.

I order strawberry banana and Taylor goes with pineapple, which makes me laugh because who orders pineapple? We drive around until we find a spot to park on the top of a hill with a view of downtown. Below us, the streets and the bottoms of trees still have a layer of mud.

"I'm sorry your house flooded," Taylor says softly.

"It's just a house; no one was hurt. Audrey saved the most important things. We lost some of Adam's belongings but she saved a lot of his memories. When no one else knew to take the flood warning seriously, Audrey was the one person who made a plan."

"It was good to meet her. It was good to meet such an important person in your life."

"I'm glad too." After a second I add, "It was pretty cool having the two most special people in my life meet."

Taylor grins. "It's going to be a good summer. I can feel it."

"Yeah." I lean in closer to put an arm around them. "I wish I could have asked you to the year-end dance. I'm actually bummed it's going to be canceled this year."

"How about we have our own celebration, one with only the people we want to be there? All of our friends from the alliance, as well as Audrey."

"That would be perfect."

Taylor ducks out from under my arm and rotates in their seat to face me. Butterflies flutter in my stomach. "Speaking of asking each other places, remember on our date when we talked about traveling together?"

I nod. The butterfly wings pick up speed.

"Well, my family is going home for a week at the end of August, and I've been telling them about you, and they said they have enough flight points that I can bring a friend if I want. Meaning you."

"Seriously?"

Taylor nods and then laughs at my expression. "Seriously."

"We're going to London! That is, if my parents let me. Considering how much they seemed to like you, though, I doubt it will be a problem."

Taylor puts their arm around me this time, and we stay like that and talk until long after we've finished the milkshakes and I start to feel guilty for not being at home to help out. "I'll come by tomorrow to help," Taylor tells me after pulling up to my house. "Just tell me when."

"I will." I give them a hug before forcing myself to get out of the car.

+ ✳ +

When I enter the kitchen, the 'rents are freaking out.

"Audrey left! She just left the house without telling us and got on a bus to Elboya," Mom tells me.

"That's like one of the safest neighborhoods in the city."

"She went to meet this Calvin boy!" Dad adds.

Oh. I smile. Good for Audrey. Except that Dad sounds ten seconds away from getting in his car, driving up there, and wringing poor Calvin's neck. "What's the problem? Remember how excited you were when he first called?"

"I thought he was a friend," Dad mutters. "I was happy she'd made a new friend at school. But then they went on a date, and now . . . this."

I can't hide my smile. "You guys need to chill. We're fifteen now. We're going to date."

Mom looks at Dad, who clenches his jaw before sagging onto the kitchen stool. "So it begins."

I laugh. "We need to start treating Audrey like a grownup. She deserves it."

"Clare's right." Mom rubs Dad's back. "We need to step back and allow her room to breathe. She probably snuck out because she knew we would say no, and at least she took her phone and called to tell us where she is."

"I'm going to go upstairs now," I say before the attention turns to me — specifically what Taylor and I did after we drove off.

At the top of the stairs, I go to Audrey's room, Adam's old room, and really look at it for the first time in years. I pick up a stuffed elephant that sits on her dresser, put it back down. She still has the assembled car from the large Kinder Surprise Mom and Dad gave us years ago. There's a paper package with the words *For Clare* written on it in black marker. I remember this package — Audrey was carrying it into the kitchen when she found out I was talking to Calvin. After that she must have decided not to give it to me.

With a glance at the door, I peel back the paper to reveal a stone sculpture of some kind. It must be the soapstone Mom said Audrey was going to carve. I pick it up and almost drop it because it's so heavy. The stone is smooth and cool, the detail nearly perfect. Did Audrey really carve this? I run my finger along the babies floating in their separate sacs with their foreheads almost touching.

This is how we were once. In the beginning, before anyone or anything came between us.

I turn it around and realize I've been looking at it from the back. Symbols are carved onto each of the babies, and I recognize them immediately as the symbols for Gemini and Taurus. There is another sign carved between the two sacs, peaks like waves, and at first I mistake it for water in the womb. Then my pinkie grazes something rough and I flip the sculpture over.

Please forgive me, Clare and Adam.

The third symbol is Adam's astrological sign, Aquarius.

My hands start to shake and I have to put the carving down before I actually drop it. I've been blaming Audrey for Adam's death for months, yet it never occurred to me she might blame herself as well. I remember telling her it was her fault during a fight, but I didn't think she took it to heart. I thought she . . . Well, I guess I have no idea what she thought because I didn't bother to ask. I've been so angry that I haven't been able to see her for who she truly is: my best friend. My sister. My wombmate.

Carefully cradling the carving, I curl up on Audrey's bed and wait. I fall asleep and don't wake up when Audrey comes home and talks to the 'rents in the living room. I don't wake up until Audrey sits on the edge of the bed.

"You found it," she says softly.

I sit up, still clutching it to my chest like a stuffed animal. "It's amazing, Audrey. I can't believe you made it. I'm so, so impressed."

She smiles and then ducks her head shyly. "Thank you. I was going to give it to you at some point."

I swallow hard. "It's really creative with the symbols. Is the third one Aquarius?"

Audrey nods. "At first it was just going to be us, but when I started carving, it took on a life of its own. For some reason I felt like Adam should be there too."

"Because he shared the womb with us too, just years earlier?"

"Mostly because I always felt like Adam held us together. Like the water in the womb."

I can't explain how proud of Audrey I am then. No one gets to know the real Audrey, the person who is thoughtful and deep and thinks about the world in wonderfully imaginative and breathtaking ways. A true artist.

"I saw the inscription," I say softly. "'Please forgive me, Clare and Adam.'"

Audrey looks away, finally breaking our gaze. "The day we lost Adam, I lost you, too."

My heart clenches. "You haven't lost me. You'll never lose me, Audrey." My voice breaks at the end of the sentence and my eyes flood with tears. All the feelings I've been shoving down and trying to avoid are bubbling up, all the memories of Adam and Audrey and me from our childhood. Why have I been acting like a jerk to the only other person going through the same thing as me?

"I'm so sorry I treated you this way," I tell Audrey when I can breathe again. "I was just so angry and messed up about Adam's death and lashed out at you."

"It's okay," Audrey says.

"No, it's not. I haven't been a good sibling to you. I've been petty and mean and you deserve so much more. Adam's death wasn't your fault, Audrey."

"Yeah." Her tone is dismissive.

"No, listen to me. Adam's death was not your fault. I'm so, so sorry I said that to you once when we were fighting. I didn't realize you actually believed that until earlier today when we were looking through the boxes, and I should have told you then like Mom and Dad did. I was too busy thinking about what a terrible person I was."

"You're not a terrible person."

"Well, I don't want to be anymore. I need you to believe that it wasn't your fault. Like Mom said, sometimes bad things just happen in life and no one could have prevented them. No one *causes* them. Do you hear me?"

Audrey nods.

"Good." I take both her hands and hold them. Our eyes lock and I give her hands a squeeze. "We're twins, Audrey. You're the most important person in the world to me and there's something I want to tell you. I'm going to tell you a secret about me and not because I'm trying to make up, but because out of the seven billion people in the entire world, you are the one person I want to tell."

Audrey's eyes widen a bit. I squeeze her hands again and she squeezes mine in return and just like that, our heartbeats sync up, beating in unison like Mom said they did in the womb. Time is unraveling, days and nights of whispering secrets in our bedroom stretching into infinity like a mirror held up to another mirror, until everything that has separated us slips away and we're no longer the estranged versions of Clare and Audrey that we've been since Adam's death — we're best friends again.

"Remember when I told you that I sometimes feel like no one understands me?"

She nods.

"Well, that's because they don't know the real me."

My body is humming now. Whether I'm excited or nervous, I'm not sure. But Audrey's hands are holding me tightly and I know I'm safe, know this is the moment I've been waiting for. I'm ready. I can do this.

"The reason I said that is because this year I've done a lot of searching into who I am. My identity, I guess. You know how I've been wearing Adam's clothes? That's not just because I miss him." I pause and Audrey waits. I take a deep breath and say, "It's because sometimes I don't feel like a girl."

"So you feel like a guy?"

"Sometimes."

Audrey considers this. "You always seemed happiest when you were hanging out with Adam and skateboarding and stuff."

"How did you know about that?"

"I saw you. Out my window."

Right. I consider how and how much to explain to her. "It isn't as simple as being a tomboy, though, or even being a lesbian. I've been wearing Adam's clothes lately, and I haven't felt like I'm being alternative — I've felt like I'm a boy. And I liked it."

"Okay," Audrey says simply, "then be a boy."

I blink at her. "You're not freaking out?"

She shrugs. "If you ask me, I don't think you've been happy for a long time. Not since we were kids, when you just did whatever you wanted to do. Before you became friends with Sharon and started acting like her instead."

"The thing is, I don't want to be a boy all the time. Sometimes I want to be a girl."

"Do you have to choose?"

Now I'm grinning because Audrey gets it. She actually gets it! "It took me a little while to figure out what term I want to use. Even though I feel closer to female on the spectrum and want to use she/her pronouns, I identify with both genders and feel like I can move between them depending on my mood or the day. So I think I might be gender-fluid."

The moment I say it to Audrey, I know it's the truth. Like Taylor, Audrey is my safe place. She's always been my safe place; I was just too afraid to admit it.

Audrey smiles a smile I haven't seen in a long time. Not since we were little kids. A memory resurfaces of a sunny afternoon and a sprinkler arching over a bright yellow Slip 'N Slide, rainbows dancing in the droplets, and Audrey grabbing my hand with the flash of a smile before we raced toward it.

"I'm glad you're going to be yourself," she says.

"I owe that to you, Audrey." I squeeze her hands again. I never want to let go. "I was in a really bad place and didn't realize how unhappy I was until I became honest with myself. I didn't like the person I was pretending to be. I used to think it was so important to fit in and be popular and couldn't see that I was turning into a complete jerk. It used to frustrate me that you never tried to be like the rest of us, but now I see that's what makes you so cool. I want you to know that."

Tears fill Audrey's eyes, but this time she doesn't try to duck her head and hide them. "You think I'm cool?"

"The coolest."

Audrey

I promise to be a better sibling, Clare says. I'm going to be there for you this time. We can help each other at school.

That's when I realize the truth.

I want to stay at Peak, I say.

Don't be scared to come back, Audrey.

No, I mean it. I *want* to go to Peak instead.

You do?

Yeah. I wanted to go back to your school when I wanted to be like everyone else. Now I'm happy being myself. Plus Peak has a better art room and it's less crazy there. Well, a different crazy. I laugh.

Clare laughs too. Fair enough.

I've been doing well there too, I say. Thriving, you might say. Monsieur Martin said I could be one of their best students. The other students look up to me.

I think about Kira. If she asked me now, I would have a different answer. I would tell her that if we're freaks, I'm glad to be a freak.

You're an amazing artist, Clare says. I've always thought that, just so you know. You and Mom are the artistic ones. To tell you the truth, I've always envied you for that.

Really? Today is full of surprises.

Definitely. I tried to find my own artistic calling to be like the two of you, but I think my talents lie elsewhere. You should go to an art college of some sort. It's your destiny, Audrey. You're going to be a really successful artist one day. I know it.

Thanks, Clare.

So I heard you went on a date with Calvin. Is everything okay now?

It is. We're dating!

Clare punches my shoulder in a gesture that reminds me a lot of Adam. Right on. How did you meet?

So I tell Clare the whole story. I don't leave anything out. I tell her he is the first friend I've had in years. I tell her about how impressed he was with my art.

He's cute and fun, I say. And he's imaginative like me. He makes me feel good about myself.

That's how Taylor makes me feel, Clare says.

I can tell.

Clare gives my hands another squeeze and she grins. This is the happiest I've seen Clare in a long time. The dark cloud above her has drifted away.

We go downstairs so I can tell my parents my decision.

I'm staying at Freak.

Don't call it that, Dad says. Then he blinks. What did you just say?

I'm going back. Thank you for the opportunity to try Clare's school but now I know where I belong.

Are you sure? Mom glances at Clare and back at me. You've wanted it for so long.

It has nothing to do with Clare. I just realized how lucky I am to have Peak.

Mom's and Dad's mouths fall open. Their chins hit their knees when

Clare takes my hand and we walk upstairs together. It will be sad to not be in school with each other, but maybe we're not meant to be. Maybe we're meant to take our own paths knowing we still have each other.

We go to Clare's room. The room we used to share. Clare peels back the covers and we climb in together, lie side by side with our heads touching. Through the open window it smells like summer. Like warm nights and freedom and the end of darkness.

You should move back in here, Clare says.

Seriously?

She laughs. You're turning into me. No, not seriously. I like having my own room. But you should visit more often.

I'll do that.

I wish we didn't have to go back to school. I wish Mom would home-school us.

Calvin pops into my mind. No you don't, I tell her. You would be lonely and so would I. From now on I'm going to make an effort to be friends with other people. I know they don't have to be exactly like me to be my friend.

What about Sirius? Clare asks.

Sirius will always be special to me. I'll keep him in my art for as long as I need him.

I like that idea.

We're quiet for a while and then she says, I'm going to tell everyone that I'm gender-fluid. If they don't get it, I don't care. It's who I am.

Under the blanket, Clare finds my hand and squeezes tight. I can just make out the glow-in-the-dark stars on the ceiling in this light. Clare had to hold me up by the waist so I could reach. I'd just finished pasting the last star when we both fell off the bed. Adam came running in to see if we were okay. Like usual.

Clare?

Yeah?

I'm happy to be us again.

Me too.

I wish Adam could be here too.

Clare bites her lip the way she does when she's trying not to cry.

Did Adam leave when the basement flooded?

The question surprises me. I thought you don't believe in ghosts.

Why did you think that?

Because you got mad at me when I said Adam was in the basement.

Clare sighs. I was scared. Because I think I felt him too, but I didn't want to admit it.

Why not?

I think . . . Clare swallows and tries again. I think I wanted him to be down there so I wouldn't have to let him go, but I was also afraid. I thought that if he could see who I am now, he wouldn't like what he saw.

I disagree. I think he'd like this new Clare. And I think he would be really proud of us both right now.

Clare smiles and shifts closer to me. I can still feel him in the house, just in a different way. He was in this room. He jumped on this bed. He slept across the hall. It sounds corny, but we will always have those memories, you know? Maybe souls leave traces of themselves in all their favorite places.

I like that. Then he can be here and there at the same time. Between two worlds.

What do you think he's doing right now?

He's probably on his skateboard.

Clare chuckles. Grinding the handrails of the elementary.

I laugh too. Then I say it.

I miss him.

I do too. Every single day.

Clare rolls onto her side to face me. She starts to cry a little and I do too. Our arms are around each other like when we were little. Soon I can hear her breathing change, and I know she's asleep. I close my eyes too.

This time when I dream of Adam, he's meeting us at the diner after skateboarding with his friends. He's sitting in the booth and ordering a coffee. Grinning. Always grinning.

It will take a long time to grieve Adam. We'll probably never stop grieving him and we'll definitely never forget him. But we'll have each other. Our best friend. And if we ever question being ourselves, we'll set each other straight. Because life is too short to be someone else.

That is the truest truth of all.

Acknowledgments

Under Shifting Stars started out as a short story centering on Audrey and her desire to be reunited with her twin at public school, but it quickly became apparent that the story wasn't complete without Clare's perspective and developed into a novel. *Under Shifting Stars* has been through multiple iterations, with many people contributing their insights, and each and every time it grew stronger. I have the following people to thank for that.

Thank you to Aritha van Herk, who read Audrey's first chapters as part of an application to enter her fiction class and encouraged me to continue.

Thank you to Heather Ezell, a Pitch Wars mentor in 2016, who read the very first draft of the novel and asked questions that led me in new and improved directions.

To my LGBTQIA sensitivity readers, including Vee Signorelli, for their invaluable insight and knowledge. I'm very thankful for the support.

Under Shifting Stars wouldn't have found a home at HMH without my wonderful agent, Hilary McMahon, who fell in love with my characters — and Audrey's lucky seven lists — and made me feel like I was in good hands.

Infinite thanks to my talented editor, Harriet Low. You are the reason *Under Shifting Stars* is what it is today. Thank you to Chan Chau for creating such a striking cover; Andrea Miller for her "stellar" design work on the title font, chapter headers, and interior layout; and copyeditor Karen Sherman and proofreader Susan Bishansky for all the good catches. I'm so incredibly grateful to the rest of the Houghton Mifflin Harcourt team for all their hard work and for bringing this book to life: Mary Magrisso, Erika West, Anna Ravenelle, Taylor McBroom, and Samantha Bertschmann.

A special thank-you to Trenton, my ultra-supportive husband, who put up with me writing long into the night and waking him up once I finally crawled into bed, and who took the kids out of the house when I needed time to work. This book was definitely a team effort.

Though *Under Shifting Stars* and its characters are fictional, the story was inspired in part by the 2013 Alberta floods, during which my childhood home was flooded. My family lost a variety of items, but the hardest part was losing objects of sentimental value: boxes of photographs; childhood stuffed animals, clothes, school assignments, and crafts; a dollhouse built by my parents' hands; my wedding dress. Having Audrey save these precious items for her family was a very healing process for me. Thank you to all the volunteers, friends, and family who helped us during that difficult time.

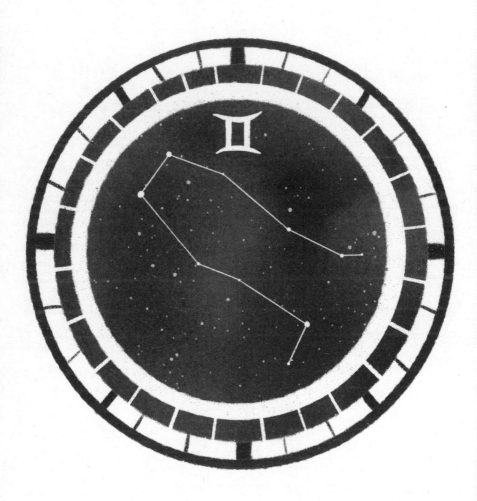